Culpepe
271 Southga
Culpepe

825-8691

MW00679067

CRIMINAL APPETITES

JEFFREY MARKS

SILVER DAGGER
MYSTERIES
An Imprint of The Overmountain Press
JOHNSON CITY, TENNESSEE

gc
cr

This book is a work of fiction. All names, characters, places, and events are either the product of the authors' imagination or are used fictitiously. Any resemblance to actual events or persons, living or dead, is entirely coincidental and beyond the intent of either the authors or the publisher.

Book design by Cherisse McGinty

Hardcover ISBN 1-57072-260-9
Trade Paper ISBN 1-57072-261-7
Copyright © 2004 by Jeffrey Marks
Printed in the United States of America
All Rights Reserved

1 2 3 4 5 6 7 8 9 0

To Ryan Paul, who has brought joy to my life.

ACKNOWLEDGMENTS

The amount of help I have received in writing this book has been legion. If I have left out a name, it is not from a lack of appreciation; it's only my faulty memory.

All I know about cooking and food came from my family. I learned to cook from my mother during our summers at home. From those humble beginnings of potato soup came this book. My family grew up in Appalachia, and without knowing it, I adopted a style of cooking and a way of life. All my favorite recipes have their roots in this shared culture. My life would be poorer and my waist thinner without my grandmother's heritage of good food.

I have to thank Rob and Robyn Perry, who have answered a million questions about cooking and recipes for this book. They are Betty, Martha, and Julia all rolled into two. The recipes are more palatable because of them.

My own family has been incredibly gracious about accepting my writing into our family. They accepted my mania and helped me with my work as they could. My parents have always loved and accepted me for who I am, and for that I am eternally and perpetually grateful. My sister is a rock of support in designer clothes, and her two boys will talk for hours with me about ideas for more books and more book parties. Of course, Tony listens to me and manages while I have my nose stuck in a book. And Ryan will eat whatever I cook, so long as it isn't barbecue. All these people mean a lot to me.

TABLE OF CONTENTS

INTRODUCTION

While it may seem a rather shocking confession as the editor of this book, I've never been much of a cook. I can make food to eat. I am a credible creator of sustenance, but it's a means to an end. Only the steps necessary to get from the refrigerator to my stomach. The beauty and ingenuity that go into preparing a good meal are lost on me.

As I read the stories for this anthology, I had an epiphany. The same artistry that whips up a four-star meal can be utilized to spin a mystery tale. These fourteen narratives have convinced me of the creativity that lies within the walls of the kitchen.

And just as the stories within the book are models of food as an art form, an analogy can be made to the writing of the stories. For mystery writers, the storyline is our stock, our bouillabaisse if you will. Plot is the base from which all the rest of the story comes. For me, I like to let the plot simmer for a while in my head before committing it to paper. I find that if my subconscious is allowed to cook the stock until it's ready, the story has a deeper, richer flavor. Then and only then can we proceed.

We have to stir in the characters for our dish. No meal is complete without a full set of characters who take the plot and give it the reasons for existing. For most authors, the characters are the meat and vegetables of the course, the vital part of the meal that adds the texture and nourishment of the dinner. No entrée is complete without them. And just as fourteen chefs could start with the same pot of beef stock and create the same number of delicious meals, authors can take the same concept, that of a meal leading to death, and create narratives as unique and rich as the chef's meals. For the meat can be beef, chicken, or seafood. The vegetables can be our old standby, potatoes, or something as outlandish as watercress or spicy as horseradish. The meal depends on the chef, just as the story does its author. I can guarantee you that no two of the tales will come close to being the same in the eyes of the reader.

You'll find that humor in this collection, no matter how dark, is the equivalent of adding the spices. Each has a liberal sprinkling of levity, which shows that the cook has been busy seasoning the meal to taste. You can't get past the Table of Contents without noticing the witty pun title from Tamar Myers.

So what is left to do? When the stories have been cooked to perfection, then it's time for the reader to put a napkin around the neck, take a sip of Chardonnay, and prepare for the feast to come. This collection will leave you sated and satisfied.

COOK'S GOOD DEED

by Joanne Pence

Joanne Pence is the author of the delightful Angie Amalfi series of mysteries that includes Bell, Cook, and Candle, *and* If Cooks Could Kill. *A graduate of U.C. Berkeley with a master's degree in journalism and a Phi Beta Kappa key, Joanne has taught school in Japan, written for magazines, and worked as an operations analysis manager. Joanne now lives north of Boise, Idaho, with her husband, sons, and a plethora of pets.*

"Believe me, Connie, you're going to love this guy," Angie Amalfi said as she logged on to her computer, her friend Connie Rogers hovering nearby. They sat in the den of Angie's penthouse apartment high atop San Francisco's Russian Hill. With a couple of clicks of the mouse, she entered the "Gourmet Gateway—A San Francisco Treat" Internet chat room and then scrolled through the list of participants. "He's not here yet."

"It figures," Connie said with a huff, her hands fisted and resting on the hips of her leopard-spotted miniskirt, one toe of her stiletto-heeled shoes tapping in irritation. "Even Internet dates stand me up. I give up! It just isn't worth it."

"Calm down," Angie cautioned, sitting back and giving a tug to the legs of her navy blue silk jumpsuit. She hated it when the knees stretched and looked baggy. "We're a little early."

Just then the words *Chagall: Hi, Connie,* scrolled across the screen.

"That's him!" Angie screeched. Her long, satin-pink manicured nails flew over the keys in reply. "Chagall is his nom de plume. Food and art. He's my kind—I mean *your*—kind of guy."

"He knows my name?" Connie asked, a tinge of worry in her voice as she tucked a blonde strand behind one ear.

"He thinks it's mine. Fear not, I have this all worked out."

At that moment, her words appeared on the screen.

GrtCook: Glad you could make it, Richard.

"Great cook?" Connie scoffed. "Aren't we humble."

"Chat rooms aren't the place for humility," Angie replied knowingly. "Anyway, I knew he was the man for you when we discussed the virtues of scorzonera versus salsify—and he gave me a recipe for potato salsify pie."

Connie's frown deepened. "I don't have any idea what you're talking about—except for pies. I love pies."

Angie busied herself making small talk with Richard as she tried to calm Connie's nerves. "They're carrot-shaped roots. Some people say they taste like oysters."

"Geez, strange stuff is supposed to taste like chicken, not oysters. Ugh! How can I carry on a conversation about such things? Aren't there guys who like apple pie? Hell, I'd settled for a MoonPie man."

"Like all men, once you get him talking, all you have to do is agree. Works every time."

Chagall: Are we still on for tomorrow night?

Connie's eyes narrowed. "How long have you been cruising the Internet, picking up men, Angie?"

"I don't cruise or pick up men! I did this for you. Like a cyber matchmaker. What can I say?" Angie lifted big brown eyes to her friend. "As soon as I realized how nice he was, I told him my name is Connie, and that I'm tall, blonde, blue-eyed, and divorced."

"As opposed to Angie—short, brunette, and single." Connie folded her arms. "Did you tell him I'm also too poor to own a computer, let alone live in this big Russian Hill apartment?"

Angie shook her head in frustration. "It's necessary to keep some secrets from a man, Connie, until he needs to know. When he meets you tomorrow night, when the time is right, you can straighten it all out."

"I don't think so."

GrtCook: I can hardly wait to meet you. See you at 7! TTFN.

"TTFN? Ta-ta for now?" Connie gawked, appalled. "Since when do you say ta-ta, Angie?"

"Richard isn't terribly hip," Angie explained. "You two will get along quite nicely."

Connie snorted.

* * *

"Oh, Angie, he's everything you said he'd be!" Connie ran into Angie's kitchen, shut the door behind her, leaned against it, and heaved a moon-struck sigh.

Angie smoothed the ruffled white apron against her plain black dress. Somehow, in the course of planning what was supposed to be a simple blind date, things had taken on a life of their own. She owed Connie big-time for a few past transgressions, and this little charade should make it all up to her. Angie looked upon the night's activities as penance—a secular three *Our Father*'s and three *Hail Mary*'s.

"He's good looking," Angie concurred, "in a Vampire Lestat kind of way."

"So he's a little pale. Maybe he spends too much time on the Internet. If he didn't, we never would have met."

"I'm glad you like him, Connie." Angie was a bit taken aback by her friend's quick surrender to Richard's charms, which she found a lot less appealing in person than on-line. She was also troubled that, when she served the canapés, her remark about vol-au-vent puffed pastry seemed to go right over his head. Of course, his mind might have been on Connie's plunging neckline. His eyes certainly were.

Connie waltzed from one side of Angie's kitchen to the other, her lemon-chiffon cocktail dress swirling around her. "If this night goes the way I think it will, after dinner I'll confess that this was our little joke—that this isn't really my apartment, and I don't even have a maid! Then, just so he won't get the idea he's out with the wrong gal, I'll let him know your very protective boyfriend is Homicide Inspector Paavo Smith."

Angie couldn't hold in her trepidation any longer. "I've suddenly got cold feet about him, Connie. Maybe I should never have told him lies in the first place. He isn't what I expected. After all, he was hanging around some chat room when I met him. What do we really know about the guy?"

"You were hanging around it, too! And it isn't some sleazy virtual sex place—it's for another appetite: food. Men who hang out there should be interesting, wealthy, mature—and hungry. In more ways than one, I hope. He's just what I need in my life. A man with taste. And now that I've met him, Richard Thompson McNab is exactly what the doctor ordered."

"As long as he's not related to Richard Speck," Angie murmured.

"Who?"

"Forget it." Angie told herself to stop being so suspicious. Just because she met the guy on the Internet was no reason to think he was a serial killer. . . .

Just because Paavo had once told her how vice cops go into chat rooms, pretending to be young girls just to catch the sickos who lurk there. . . .

Just because some women who met men on the Internet ended up in shallow graves. . . .

And, to be fair, just because some Internet Romeo ended up in his Juliet's freezer. . . .

Connie fluttered back into the living room, her hands folded beneath her chin. "Dear Richard, I'm sorry to have left you so long. I just wanted to make sure Angelina would lock up for me when she leaves."

Angelina was ready to barf.

"I understand," Richard's sonorous radio-pitchman tones wafted into the kitchen. "Reliable help is hard to find these days. You have to explain things to them over and over. Your girl seems brighter than most, I must say."

"She's a treasure," Connie twittered.

Angie clutched her throat, silently gagging as she stepped closer to the door to listen.

"Do you use her full time, or might she have a few hours to spare on my place each week?"

It was nails on the blackboard time.

"I need her full time, I'm afraid," Connie answered with a chuckle. The woman was so besotted, Angie wouldn't have been surprised if Connie didn't send her over to scrub dear Richard's toilet bare-handed.

"It must be wonderful to be able to afford such help," he said, his voice oilier and more cloying with each word spoken.

"You don't know the half of it."

The door closed and the apartment was quiet.

Angie whipped off the apron, tossed it onto the counter, and stormed into the living room to pick up the hors d'oeuvres she'd made to impress him—artichoke hearts stuffed with mushroom puree, chicken livers in aspic, and beluga caviar. The caviar demanded champagne, so she had popped the cork on a bottle of Perrier-Jouet Fleur de Champagne. Although she'd made quite a few hors d'oeuvres—she didn't want the plates to appear sparse and ruin the well-to-do impression—since Connie and dear (gag) Richard were going to one of the city's finest restaurants for dinner, she was sure they'd only nibble at the food.

She'd invited Paavo to come over. No sense letting good champagne and caviar go to waste. After all, no one is *that* rich.

To her surprise, the plates had been practically polished clean. Not even a crumb was left. Connie had been too nervous to eat, so dear Richard must have been half starved.

How could he have talked—on and on—and eaten so much too? Garrulous glutton.

Now she was sure she didn't care for him.

She had just finished straightening the kitchen when she heard a loud, familiar knock on the door.

"Are you in mourning?" Paavo asked as he entered. She glanced down at her shirtwaist dress and chunky shoes. He was right. Black wasn't her color.

"It'll just take me a minute to change, then we're out of here."

Paavo sat down on the sofa. He was a big man, with dark brown hair, blue eyes, and a high-cheekboned, chiseled face. It was a stern face that gave crooks pause, but Angie found it handsome.

In a short while she came out wearing a red silk Donna Karan sheath with matching four-inch heels and ruby earrings—as far a cry from a scullery maid as she could get.

"You look beautiful, Angie," Paavo said. "But I thought we were staying here this evening."

"All my food disappeared into a human Hoover. We'll have to eat out, but first we need to make a quick stop at Ernie's."

"The restaurant?" He helped her with her coat.

"Yes. You've got to run in and make sure Connie's in there. I don't want her date to see me."

Paavo gave her one of those what-in-the-world-are-you-and-Connie-up-to-now looks. "What's going on?"

"Nothing really. She's gone out on a blind date, that's all." Angie tried to sound casual, carefree, and composed, as they walked toward the elevator. "I just want to make sure she's okay."

"A blind date? That doesn't sound like Connie. She's usually cautious about men."

"I know. I sort of fixed her up."

"Why are you worried, then? You must know the guy."

She didn't answer until the elevator arrived and they got on. "Not all that well, I'm afraid."

"I'm sure she'll be fine. The only blind date I'd worry about these days is one off the Internet. Some con artist is working it, finding rich women, charming them, and then he gets them out of the house and while they're gone, he enters the home and robs them. The last victim returned home while he was still there. He killed her."

"Oh, no! Do you have any idea who he is?"

"Not really. The guy changes his name and identity, and even his looks to some degree. We're working with vice, putting the pieces together and getting closer."

Once in the basement parking garage of her apartment, she handed Paavo the keys to her Ferrari. He adored driving her car. She asked, "You're sure the Internet is involved?"

"The common thread is that the women met him in a chat room. Come to think of it, you might have some acquaintance with it yourself—it's a San Francisco-based Web site called Gourmet Gateway."

She made small talk and waited until they had almost reached the restaurant before saying, "Paavo, there's something I've got to tell you."

A click of the dead bolt told him he'd unlocked it. A toothy smile smeared across his face. The apartment was his.

He flicked on his flashlight and made a quick check of his watch. Nine o'clock. Dan would keep the babe yakking till ten or so, then split. She'd wait a while, expecting him to return, and finally head for home. Even if she had luck and found a cab fast, it'd be ten-thirty, easy, before she got back.

He had plenty of time.

The flashlight panned the room. Classy. One of the best yet. Dan had been right. "Don't quit yet," he'd said. "Just one more hit."

One more, then they'd head for Vegas, fence everything, and enjoy life. This line of work was beginning to make him nervous—especially after the last babe saw him and started screaming. He had to bash her head with his gun until she stopped. Not his fault she died. She could've kept her yap shut.

It was a sign. "Luck runs out when you most need it," his momma used to say. Long as it didn't split on him before he was out of here, he'd be okay.

He shined his light on the small watercolor over the stereo system—the Cézanne original Dan was so hopped up about.

He knew from nothing about paintings, turned his back on it, and headed for the bedroom. Go for the jewelry. It was easy to carry, easy to sell, not traceable like some damn picture that could spell nothing but trouble.

His eyes zeroed in on a framed painting in the middle of a wall, with no furniture under it. He chuckled under his breath. Didn't these schmucks realize what a dead giveaway that was? A spot where a person could stand close to the wall to work the combination? Jerks.

He lifted off the painting. Bingo!

Concentrating hard to hear the click or feel the catch of the tumbler, he almost missed the much louder sound of the door opening, followed by voices in the living room.

"Oh, no, no, no!" Angie dropped her purse on the drum table by the door as she walked back into her apartment. She hurled herself into the living room, hands clutching her hair, spinning around and around, and lamenting her friend's disappearance. "Why, why, why did I get involved in Connie's love life? Where can she be?"

"Don't worry, Angie. It's probably a coincidence. She's likely to be just fine. The Greedy Gourmet—that's what vice calls him—has to know we're onto him. He shouldn't try anything this quickly unless he wants to try one last big one."

"Ah!"

"Relax. I called vice plus Calderon, who's in charge of the murder case." Paavo caught her, put his arms around her, and tried to draw her close. "They're working on the case right now. I really doubt Connie's involved."

A bit dizzy, she clutched his lapels. "You always said there's no such thing as pure coincidence."

"I could be wrong." He placed a light kiss on her brow, then her nose and her cheek. "She'll turn up, and we'll be here for her," he murmured as he lowered his mouth to hers.

She drew back. "You've got to go find her!"

He froze. "Now?"

"Yes! She wasn't at Ernie's; she isn't home!" Angie headed for the windows that faced the bay and Alcatraz. "She's out there, alone in the city with a phony food fanatic. What if—when he finds out she isn't rich and has nothing for him to steal—he slits her throat?"

"Stop being melodramatic. I'm sure there's nothing to worry about."

She clenched her fists. "Talk to vice again! Do something! She's my friend, and I'm responsible. Oh, Paavo, please." Tears filled her eyes. "I promise, I'll never, ever mess with anyone's love life again. Just find her. Make her safe."

He nodded. "I know when I'm beaten. All right. I'll see what I can do."

"Thank you." She kissed him lightly. "Now go get Connie and nab that rambling Lothario!"

Earlier, she'd given him a description of Richard, which he'd passed on to vice and Inspector Calderon.

"I'll try. And you lock your doors," he said. "I can't imagine he'd show up here, but if he does, call my cell phone. Don't let him in. Even if he swears it's all a mistake, remember he could be lying. Understand?"

"I thought you weren't worried about him?"

"I wasn't worried when I thought I'd be here with you. With you alone, it's another story."

She nodded.

"In fact, don't let anyone in. Is that clear?"

She nodded again.

"Go to bed. I'll find Connie."

She locked the door behind Paavo. This evening hadn't turned out at all the way she'd planned. All she wanted was a little love in Connie's life, and a lot of it in her own. Instead, she headed for an empty bed.

At the doorway to her bedroom, she stopped. Nothing in the room was out of place, and yet, it felt wrong . . . strange, somehow.

It was her imagination. This business with the Greedy Gourmet and Connie had creeped her out, that was all.

He couldn't make it. The ledge along the side of the building was too narrow to balance on while trying to reach the rooftop. He was too old, stiff, and clumsy for cat burglary, anyway. The only other nearby window was the bathroom, then a blank wall—probably where the elevator shaft was. He was stuck.

No building was across from him, so no one could see him now, especially at night. He was at the back of the building, and the neighboring houses opposite him were only one or two stories tall, far, far below.

He had to go back inside, wait until the guy left or the two were otherwise engaged, maybe watch some of the action, and then sneak out of the apartment.

He began to sidle along the ledge toward the open window.

Angie was halfway to the kitchen—she'd decided to make some hot chocolate to help relax before bed—when she felt a breeze in the hallway.

Warily, she moved toward her den. The draft was coming from inside.

The den window was open wide. That was strange. She lived on the twelfth floor and rarely opened the windows. She remembered seeing Richard pat his breast pocket in the way of smokers. Could he be a surreptitious smoker, to boot, who perhaps had tried to sneak a puff or two? That must be it.

Finally, the window opening was within reach—it still seemed miles away—and he could kiss this damn ledge good-bye. He was feeling dizzy. He could hear his own racing pulse. Spots danced before his eyes, and his legs seemed to belong to someone else. He reached for the window frame to steady himself.

Angie slid the window shut, then flipped the lock in place. She paused. Was that a cry? A kind of yelp? But it came from outside the window. Her imagination was definitely working overtime, and she headed back to the kitchen.

The chocolate made, she sat in the living room with it in front of her on the coffee table, contemplating the phone and wondering if she should call Paavo, when she heard a knock on the door.

Peering through the peephole, she saw Connie. "Are you alone?" she called.

"How did you guess?" Connie snarled.

Angie opened the door, grabbed Connie's arm, and yanked her into the apartment, then shut and locked the door. "How did you get away?"

"Get away? He left me!"

"He what? Paavo and I went to Ernie's. We didn't see you."

"We went to The Top of the Mark instead—and he dumped me! I might not know much about gourmet food, but, believe me, I now know all about the price of seared foie gras, Kobe beef, and poached abalone. He ate and ran!" Suddenly, she began to cry. "My credit card bounced, and I had to leave my watch before they'd let me leave. I'm sure they know the watch was only thirty dollars at Target, but they took pity on me." Her sobs grew heavier.

"Oh, Connie." Angie put her arms around her. "I'm sorry. But it could have been worse. I was afraid he was a murderer! Paavo told me some guy was hanging around the Gourmet Gateway looking for rich women to steal from, and he even killed one of them. Frankly, I'm relieved Richard was only a dinner snatcher—not to mention the way he scarfed down a hundred dollars worth of beluga caviar."

Connie pondered Angie's words a moment. "What if he came back here to rob the apartment after sneaking away from me?"

"He couldn't have. I've been here over an hour, and Paavo was with me part of the time."

"Ah. That's good. I guess." Her face fell. "All this means he didn't abandon me because he had some nefarious plan. He left because of me! Because I was so boring . . . or dumb . . . or sexless." Her tears welled again.

"Forget him!" Angie ordered. "Stay here tonight. You can use the daybed in the den. I'll even make us both some hot chocolate—mine got cold, I'm afraid."

"Hot chocolate?" Connie's voice was tiny.

Angie nodded.

"I'll stay."

Hot chocolate. He nearly cried at the thought of something warm and comforting. His momma used to make him chocolate before he was sent up to stir the first time. Oh, for some hot chocolate laced with Irish whiskey. . . . His fingers were nearly frozen, clawing into the sides of the building as the temperature dropped and the breeze from the bay grew stronger. He could hear it howling as it whipped around the building and lashed around him!

Come and bail me out, Dan! Dan—damn his bright ideas!—should show up here looking for him soon. Maybe they'd have to whack two broads this time. For making him suffer like this, they deserved it!

Angie called Paavo and told him Connie was fine. The two had their chocolate, and soon retired for the night.

It was one in the morning when Angie heard a piercing scream. "Connie!" she cried, and ran down the hall.

Connie sat up on the bed. "Out there! There was a man outside the window. Trying to get in."

Angie sat next to her and patted her shoulder. "We're on the twelfth floor, Connie. Nobody is outside the window. You had a nightmare."

"No, really. I heard a scratching noise. It woke me, and then I saw him. He had the ugliest face I've ever seen. Sort of like a bulldog with gray hair that whipped round and round his head. I guess it's windy out."

Angie almost laughed. "It's always windy at the top of this hill. Your dream was certainly vivid."

"It was no dream. Look out there."

Come on, you stupid cow! Open the damn window! He pressed himself flat against the wall and waited, ready to swing and hurl himself inside.

Angie went to the window and peered from one side to the other. "I don't see anyone."

"Open it."

Yeah! Listen to her, you bitch!

"Are you kidding? It's cold and foggy out there."

"Open it and look out."

Come on, come on, come on!

The sound of the lock being flicked back was music to his ears. He braced himself to bound into the warm room.

Angie slid the window ajar and immediately slammed it shut again. It seemed to hit something and not quite close, so she slid it open and slammed it even harder against the frame and turned toward Connie.

"Other than it sticking, it's fine."

His smashed finger hurt so badly he couldn't even scream. He jerked his hand free, and the force of his action pulled one foot off the ledge. As he teetered on the air, struggling to find his balance, he thought how much he'd enjoy killing that broad. Where the hell was Dan?

"You didn't even look," Connie complained.

"No, I didn't. Because we're twelve stories up, and unless The Fly has come to life, and Jeff Goldblum is clinging to the side of the building, I'm not wasting any more time. Go to sleep." Angie drew the heavy drapes over the window.

"Didn't you hear a cry at the same time as you shut the window?"

"All I heard was the screech of the window frame."

Connie snuggled back under the covers, her eyes wide. "Not a screech. What I heard was more like a whimper."

"There was nothing."

"If you say so."

"I do. Listen to Auntie Angie. She always knows best. Good-night."

At 2:00 A.M., Connie heard a rapping on the windowpane. After a quick glance at the fluorescent clock numbers, she pulled the covers over her head and squeezed her eyes tighter. *It's only my imagination,* she thought. *Just the raven. Nevermore.*

Angie slowly crept into the den. "I heard a sound," she whispered.

"No, you didn't," Connie said. "It was my imagination."

"He might be hiding in the apartment somewhere."

Connie sat up like a bullet. "Do you think it's . . . him?"

"It's got to be. He must be here trying to find my jewelry."

"Or your Cézanne. He said he loved it."

"What nerve!"

Connie squeezed the covers to her chin. "What shall we do?"

"I'll call Paavo," Angie said.

"But he lives thirty minutes away. We could be dead by the time he gets here!"

Angie reached into the bottom drawer of her desk and pulled out a heavy, clear glass paperweight with a carving of the Golden Gate bridge inside. "I knew this would come in handy someday." She handed it to Connie then picked up a silver letter opener for herself. "Let's get out of here."

Clutching their weapons—Angie in the lead, Connie right behind her—the two crept toward the living room. As they neared it, Angie heard a light scratching sound outside the front door.

"Thank God he's not in the apartment yet," she said to Connie as they huddled in the hallway.

"But how did we hear that little noise from the den in the back?"

"It must have something to do with the way sound waves carry," Angie replied. "Let's go out the back door—there's a fire escape." They stepped into the living room to make a dash for the kitchen just as the front door opened.

Richard stood in the doorway, the hall light framing him and casting a ray of light onto Angie and Connie, now huddled against the wall. "We meet again," he said and pulled out a gun. "All right, where is—"

"Freeze! Drop it!" From two sides, police rushed him, grabbed his arms, and yanked them behind his back. He was dragged away as Paavo stepped into the room and turned on the living room lights.

"What are you two doing up?" he asked, shocked.

"What are you doing out there?" Angie cried.

"Thanks, Paav!" a plainclothes policeman waved at him. "Sorry to bother you this way, miss. We had to catch Starkey in the act, and we did."

When the others left, Angie and Connie turned to Paavo. "Vice had an eye on the guy—Dan Starkey is his real name—all night. They followed him to the restaurant with Connie and were continuing to go after him when I called, trying to locate them both. We tailed him to a flop-house in the Tenderloin, but for some reason, he headed back here. We couldn't figure out why. Vice was hoping he'd try to break in and we'd catch him in the act. I figured you two were safe asleep and wouldn't be in harm's way."

"We were, except for the noise he made trying to break in here."

"Noise? He was almost completely silent. The guy's a pro. What do you mean?"

"Good ears, I guess," Angie said. "Let's get out of here, Connie." She went into her bedroom and quickly grabbed some clothes and under-wear. "This has made me too nervous. We'll drop you off at your place, and I'm going home with Paavo." She faced him. "Is that okay?"

He grinned. "Sounds perfect. A couple of days, at least, will be needed to get over the trauma of all this."

"My thoughts exactly," she said with a smile.

He looked around. "Hmm. There was some thought that two guys were working together to pull off this scam, but I guess not."

"Richard—or, I should say, Dan—was the only one we saw," Angie said.

"Guess you're right. Let's go." Paavo held open the door and the two women left.

"Help!" he cried. "Can anybody hear me? It's freezing out here. Damn those two broads! They'll pay! When I get hold of them I'll put my hands on their scrawny necks and I'll. . . ."

Splat.

POTATO SALSIFY PIE

Walnut Pastry (Single 9" by 2" Shell)

½ cup walnuts

1⅓ cups all-purpose flour

1½ teaspoons sugar

¼ teaspoon salt

4 tablespoons unsalted butter, chilled and cut into ½" dice

1 large egg whisked with 1 tablespoon iced water

1-2 tablespoons iced water

1½ teaspoons softened butter

1 egg white

pinch salt

Pulse the walnuts in the food processor with a small spoonful of flour until the nuts are coarsely chopped. Spread on a baking sheet and toast in a 350F oven for 5-7 minutes, to brown lightly. Remove half and reserve for final decorations. When completely cool, scrape remaining walnuts into the food processor. Add the rest of the flour, sugar, and salt. Pulse the chilled butter into the flour mixture, but only until it looks like very coarse meal. Process in the egg-water mixture, then add droplets of iced water just until the dough masses; be careful not to overmix—the dough should not ball up on the blade. Turn the dough onto a lightly floured board, hand-knead briefly, and wrap in plastic wrap. (If you are making two pies, cut in two and wrap separately.) Refrigerate for 2 hours.

Ahead of time: Dough may be left in refrigerator for 2 days, or frozen.

Grease tart pan with softened butter. Roll dough into 14" circle and line it into the buttered pan. Refrigerate for 1 hour.

A half hour before baking, preheat the oven to 350F.

Line the crust with aluminum foil and fill with dried beans or pie weights (to weigh it down during baking). Bake in preheated oven for about 15 minutes or until set. Remove the foil and beans. Whisk the egg white with a pinch of salt until foamy, and paint the shell with a light coating, then return to the oven for 10 minutes.

Filling

½ cup olive oil
6 large cloves of garlic,
    smashed and peeled
2 cups chicken stock, more
    if needed to cover
    ingredients
1 bay leaf
¼ cup white wine vinegar
1 teaspoon kosher salt

5 sprigs fresh thyme, plus 1
    tablespoon finely chopped
    thyme leaves
1 teaspoon coarsely chopped
    rosemary leaves
1 pound salsify, peeled and
    sliced lengthwise into thin
    3" sticks (if not available,
    substitute more potatoes)

Bring the olive oil, garlic, chicken stock, bay leaf, vinegar, salt, thyme sprigs, and rosemary to a boil in a large saucepan. Simmer for 10 minutes, then add the salsify, and simmer until it begins to soften. Remove the pan from heat and allow salsify to cool in the liquid. Strain and reserve leftover liquid for soups and stews.

Ahead of time: Cooked salsify may be refrigerated up to 3 days.

2 cups heavy cream
½ cup lamb or chicken stock
1 teaspoon salt
½ teaspoon freshly ground pepper

⅛ teaspoon minced garlic
¼ pound boiled potatoes,
    unpeeled and sliced ¼"
    thick

Bring the cream, stock, salt, pepper, and garlic to a boil in a large saucepan. Add the potatoes and simmer several minutes until just tender—taste slices to be sure.

Use a slotted spoon to transfer the potatoes from the cream to the walnut crust. Spread the cooked salsify neatly over the potatoes, trimming to fit if necessary. Pour enough of the potato-boiling cream mixture over the vegetables to coat. Bake at 425F for about 20-30 minutes until bubbling hot. Toss the remaining walnuts and chopped thyme together and strew over the top. Cut the warm pie and serve.

STEAK BLUES
by Tim Hemlin

Tim Hemlin is the author of such delectable mysteries as A Catered Christmas *and* Dead Man's Broth. *His sleuth, Neil Marshall, is a graduate student in creative writing, a struggling poet, and part-time chef and caterer in Houston, Texas (where Tim and his family also live).*

"On a random note," Leslie-Alice Crawford said, "Aunt June-Ellen saw another dead body."

Harry scooped out the last of the ash into a coffee can, then poured fresh charcoal into the barbecue. Without looking up he responded, "And has Elvis left the building?"

Leslie leaned a slender hip against the doorframe and sipped wine. "You've beaten that line senseless, Harry."

"Yes, but it still applies."

"Well, this time it's a little different. First off, she called the police."

"Why was she allowed to bother the police? Those poor people aren't paid enough to deal with the likes of June-Ellen." Harry met his wife's sea-green eyes. Even now, after all these years of marriage, he could still find himself lost in her crystalline gaze. Her eyes were the finest he'd ever seen on either side of the Atlantic, and they, along with her superior endowment, were what first attracted the displaced Englishman to the American, an East Texas woman.

As for June-Ellen, the old bat was always spotting dead bodies. Usually men, professionals. A banker who'd been force-fed twenty-dollar bills until his eyes bugged and he was as blue and cold as dry ice. A lawyer bludgeoned to death by a judge's gavel. A publisher found crushed like a dried leaf beneath the weight of all the marvelous books he'd rejected for the sole reason they weren't mass marketable. Or—and this was the old crone's all-time classic—an oil and gas executive discovered fossilized, hard as his greedy heart, heavy as his massive ego. June-Ellen's estranged husband, Bertrund, had been an oil and gas man.

Granted, though, as rampant as her imagination ran, she never actually reported any of these delusions to the authorities. Until now.

June-Ellen herself was a natural-born storyteller, and for years her family had encouraged her to pen the tales. Most everyone claimed she had Agatha Christie-like potential. However, as that wise American football coach Bum Phillips once said, "Potential means you just ain't done it yet." And June-Ellen never did do it, especially after her husband ran off on her and she went nuts.

"Well, Harry Crawford, I do believe you've become as hardened as my cousin Jasper in your old age," Leslie commented, breaking his reverie. She scuffed the toe of her boot against the patio pavement. "No one allowed Aunt June-Ellen to phone the cops. Besides, Molly and I can't watch her every move."

Harry bristled. Not at being reprimanded or even at being compared to a small-town undertaker who drank too much, as Jasper was and did, but at the slight upon his age. Only in his forties, Harry worked diligently to stay in shape. Jogging, weight lifting, rope jumping, and such. The routine was the sole surviving habit from his private-investigating years.

"I am not hardened," he replied, "like your cousin Jasper—whose hardening, I may add, deals mainly with his liver. It's just that it must have been obvious June-Ellen was worked up more than usual."

"So Molly should have seen it coming?"

"Yes, Les-darling, I'd think so."

Harry failed to notice that it was his wife's turn to fume, as she always did, at the nickname—one that he unconsciously used when irritated by her. And one that she had never quite learned to dismiss. She was Leslie or Leslie-Alice, not Les, a term that implied a lack thereof. No, instead of watching his wife check her temper, Harry gazed at the ashen sky and wondered if the humid fall evening would wash out his grilling. He also regretted not calling in the yardmen. Damp brown leaves were matted like a patchy oil slick across the dying grass.

Leslie took a drink of wine, then cleared her throat. "Nevertheless, this is what happened. June-Ellen was on the way back from Nacogdoches. Molly was driving, and you know dear Molly. No word out of June-Ellen's mouth raises her eyebrows, anymore. So when Aunt June-Ellen points to a stand of huisache and promptly announces there's a body out there, Molly kindly comments on what a shame that is. It's only when she says, 'And I know who it is,' do Molly's ears perk up." Leslie paused, believing the suspense sufficiently built to garner Harry's full attention.

However, he muttered, "Bloody busman's holiday," and tossed lit matches on the charcoal. Flames rose quickly and high, bright as the marks of a child's crayon against an unused page in a coloring book.

"Oh, for crying out loud, Harry, I don't want to hear about how you spend all your time cooking. Least not while I'm trying to tell you a story."

Harry was part owner and head chef of Café Noir, a swanky eatery with a cloak-and-dagger theme that demanded much of his time and energy. Leslie and her social demands usually claimed any leftover time and energy.

"What's to tell?" he asked. "June-Ellen spied a body by some gnarly shrubbery. Claimed to know who it was, when, of course, there was no body there. Except, for some reason, she found it necessary to pester the police."

"Aunt June-Ellen declared it was Bertrund," Leslie stated. "Even Molly's mouth dropped, and the poor thing nearly drove right off the road."

"All bodies the old gal sees are forms of Bertrund in one way or another."

"You know that, and I know that, but she's never said as much before. No, she really thinks she saw Bertrund."

"Like Hamlet's father's ghost?"

Leslie shrugged off a shiver. "Be serious."

"Sorry, dear."

"You think the police drove out there?" she asked.

"I imagine they gave the area an obligatory once-over."

"You don't think—"

"Of course not."

Before Harry could move to embrace his wife, Leslie stepped over to the patio furniture and eased her thin frame onto one of the deck chairs. The south wind rose and tussled her short, dark hair. "Now, why do you suppose Aunt June-Ellen would say a thing like that? She hasn't allowed anyone to mention that bastard's name in eons."

"If I even tried to figure your dotty old aunt's mind, I'd go crazy." When the flames dropped, Harry added chunks of mesquite to the coals.

Smoke billowed immediately. He closed the top, cracked open the vents.

"Why don't we get a gas grill?" Leslie asked.

"I don't like gas. Not for this. The food won't taste the same." With Harry, everything came down to taste. Whether or not it was true that the taste was different didn't matter. Only the fact he thought it did.

Leslie sighed. "Well, you think I should ask her?"

"Ask her what?"

"Oh, Harry, you're dense as a box of rocks sometimes. Ask Aunt June-Ellen why she resurrected her runaway husband."

"I don't care. Give her a ring."

Leslie pinged her empty wineglass with her forefinger. "No need to call."

"What?"

Leslie pinged the wineglass a second time.

Harry caught her eye, understood. "You didn't."

"I most certainly did."

"You're as batty as your old aunt."

Leslie thrust herself up. "Harry Crawford, you're impossible," she proclaimed and marched back inside.

At the closing of the door, however, Harry smirked. Might not be such a nasty idea, after all, he thought. June-Ellen's presence quite possibly could have a limiting effect on future soirees. Most certainly, once word got around.

Harry completed stuffing the twice-baked southwestern potatoes—the whipped filling flavored mainly with chives, cilantro, chopped pecans, minced jalapeño, asadero cheese, and a sprinkling of chorizo sausage on top—then covered them with foil to hold before a final run in the oven. Using an ivory colored kitchen towel bearing Café Noir's insignia—the silhouette of a Bogart-like figure, trench coat and hat, head bowed—Harry dabbed the sweat off his forehead. As usual, he vowed that next time Les-darling pulled a last-minute dinner party on him he'd ring the restaurant and have one of the boys toss together the fete. However, when push came to shove, pride would, of course, take over, and he'd find himself laboring at the last minute on one of his signature dishes.

Leslie's heels glided across the tile floor as she waltzed into the spacious kitchen. "Smells marvelous," she announced, the saloon-style doors swinging closed behind her.

Harry grunted as she wrapped her arms around the back of his neck and nibbled at his ear.

"It never ceases to amaze me that a brute like yourself from a culinary-challenged country can cook so damn good," she added.

"Your flattery is overwhelming."

"Oh, you love showing off." Leslie let go and walked around the island. "And for some reason, you love bitching about it, too."

Harry leaned his thick hands against the butcher-block table. The muscles of his powerful arms rippled beneath the denim shirt he wore. Leslie had adorned herself with a tan, fringed blouse and long leather skirt the color of doe skin. There was also fringe on her tall, brown boots. Feather earrings the shade of copper complemented the outfit.

"But I must say, you look delicious," he told his wife.

"I had to in order for you to forgive me."

"Oh, I didn't say I forgave you."

"Louse."

Harry stared down at his scribbling. There was fruit, a good block of Gloucester cheese, and biscuits to set out. Bite-sized circles of mushroom strudel and mini crab cakes to pass hot. Creamy tomato soup with a dollop of spicy corn hash as a starter. The entrée of lime-tequila marinated steak with red-pepper sauce, the potatoes, a medley of steamed veggies, and a freshly baked loaf of sun-dried-tomato bread. This would be followed by watercress salad with a pecan vinaigrette and, finally, individual raspberry trifles for dessert. Everything, he noted, was either ready or required only a last-minute touch. He was satisfied.

Glancing up, he stated, "Don't suppose for a minute June-Ellen really saw the old boy's apparition. Although, I hear tell that crazy people can tap into sources the rest of us only read about in Edgar Allan Poe stories."

"You're not helping, Harry. In fact, I think my family has finally driven you off your little Tory rocker. No, I've convinced myself that the bastard's simply another face amongst the crowd in Aunt June-Ellen's head." Leslie hesitated, smiled, and brushed a strand of hair from her eyes. "Pour me some wine, dear."

Harry retrieved a bottle of Kendall-Jackson Chardonnay from the refrigerator and joined her in a glass. Doubtful his wife remained unshaken, he nonetheless said, "Splendid. One would think we'd all be used to June-Ellen's demented rubbish by now. Earlier I was afraid you thought it some sort of revelation."

"I didn't say diddly-squat about any revelation. My curiosity's piqued, is all."

"Is all," Harry drawled, then hid his smirk by drinking.

Leslie peered at him over her glass. "You know I despise it when you mock my speech. You may sound like Michael Caine, but you're not exactly descended from royalty."

"Thank God." He set his glass down. "By the way, who are the other poor victims of June-Ellen's ravings to be?"

"I told you last night."

"No, dear," Harry said, walking up to her. "As I was nodding off, you informed me there'd be six to dine tonight. Now, of course, eight."

"You do have enough food, don't you?"

"Yes, Les-darling."

She pecked his lips with hers, patted his cheek. "I'll introduce them as they come through the door."

"Leslie-Alice."

"Well, you shouldn't fall asleep so quickly after sex. If you hadn't been snoring, you'd have heard all you'd cared to about each and every one of them."

Harry had retained a waiter from the restaurant to pass hors d'oeuvres, serve dinner, and pour wine. At the moment, the young man was offering mushroom strudel rounds and mini crab cakes to Franklin Light-feather. A Lakota artist of Oglala descent, Lightfeather, contrary to his name, looked more like he should be snapping a football between his legs rather than holding a paintbrush.

"I only know your work by the piece my wife purchased," Harry told the artist. "I admit I find it intriguing."

Lightfeather nodded. "Intriguing. Good. Implies mysterious." He held an unlit miniature cigar between his forefinger and thumb.

Together they strolled from the den, where Harry had been showing his guest the Native American art Leslie had collected over the years, the new focal piece being Lightfeather's painting.

"Mysterious," Harry echoed. "As in spiritual, perhaps?"

Lightfeather shrugged. "Perhaps."

"You are a spiritual man," Harry said, not asked.

"Less than some, more than most. And you?"

"I rather believe we're all like a bunch of kindergartners jumping up and down, hands raised, and speaking out at the same time, trying to get the great teacher's attention. We have quite a long way to go, I'm afraid."

"Not your normal Anglican view," Lightfeather observed.

"Doesn't my poor old dad know it. He rues the day he accepted the job that brought him here, believe me. In the '70s with the oil boom. He did his time and left. I completed my education and stayed."

The blues of Ruth Brown and Mongo Santamaria, Harry's choices, alternated with the likes of Leslie's ethereal Coyote Oldman across the stereo. In the living room Leslie entertained Colin Miller and Russell Townsend, two prominent Houston-area designers, and Sara Wallace, owner of the gallery that featured Lightfeather's work. June-Ellen and Molly had yet to arrive.

Harry opened the back door, and the two of them stepped outside. He wanted to check the barbecue and allow his guest the opportunity to smoke.

After offering a tiny cigar to his host, who refused, Lightfeather lit up. The sky was the color of a damp wool blanket.

"Smoking inside is quite all right," Harry said.

"There's an absence of ashtrays. Obviously you have a smokeless house. I respect that."

"Very well." He lifted the lid on the grill. The coals were good and hot; the tantalizing scent of charred mesquite wafted from the heat. Harry poked and spread them out even with a long-handled fork.

"What do you do now that you're no longer a private investigator?" Lightfeather asked.

Harry slowly lowered the lid. "How did you know that I was an investigator? That was a number of years ago, now."

"Word gets around." He puffed on the cigar. "And there aren't too many British detectives in Texas. The Donovan case was the big one for you, if I recall correctly."

"You do."

Caesar Donovan, CEO and president of the independent Donovan Oil, had hired Harry to determine if suspicions concerning his wife's fidelity were grounded in truth or not. Harry had grown to hate this aspect of the job, but he was too broke and the money was too good for him to reject the offer. During the course of his work, however, Donovan's wife disappeared. Through some twists and turns and after dodging numerous barbs from the authorities, Harry discovered that Kirby Donovan had been kidnapped by a disgruntled employee who not only planned to extort large amounts of money from Donovan but, in the end, eliminate his dear wife—who, it proved, had been quite faithful to her husband. Harry was rewarded well for his efforts. In turn he used his spoils to buy into Café Noir. And retire from investigating.

Harry set the fork down on the wrought-iron table and crossed his arms over his thick chest. "Pray tell, how does word get around? Are you in the business?"

"I did a little field work for the FBI."

"Oh, really? The big boys."

"Some small-time drug operations, a stolen-car ring. Nothing as flashy as the Donovan kidnapping."

"You are, then, no longer with the Bureau?"

"I ended up with a supervisor named Holcomb, who liked to call me Breed."

Harry cocked an eyebrow.

Through a cloud of smoke, Lightfeather explained, "My mother's pure Oglala Lakota, but my father was descended from your country. My full name is Franklin Lightfeather Suppleton-Greer. I suppose if I'd dropped the Lightfeather instead of the white man's surname, I'd have had less trouble with supervisors like Holcomb."

"But obviously that's not the heritage you identify with."

"My father died when I was very young. My mother and her family raised me on the Pine Ridge reservation. Still, I was quite interested when you broke the Donovan case. Many were angered by you."

"I imagine they got over it."

"Maybe. It's one of the main reasons I'm here tonight."

"How so?"

"I don't usually accept dinner invitations of this nature."

"And what nature is this?" Harry inquired.

"Native artist on display. Feels too much like the Old West medicine shows."

"I see. But this time curiosity got the better of you."

"Yes."

"Over the Donovan case."

"Among other things."

"But you're no longer a member of the Bureau? I mean, you quit and became an artist."

Lightfeather's eyes sparked. "I've always been an artist. Only now, painting is the focus of my day."

"Much the same as my culinary endeavors, I suppose. After all, I didn't simply awaken one morning after a windfall and decide to become a restaurateur."

Lightfeather puffed on the cigar and nodded.

"Still, you haven't exactly addressed my question," Harry added.

Lightfeather's dark eyes met Harry's. Be it stereotype, or active imagination, or maybe even guided hypnoses, for a split second, Harry felt as though he were looking into night itself, through a break in the woods, at a large fire sparking upwards with a solitary figure in shadows thoughtfully circling, circling—then Lightfeather spoke, calmly, almost innocently, "Haven't I?" And broke the bond.

Harry drew a deep breath, blinked the image from his mind. "Well, I suppose you could call it the jitters from the past, but active lawmen, especially Feds, make me jumpy."

"I foresaw my death if I continued on that path."

"Really?"

Lightfeather dropped the cigar butt to the ground and toed it out. "I sense the skepticism in your voice, and I must admit, at times even I doubt my own intuitions. Comes from the Anglo side."

"Perhaps June-Ellen was destined to dine here tonight," Harry mumbled to himself.

Though unsatisfied with Lightfeather's responses, Harry dropped the subject. Besides, what did it matter if the burly Native American maintained ties with the Feds? The artist might be adept at evasion and confusion, but the only thing he'd learn this night would be how the mind of a crazy woman worked.

"What exactly does your wife do?" Lightfeather asked.

Just then the back door opened and out stepped Leslie, leading Colin Miller and Russell Townsend. Close behind, sipping off a full glass of wine, was Sara Wallace.

"Ah," Harry said, "ask her yourself."

Before Lightfeather opened his mouth, however, Leslie announced, "Aunt June-Ellen and Molly are here."

"Here?" Harry said. "Is that why you all darted out of the house so quickly? Pretending there's nobody home? Is the poor dear around front still ringing the bell?"

Leslie stiffened. "No, darling. Aunt June-Ellen's freshening up. Then she'll be straight out."

Though Lightfeather appeared as noncommittal as a brick, Harry took it upon himself to offer further commentary on his wife's aunt.

"June-Ellen sees specters," Harry explained.

"Specters?" questioned Miller. Caught with honest astonishment, he abruptly halted the rise of his wineglass to his lips in order to speak, causing a few drops to slosh over the rim and onto the cuff of his black silk shirt.

"Ghosts," Townsend defined, dabbing at the spilt wine with a cocktail napkin.

"I know what specters are, Russell," Miller chided, though he allowed his companion to dry his cuff. "I've just never met anyone who has seen them before."

Miller and Townsend had been to at least a dozen of Leslie's orchestrated dinners, and Harry had grown quite fond of them as if they were a couple of favorite uncles. Townsend, the elder of the two, had recently hit fifty and, though he remained trim, was at least a head—balding, at that—shorter than the blond-haired Miller, who was about Harry's age. Usually an invitation from Leslie meant she was touting, with her philanthropic zealousness, another artist, but Miller and Townsend—who placed art, especially to corporations, through their interior-design firm—adored Harry's wife to the extent they'd accept even if the artist of the hour painted images of soup cans or celebrities.

"I dare say that, even after June-Ellen's acquaintance, you'll be disappointed," Harry told the designer.

"I beg to differ," Leslie interjected. "Aunt June-Ellen rarely fails to entertain."

"If one manages to keep her enthusiasm in perspective," Harry offered, though he was thinking he needed to get the steaks on while the coals were primed.

"Her estranged husband is the latest ghost," Leslie volunteered to the guests. Harry noted the twitch in her smile.

"Yes, Bertrund Alexander," Lightfeather stated. "Reported missing, ah, how many years ago?"

"Enough that I should say you have a remarkable memory, sir." The surprise in Harry's tone was genuine.

"Only because of the Donovan case," Lightfeather replied plainly. "To crack a job like that, yet be unable to locate a missing man. A relative whose habits you know. Interesting."

"You mean intriguing—mysterious."

"Perhaps." Lightfeather drained his wineglass and signaled the waiter, who'd discretely followed them outside, to provide a refill.

"You, of all people," Harry said, "are quite aware of the difficulty of locating someone who wishes to remain lost."

"Yes and no. Did he have a stash of money to help him stay lost?"

"Every penny we had," an old woman declared from the back door. Standing as if her frail four-foot-ten-inch frame matched Harry's six-two build, she stared forward defiantly, daring disagreement.

Lightfeather nodded politely. "And how much was that, ma'am?"

"Drained the whole damn account," June-Ellen reiterated. "Close to a hundred thousand. Didn't even leave enough to feed the dog." Her voice crackled like an old 78 record.

A tall, thin woman slipped up behind the ancient crone. Her freckled skin was fair, almost matching the tone of June-Ellen's white hair, and her own hair showed but a hint of its former red within the now prominently silver shade. Leslie stepped over to them, giving each a gentle hug before introducing Aunt June-Ellen and Cousin Molly to the guests.

"A hundred grand," Lightfeather thought aloud. "A nice piece of change. But not enough to live off of for life. Not all these years."

Harry locked eyes with Lightfeather. "Oh, I concur. Unless it was invested quietly and wisely. Or used as start-up money. Though, I never caught wind of anything remotely related to Bertrund starting up."

"Your conclusion?"

Harry wanted to shrug, but he knew what Lightfeather was leading to and played along. "Skipped the country? Went someplace where a C-note was a half a year's pay?"

"Perhaps."

Molly guided June-Ellen to a deck chair that Miller had pulled away from the table. As the old woman gingerly sat, Harry realized she'd dressed in black. He turned to Molly, whose eyes averted from his and who also wore black. *Poor dear*, he thought of his wife's cousin, *allows the old hag to browbeat her into anything.*

"Well, I'm tickled to know the rascal's dead," June-Ellen cackled. "Now I can get on with my life."

Harry's mouth opened, but Leslie's glare disengaged the vocal chords, thus stopping him from pointing out to June-Ellen that, at seventy-three, if her ship hadn't yet sailed, it was, at best, dry-docked.

"And what do you intend to do?" Lightfeather asked her.

"I believe I'll write the murder mystery I've always been meaning to," she replied. "People round here say I spin a good yarn."

Miller murmured something to Townsend, who laughed quietly.

However, what caught Lightfeather's attention, Harry observed, was Molly's white face paling even more.

"Does it upset you—your mother writing a book about murder?" Lightfeather asked the quiet woman.

Molly, startled when she realized he was addressing her, glanced at Leslie.

"Oh, Molly's not Aunt June-Ellen's daughter," Leslie clarified.

"No, no." Molly forced a smile. "She's my aunt, too."

"The dear has looked after me since Bertrund left." June-Ellen patted her niece's hand. "That was shortly after Jean-Jean died, wasn't it?"

Molly nodded.

"Aunt Jean was the oldest of the three sisters," Leslie explained.

"I'm the only one left." Almost a whisper. For a moment June-Ellen appeared deflated, then suddenly the life percolated through her veins again. "Can't an old woman get some booze?"

"Most certainly." Harry raised his hand and caught the waiter's attention. "White wine, Auntie?" he teased.

June-Ellen's face soured. "You know better."

"Mint julep for Aunt June-Ellen," he told the young man.

"Don't be shy with the bourbon," the old woman ordered.

The waiter nodded.

"And white wine for Miss Molly," Harry added.

Lightfeather lit another cigar. "Tell me about your book," he addressed June-Ellen. "To me, working with words is much more difficult than working with colors."

"Even after all those years of practice on crime reports?" Harry asked.

"A hacking, two-fingered practice that never improved. Besides, I'd like to hear the dear lady spin one of her yarns."

June-Ellen cleared her throat and grinned like the Queen Mother. "I'd be pleased to tell you about my story."

Molly gently lowered herself to a chair and stared at the table. The waiter returned with the drinks, which only widened June-Ellen's grin, and

Harry instructed the young man to fetch the marinated steaks. Light-feather puffed quietly on the cigar.

"Of course, my book begins with what I know, or knew, and what I knew was a scoundrel. So first I had to ask myself, why would the old coot disappear?" June-Ellen hesitated. "Naturally he ran off with his floozy secretary."

"A good-looking bird, too, as I recall," Harry broke in.

"You asshole." Leslie-Alice tapped a foot.

"Well, if you like them that way," he said.

"And what way is that?"

Blonde, buxom, and beautiful, Harry thought, but he hadn't lost all his senses to say so. "Shallow and superficial, dear."

"And who would fall for anyone like that?"

"Only a man like Bertrund." Harry opened a palm toward June-Ellen to continue.

But Lightfeather spoke first. "Is that a fact? The part about the secretary?"

"In my book it is." She slugged down a healthy portion of mint julep. "Of course, the wife, our heroine, hires a private investigator. A bumbling sort of chap—"

"Purely fictional," Harry commented, though he inwardly winced.

More bourbon slid down June-Ellen's throat. "Yes, the kind of gumshoe who needs the Lord's hand upside his head 'fore he'd recognize a clue."

"Aunt June-Ellen!" Leslie cried while attempting unsuccessfully to sti-fle a short snicker. "I do declare."

The waiter appeared with the steaks.

"Very funny," Harry began. "Now, how would you like your beef, dear? Medium rare or over your eye?"

"Brute."

"Hush—the both of you." June-Ellen drained her glass and shook it.

"I believe Aunt June-Ellen requires another drink," Leslie observed.

Harry doubted the wisdom of that request but still directed the waiter to provide a refill.

"At any rate," June-Ellen continued, unaware of the subtleties sur-rounding her, "the gumshoe charges a small fortune and comes up with nothing. It takes the heroine to dig up the first big break."

"Naturally," Harry muttered dryly. A thunderclap rattled the sky. The air went deadly still.

"Is our ego hurt, darling?" Leslie then turned to Lightfeather. "After enough wine, he'll admit it anyway, so I'll speed up the process. The fact that he never discovered what happened to Bertrund is his unfinished business. Almost kept him from retiring."

"That so?" Lightfeather browsed the darkened sky. "I understand how unfinished business can haunt a soul."

"I'm not finished, either," June-Ellen objected.

Leslie drew a sharp breath. "Fortunately Harry was able to let go."

"Fortunately," Lightfeather agreed.

She cocked her head to the side. "You don't strike me as a haunted man."

He shrugged. "We all go through life with ghosts in our shadow. Some you exorcise, some you don't."

"I suppose that's true."

June-Ellen rattled her empty glass of minty ice. "And another truth is for you to hush up so I can finish."

"Yes, please continue," Lightfeather stated. "This is very interesting."

Harry raised the barbecue grill's lid. A nearly smokeless heat slipped out. "Contrary to conventional belief, fiction's always much spicier than real life."

"Some time passes," June-Ellen rambled, "and come to find out, everyone's much happier without Bertrund's bullying, selfish ways. Unfortunately, much poorer, too."

"Gone but not forgotten," Lightfeather commented.

"Precisely. Until one day the heroine answers the doorbell, only to discover the floozy standing there looking a lot rougher around the edges. Certainly not the Barbie doll she once was."

The waiter returned with June-Ellen's new drink on a tray.

"And how much time passed between when she ran off and then paid this unexpected visit?" Lightfeather asked.

"Oh, a couple of years."

"That's her big break?" Harry hesitated, a thick steak hanging from a two-pronged fork, its juices hitting the hot coals in sporadic sizzles. "You call that uncovering a clue? I'd say that's more like having the clue come up and give you a big old sloppy kiss." He felt Leslie's eyes boring in on him and half smiled. "For old times' sake, of course."

"Of course," mimicked Leslie. "If this were your story, that's certainly the way events would unfold. The old flame who left the detective for her rich boss only to discover she'd gotten herself into something deeper than she could handle. Thus she runs back to the only man whose big, strong arms she feels safe in."

Harry blushed, placed the steak down. "Has a nice ring to it. Unfortunately, it isn't my tale."

"Anymore," Leslie muttered.

Harry said nothing.

Lightfeather squinted his eyes over his wineglass, took a sip. "And what news did this blonde bombshell convey?"

"As you would expect, the scoundrel dumped her, too," June-Ellen replied through a self-satisfied smile. "Took up with some nightclub dancer. A Latino beauty that he himself had hired. You see, after he had ducked out on our heroine, he and the floozy made their way down to Argentina. Seemed he had some connections there due to his dealings in oil and gas."

"One would think our brave private investigator would have uncovered that," Lightfeather observed.

"I'm quite sure he did," Harry put forth. "But imagine all the misinformation going around. And, as it was made clear earlier, funds were limited. Difficult to follow all leads." He lowered the lid on the mass of hissing beef.

"This sounds like a story of misinformation." Lightfeather drained his glass, placed his palm over the mouth to indicate enough for now.

"Of course it is. Fiction is a quilt of rumored truths. And it gets better," June-Ellen added. "After our dreaded scoundrel settled in South America, he quietly invested in a number of ventures, including a nightclub which was called, I do believe, *La Casa del Toro Azul.*"

"The House of the Blue Bull." Lightfeather nodded. "Good name."

June-Ellen narrowed her eyes, worked on her latest drink. "The only good thing remaining in this story."

"Our tale turns dark?" Lightfeather played along.

"It's been dark," June-Ellen responded. "Our heroine has simply chosen to ignore it. Until now. Turns out, she actually feels sorry for the floozy, whose name is something like Diane. She has been used by our scoundrel just like all the other women he's come across. But that's not the worst of it.

"Involved in our subplot," June-Ellen continued, "is another woman, a young woman. Someone like a good family friend or perhaps even a cousin or niece. Normally pleasant and vivacious, this young lady pleads passionately to the heroine that she should let go of the scoundrel and get on with life. Her words are something like 'Let the bastard rot in the jungle.' Quite a shocking statement, especially from such a staid Christian woman, mind you. She even curses out Diane the floozy for bringing the scoundrel back to life.

"This plays on for a while in a Tennessee Williams-ish manner until our heroine uncovers the horrid truth. Right before the scoundrel disappeared, he forced himself on our young woman. An occurrence she's kept bottled up for all this time."

Harry regarded June-Ellen sharply, then softened as he viewed Leslie. A chill rippled through her, and she chewed a nail. Cousin Molly, who'd been staring at the table the whole time, raised her head slightly, then rested a hand on Leslie's arm. Leslie smiled faintly, though warmly.

Lightfeather focused on June-Ellen. "Where does the story end?"

"With a mess of scorned women, of course."

Suddenly, large drops of rain began to pelt the party. At first they were singular and spread apart like someone was tossing balls of water at them.

June-Ellen gazed up. "In the rain," she added.

Harry raised the lid and flipped the steaks. Leslie-Alice ran to the house, Molly at her side, followed by the two designers and the art gallery owner. The waiter opened the door.

"Over a shallow grave by a stand of huisache," the old woman concluded.

"Is there huisache in Argentina?"

"I don't know," June-Ellen told Lightfeather.

"Might need to research that."

Leslie-Alice reappeared, followed by the waiter, both opening large umbrellas. "Go inside, you two," she called, then huddled close to her husband. The waiter did his best to spread the umbrella over the two guests.

"Why did you tell me this?" Lightfeather gently directed the young man to hold the parasol over the old woman.

"Because you wanted to know," she replied.

"Isn't this among the other things as to why you came?" Harry asked him. The sluggish rain began to intensify.

"Perhaps. Who gets credit for pulling the trigger?"

"I suppose any one of them could have," Harry said, "and had a damn good reason, too."

Lightfeather scratched his chin, oblivious of the building torrent. "Is that the case, ma'am?"

"Another Orient Express? I'd be a damn fool to copy Agatha like that," she scoffed.

"Then who?"

"I haven't figured it, yet. And that whining fool Bertrund won't tell me."

"You really do see Bertrund Alexander, don't you?" Lightfeather asked.

"See him? Hell, see right through him." The old woman cackled again, touched her hair.

"And you really don't know, do you?"

"What's the difference?" called Harry. "It's all fiction."

Lightfeather smiled easily. "Perhaps."

"So you were pissed off about the Donovan case, after all."

Again Harry and Lightfeather locked eyes, as the Native American repeated, "Perhaps." This time, however, there was no dark night, no fire, no solitary figure dancing within the shadows. Instead Harry saw a man, like himself, who'd taken his hits, lived a little close to the edge, and was now working to bring a sense of peace back to his life.

Without a word, Lightfeather offered his arm to the old woman. The rain had worked into a full-scale pounding. "Let us go inside."

June-Ellen took his arm. "You think my story has a chance?"

"Yes, ma'am. It has all the makings of a perfect crime."

Casually, indifferent to the rain, they headed toward the house. Lightfeather glanced back only once to see Leslie-Alice drawn tightly against Harry. Umbrella, gripped with both hands, a loving yet almost futile gesture as the liquid bullets bounced off in rapid fire. Harry hunkered over the grill, his expression pensive, an arm around his wife's slender waist. A quick glance between them, eyes deep with history. The stirring smell of meat charred the air. And for a moment Lightfeather almost thought he heard singing. A sonorous, muscular voice. Soothing. The tune vaguely familiar.

Intimate and bluesy.

LIME-TEQUILA MARINATED STEAK
WITH RED-PEPPER SAUCE

a 2½- to 3-pound beef tenderloin, trimmed and cut into 2-3" steaks

Marinade

½ cup olive oil
⅓ cup fresh lime juice
⅓ cup tequila
¼ cup Triple Sec
1 jalapeño pepper, seeded and
   minced

1 bunch minced fresh cilantro
1 bunch chopped chives
2 minced garlic cloves
the zest of one lime and one
   orange
ground black pepper

Red-Pepper Sauce

2 minced garlic cloves
1 small onion, chopped
1 jalapeño pepper, seeded and
   minced

2 tablespoons olive oil
1 16-oz. jar roasted red peppers
heavy cream
salt and pepper to taste

Mix all marinade ingredients and pour into a shallow glass or other non-aluminum pan. Add steaks and coat thoroughly with marinade. Cover and refrigerate for 3-4 hours, turning steaks occasionally.

To make sauce, sauté garlic, onions, and jalapeño pepper lightly in olive oil. Add red peppers and sauté a couple of minutes. Remove from heat and puree in a blender until smooth. Add cream until desired thickness is reached. Add salt and pepper to taste.

Light a fire in a grill or preheat a broiler. Allow steaks to sit at room temperature 30 minutes, then remove them from marinade and grill approximately 5-6 minutes per side for medium done.

Serve steak with 1-2 tablespoons of red-pepper sauce. Garnish with a sprig of fresh cilantro and a slice of lime.

TRUTH SERUM:
A MARIE LIGHTFOOT STORY

by Nancy Pickard

Nancy Pickard is the Agatha-winning author of the Jenny Cain mystery series and the more recent Marie Lightfoot series. She is also the coauthor (with Lynn Lott) of Seven Steps on the Writer's Path, *where she extols the virtues of coffee.*

Not every crime merits its own book, I can tell you from my experience. Some are worth a brief story, but that's all. That's why, for every thousand murders that occur in this country, there's probably only one that qualifies for retelling in a full-length book of the sort I write. I know this sounds cold-blooded, but it's the truth. For me to select a homicide to write about, there has to be an appealing victim, a heinous and fascinating killer, a glamorous setting, and an unusual method or motive for murder. There also has to be a complexity that you might call "plot turns" if I were writing fiction, instead of truth. Considering some of the awful crimes I've covered, it's too bad they *weren't* fiction instead of truth.

My name is Marie Lightfoot, and I write books about true crime.

Maybe you've heard of or read some of them—*Anything To Be Together, The Little Mermaid, Betrayal*. Or, you may have seen the movies made from others of them.

You'll never see this story put to film, however, unless maybe it's picked up by the French and transformed into a little art-house flick. I think it has that feeling to it—interior, intense, intimately wicked—that makes it seem as European as the Mafia.

It will never make it into one of my full-length books, though. The victims in this story aren't the vulnerable sort that appeal to readers of true crime, the setting is more cozy than glamorous, the method of murder is too ordinary, and the motive is as old as time—but then, at heart, aren't most of them?

So why tell it at all?

Well, in part because even ordinary victims leading ordinary lives deserve attention. So I want to say: take note of their fate. But also because, in its own small way, this true story is rich with the flavor of evil; I can almost smell it wafting off these pages as I type—an aroma as sharp and bitter, as pungent and pervasive, as roasting coffee beans.

After three men were killed in Spokane, Washington, in a relatively compressed period of time last year, the police traced no similarities among them save one: all had frequented the Qahveh Khaneh, which literally means "coffee house" in Arabic. This particular coffee house was, however, no A.D. 1000 gathering place dating back to when the Arabs controlled coffee as they now control oil. This was merely an ordinary little coffee shop in an ordinary little L-shaped corner shopping mall, like thousands of such shops and malls. This one happened to be in Spokane, which is a nice place to live and a great place to raise a family. I think even the locals would be the first to acknowledge that there's nothing glamorous about their hometown. Though it's a pretty city, Spokane is no Chicago or L.A., and I suspect that suits most of its citizens just fine.

If the shop was unique in any way, it was only that the proprietor of the Qahveh Khaneh, Quentin Reynolds, tended to take things to delicious excess when it came to coffee products. For instance, there was no tea of any kind sold on the premises, not even the fashionable chai.

"You want tea, go to England," was Quentin's rule.

He says that it was the *Q* in his own name that attracted him to the name for his shop—"I envy the Arabs who don't have to have that damned *U* after the *Q*," he claims. It was for that quirky—pardon the *Q*—reason that he named the shop something that no two customers ever pronounced the same, and also because of his love for and encyclopedic knowledge of anything having to do with coffee, especially its history.

"How *do* you pronounce it, Quentin?" people asked him.

"Coffee," he told them. "Just pronounce it coffee."

Where other coffee shops might sell bagels, muffins, and cookies on the side, Qahveh Khaneh did, too, but they took it one step further by selling only food with coffee in it. In the glass cases and the see-through

coolers, there were Coffee Mint Balls and Mocha Cookies; there were Coffee Truffles and Coffee Fudge; there were thin, scrumptious slices of a
coffee almond sponge cake with an icing made of chocolate, heavy cream,
powered coffee, confectioners' sugar, and chocolate vermicelli. There were
coffee macaroons and a Coffee Fruit Loaf that was similar to a fruitcake
and served warm with butter. Some days Quentin's wife, Norma, made
Coffee Carrot Cake or Coffee Scones in the kitchen that adjoined the
office in the back. Her Whole Wheat Coffee Bread, which she made for
holidays, was famous in the neighborhood. When she and their teenage
daughter, Rosie, baked one loaf after another, the aroma filled the shopping center. The scent gave people a sudden, irresistible urge to stuff their
groceries in their cars and follow their noses to Qahveh Khaneh to find out
what smelled so good. Suddenly, smelling that fragrance, they just had to
have a cup of coffee or die.

Three men did have a cup of coffee there and die.

Upon arriving in Spokane, I visited the police first to get the general lay
of the case and also to get more local feeling for it than I could pick up
from news accounts.

"The victims' names were Jason Moran, Theodore S. Allison, and
Courtney Hannerman," a homicide detective told me, ticking off the facts
from memory without even having to refer to his case file. "Nineteen years
old, fifty-two years old, and twenty-five, respectively. One divorced, one
married, one single, although not in the order you might think. The
youngest one was the married one, the oldest one was the single one, and
Hannerman, the twenty-five-year-old, was divorced. Moran, the young
married one, was Asian-American. The other two were white. These guys
were as different from each other as you can imagine, Marie. Say, is there
any chance I could get you to sign a book for my wife?"

There was a very good chance of that, and since I always travel with a
few paperbacks to sprinkle about as gestures of good will, I was able to
pluck one out and autograph it, "To Susan, With Best Wishes, Marie
Lightfoot." I signed another one to him, "To Detective Jay Choat, With
Many Thanks for All Your Help, Marie."

"This is great," he said, grinning at me.

"My pleasure," I told him, and it was. It always is.

At the time, I didn't know if this case would turn out to be one of those
special ones that might qualify for a book. The detective was so hand-

some it would break my heart if I didn't get to use him as a "hero." He looked the part in spades. On his desk he had a photograph of a pretty woman with three pretty children; oh, I could just see the paragraph I could write about this gorgeous, dedicated cop and family man. I crossed my fingers that the victims and perpetrators would measure up as well.

"What else you need to know?" he asked me.

I'd already warned him that his case might not turn out to be material for a book, but he seemed pleased anyway, just at the idea that he might get to star in one of my books. It would give him bragging rights: "Hey, you'll never guess who came all the way from Florida to interview me." Most cops make my job easy; a lot of them are natural talkers and story-tellers, so all I have to do is take good notes.

"Anything you want to tell me," I encouraged him.

It was a simple story, the way he told it. The three victims had the bad luck to visit the Qahveh Khaneh on days when their innocent paths crossed with the less-innocent paths of a band of five local high school kids who loved to participate in a role-playing game similar to Vampire the Masquerade. Too smart and too bored for their own good, the five eventually picked out random living human targets for their play. One, two, three.

"If they'd just done one, they might have got away with it," Jay admitted to me. "But doing three, they made it easy. They shot each victim in his own driveway at night when there were no witnesses. Same gun. Same caliber bullets."

"You have the gun?"

"No."

"No witnesses, no gun . . . how'd you catch them, Jay?"

"Too much coincidence, Marie. It was a combination of the game they played—they pretended to stalk and kill people—and the fact that they were in the coffee shop when those three men were there. Since that was the only thing tying the three victims to each other, we knew it had to be the kids."

"That's pretty circumstantial," I observed. "Isn't it?"

"Yeah." He nodded, looking comfortable with his own conclusions. "But I'm not worried. We'll get the evidence."

The "kids" were all sixteen and being held in juvenile detention, await-ing their trials. None of them had confessed to anything. The detective described them as "tough little bastards."

You'd think there might be a book in this, about how five kids in an all-American city had gone bad, right? But the truth is, stories about kids who role-play games are passé. And not very many people want to read about kids who dress in black and grease their hair into spikes and stick metal studs into their lips. Kids like that don't make "attractive" or sympathetic villains. When most people see kids like that, their natural instinct is to cross to the other side of the street.

It's my job to sell books. I can't afford to write them about people who turn off readers. Hell, even *I* didn't want to meet these kids. The idea of trying to interview kids like that, kids who are resistant and uncommunicative with adults at the best of times, sounded like hard work to me. But I thought I could still squeeze a short story out of it, maybe based on sympathy for the victims, like that poor nineteen-year-old married kid with his whole life ahead of him.

I set out next to interview the families of the victims.

But by the time I finished with that, I wasn't encouraged that this would even make a short story. Although I felt as sorry for the families as anybody would, the detached part of my brain that evaluates such things knew there was nothing really interesting there. They were ordinary guys living ordinary lives. One of them went skiing in the nearby mountains every chance he got. Another one wrote crossword puzzles and entered them in contests. The married one had been on the edge of divorce. It was all the normal stuff of normal lives. Oh, sure, I could jazz up my accounts of those lives in a way that might tug at the heartstrings of my readers, but that smacked too heavily of manipulation to me, instead of genuine storytelling. Hey, if it's not there, it's not there.

I decided to buy a cup of coffee and then fly home.

What the heck; it's all tax deductible.

"On the house," Quentin Reynolds announced, placing in front of me a steaming cup whose contents looked richer than El Dorado. He was a man in his late fifties, I decided, though he looked a little older than that because he was heavy for his short stature and because there was a certain gravity to his personality. He had a beefy face that looked as if it had been permanently reddened by all the water he'd steamed to make his many kinds of coffee. "It's Café Mexicano."

"Thank you, Mr. Reynolds. What's in it?"

"Heavy cream, cinnamon, nutmeg, sugar, and chocolate syrup."

"And coffee?" I joked.

"Of course, coffee," he said, looking offended. "Want something to eat?"

Afraid he'd insist on giving the beverage to me rather than letting me pay for it, I said, "I'm not really hungry."

"Sure you are," he told me and came back shortly with a full plate. "Have an orange-coffee scone with some butter. I promise, you're gonna love it."

I cut into the steaming round confection with my fork and took a bite. "Mmm, I do love it. Thank you. You make these here?"

"My wife does, sometimes my daughter, Rosie. Me, I can't cook."

"What *can* you do?" I asked him, slightly teasing.

"I make damned good coffee," he replied, looking as serious as if he were telling me he did damned good brain surgery. "You know the story of how coffee came to be?" Without waiting to learn if I did know it, he launched right in. "There was this goatherd in Abyssinia, see, and one day he noticed that his goats were jumping around like somebody'd goosed them. He found out they were eating some red berries off a plant. So he tried eating a berry himself, and it made him feel great. So he takes some berries to the local monastery and tells the monks all about it, but the head monk says it's got to be the work of the devil, and he throws the beans into the fire to burn them up. But this great smell comes out of the fire, and the head monk changes his mind and says only God could make something that smelled that good. So he gets the beans out of the fire—they're nice and roasted by now—and puts them in water, and voilà, you've got your first cup of coffee."

I took a sip from my cup. "Thank you, Abyssinian goatherd."

"Want a refill?"

"No, I—"

"Hey, Rosie," he called, "bring us another Café Mexicano!"

She was everything in physical appearance that her homely father was not—a pale beauty with lustrous dark hair and a luscious red mouth, a mature figure, and great dark passionate eyes. All features would have looked right at home on an Italian opera singer but were startling to find on a sixteen-year-old high school girl working in her parents' shop after school.

Every now and then her busy mother popped out of the kitchen or the office to help make coffee for a customer when the line got long. Mrs.

Reynolds—Norma—was a "hoverer," it seemed, constantly taking over her daughter's jobs. "Mom, I can do it!" was a constant refrain behind the counter.

"Let her do it!" her husband commanded more than once.

"I can do it faster," was Norma's reply each time.

"My wife didn't used to have to come in for this shift," Quentin told me, looking aggrieved. "But after what happened, she didn't want Rosie here alone if I ever had to step out for any reason. I told her I never left Rosie alone in here, never. Norma just had to come in anyway." He looked disgusted, especially as he repeated what his wife had just said. "Fast! Who needs fast? Quality, that's what this world needs more of, not more speed."

I thought it was an amusing thing to be said by a man who purveyed one of the most effective kinds of "speed" on the market. If his other customers felt as I did after imbibing one of his coffee and chocolate concoctions, they could have raced home without their cars. But the man who said it didn't seem to get the irony.

As Rosie waited on a businessman who looked dumbstruck by her beauty, her father regaled me with more "coffee lore," whether I wanted to hear it or not. Fortunately, I did and found it fascinating. If only this case were "big enough" for a book, I might be able to use all the historical stuff he was giving me.

"The Arabs were after quality control, clear back in the seventeenth century," he told me, while keeping an eye on the man's behavior with Rosie. I thought the businessman looked on the verge of asking her on a date; I thought her father looked on the verge of jumping up and telling him he was twenty years too old for such ideas. "They had a lock on the world's coffee supplies and they guarded the seeds with their lives. They wouldn't let any of the seeds out unless they'd been roasted first."

"Really? That seems strange. Why?"

"Because you can't plant a roasted seed, that's why. They didn't want any foreigner taking their coffee seeds to another country and germinating them."

"That must have been hard to control."

"Damned hard. They wouldn't let foreigners onto their plantations, but some Dutchman managed to steal some plants and take them to Java and plant them."

"Java!" I exclaimed. "So that's where that came from!"

All my life, I'd heard the phrase "a cup of Java" to mean coffee, but I thought it referred only to the fact that coffee is grown there. Now I realized there was more to it than that. Quentin had his gaze locked on the next person doing business with his daughter at the counter, so he didn't even smile at my delighted response to his history lesson.

"Worth its weight in gold, coffee was," was all he said, but then he got interested again in telling me more. So far, we had only slightly touched the subject of the killers who used to be habitués of his shop; mostly, all we'd talked about was coffee. Now he took up that tale again. "That happened in the late seventeenth century. In the next century, a Frenchman stole a coffee plant—a seedling—and took it with him to Martinique. Fifty years later, there were 80 million coffee plants on Martinique."

Rosie had brought over my refill by then, and, against my better judgment, I began to sip it. The orange-coffee scone was long gone and every bit of butter with it. I could only hope that the proprietor didn't have another burst of generosity and force on me a piece of the yummy looking coffee cake I spied on the counter. If he did, *I'd* burst. It was clear, as I licked whipped cream and chocolate powder from my upper lip, that I didn't possess a shred of self-control.

Now a couple of teenage boys stood at the counter, flirting with Rosie. They were cute guys, and she was flirting right back at them. I saw one of them lean forward and say something to her. She cracked up laughing, which made both her mother and her father look up sharply. Her mother edged Rosie out of the way and held out her own hand for the boys' money. I couldn't hear the girl protest, but I saw her mouth shape a disgusted "Mom!" Rosie flushed and looked embarrassed as the boys moved on, one of them casting a longing glance back at her.

The teens walked toward us as if they would take the little table next to us, but Quentin suddenly pushed the chairs in toward it and brusquely told the two boys, "This table's reserved. There are to-go cups up front."

The boys looked around, saw no other empty tables, and retreated.

"Punks," my host muttered. "I don't need any more punks."

The two teens hadn't looked anything like punks to me, but at least we were edging closer to the reason I was supposedly here. I opened my mouth to ask him a question about the five boys who used to come in, but he beat me to speech.

"You want to hear how Brazil got coffee?"

"Sure."

"French Guiana and Dutch Guiana both had it already, and Brazil wanted it. So they sent a handsome young fellow to seduce the Governor's wife and get some plantings from her. She hid some in a bouquet of flowers and gave it to him in front of her husband and everybody. And that's how coffee first got to Brazil."

"Amazing," I said. "It's incredible, what people and countries will do to get something they want—"

A shock like electricity shot through me.

I thought, *And to guard something they don't want anybody else to have.*

Three men, one single, one divorced, one on the verge of divorce, and all they had in common was that they visited a coffee shop and were served by the landlord's black-haired daughter. Five young boys, hanging out in the same coffee shop, where they were served by the landlord's dark-eyed daughter, carefully watched by her obsessive, excessive, protective, controlling father and her interfering mother. They were teenagers; they would have come in after school was out, just as Rosie did to come to work. Norma hadn't always worked this shift; her husband had told me so.

But he was always here.

Adrenaline surged through my body, and I knew it wasn't because of the caffeine.

"How about trying a Hot Mocha?" Quentin asked me.

"No." I stood up so abruptly that it made the table wobble. I suddenly couldn't bear to drink another thing from this shop, eat another thing made by their hands, or remain in this man's presence another moment. "Thank you. No. I have to go."

"What about your book, we going to talk about that?"

"Maybe," I told him. "In another time and place."

The time was one month later, the place was the Spokane city jail, where Quentin Reynolds was awaiting arraignment for the murder of three men. But I knew, as did everybody else including Detective Jay Choat, that Quentin had nearly been responsible for ending five other young lives as well, if the original defendants had been tried as adults, convicted, and sent to prison for the rest of their lives. Their worst crimes had been to be in the wrong place at the wrong time and to look like kids that other people didn't trust. But at least they lived to tell about it. For the three men who had merely bought their cups of coffee and come on too strong to Rosie, there'd been a harsher fate.

The time and place for me to talk to her father again was set, as I said, for one month after my first visit. But at the last minute, Quentin decided he wouldn't see me.

It must have been the first time in his life that he didn't want to talk.

Until he refused to see me, I almost thought I'd get a book out of it. But I've had bad experiences in writing books in which a perpetrator didn't want to talk to me, and I wasn't going to do that again. And besides, it just didn't meet my criteria for a full-length work.

So I didn't get a book out of the Spokane coffee shop murders, but I have to admit that I got a hell of a good cup of coffee.

SPICED COFFEE COOKIES

1 heaping teaspoon baking soda
2 teaspoons instant coffee
1 cup sugar
½ cup molasses
1 egg
1 teaspoon salt
¾ cup shortening
1 tablespoon spices (a mixture of cinnamon, cloves, ginger)
5 to 6 cups all-purpose flour (or enough to make a stiff dough)

Dissolve baking soda and coffee in ¾ cup hot water. Mix together all ingredients except flour. Add flour gradually until stiff dough forms. Chill dough for one hour. Roll dough about ¼ inch thick. Cut cookies, using 3-inch round cutter. Bake in preheated 375F oven on ungreased cookie sheet until barely done. Remove from cookie sheet.

Best if frosted. For coffee frosting, use any confectioners' sugar frosting recipe, with the addition of 2 teaspoons instant coffee dissolved in the liquid that is used.

For delicious coffee-based recipes and fascinating stories about coffee, I highly recommend the gorgeous tome from which I got most of my information: The Coffee Book *by Jacki Baxter, 1993 edition published by Chartwell Books, Secaucus, New Jersey.*

Thanks to Jean for a recipe that I adapted to give it a coffee flavor.

WHEN HARRY MET SALAD
by Tamar Myers

Tamar Myers is the author of two successful and very humorously titled mystery series. One is set in the Pennsylvania Dutch Country and features Magdalena Yoder as the sleuth. Miss Yoder recently crossed over for an appearance in Bubbles in Trouble *by Sarah Strohmeyer. Myers's other series is the Den of Antiquity series with the feisty Abby Timberlake.*

I was in the bank cashing a check when an Amish man wielding a gun burst into the lobby. We all stared in disbelief. The Amish are a peaceful, law-abiding sect, dating back to the sixteenth century. An armed Amish bank robber was about as likely as lasting peace in the Middle East.

"Get down on the floor!" the errant Amish man barked. "Everyone down or I'll blow your heads off." Actually, the man used an adjective I'm not about to repeat.

I knew then it was no Amish man. Even an Amish man gone bad would not use that type of language. And another thing, the robber had a mustache. A *real* mustache. Not the kind you stick on with glue. The Amish church forbids mustaches, as they are a symbol of the European military officers of the sixteenth and seventeenth centuries.

At any rate, we did what we were told and lay on the cold marble floor. Mercifully, the robbery was quick and the loot taken only from the tellers. Shouting another vicious threat, the evil man fled but without firing a shot. For a few seconds we lay on the floor shivering, then, one by one, we staggered to our feet. Yours truly was amongst the first up.

"After him!" I cried.

The others regarded me with looks that ranged from dumbfounded to horrified.

"We can't let him get away!"

Their wide eyes told me they were perfectly willing to do just that.

Never one to fiddle while Rome burned, I mustered my anger into courage and charged out the door, just in time to see the robber drive away. In an Amish buggy!

"Don't be ridiculous, Yoder," our Chief of Police said. "There were eleven other witnesses. They all said the man was Amish."

"But he wasn't!"

"Don't be an idiot, Yoder. Why would somebody dress like an Amish man, if he wasn't Amish?"

I prayed for a civil tongue. "To fool us."

"You're nuts, Yoder, you know that?"

I shook my head sadly. The Chief of Police is Melvin Stoltzfus, my brother-in-law. He is also the stupidest man God ever created, and I say that with Christian charity. Melvin once *mailed* his favorite aunt a gallon of ice cream. Rumor has it he was kicked in the head while trying to milk a bull. Need I say more?

I, on the other hand, am a middle-aged Mennonite woman with a good, but rather horsy, head on her broad shoulders. I run a thriving full-board inn in the charming town of Hernia, Pennsylvania, and I know my Amish. My Mennonite forebears were all descended from Amish. My cook, Freni Hostetler, is Amish. I knew that the bank robber was not of the faith.

"Melvin, dear," I said—careful not to let the sarcasm, which dripped from my lips, stain my shoes—"were you right about the Agnes Schlabach case?"

My nemesis squirmed. "Well, she had thirty-two cats!"

"Which didn't make her a cat burglar, now did it? Look, Melvin, I'm telling you, this guy was not Amish. That he thought he could pass himself off as one was as dumb as—well, never mind. The point is, he got away, and you need to do something about it."

"What do you want me to do? Put out an APB on a horse and buggy?"

"No. There's more to it than that. I was the first one out of the door, Melvin, and I saw that guy drive off in a buggy. But I also chased after him. He turned right on North Main, then left on Elm. But when I got to Elm, he was nowhere in sight."

"So?"

"So, Elm is a long street, without any cross streets until you get to Woodbine. I'm telling you, Melvin, that buggy just disappeared."

I'm convinced that Melvin Stoltzfus is a praying mantis posing as a human. His knobby head sports bulging eyes that move independently of each other.

He trained his left eye on me now. "Are you suggesting magic?"

"Of course not!"

"Then what?"

"I don't know!" I wailed. "That's for you to find out, not me."

The miserable mantis arranged his mandibles in a sneer. "Now you want me chasing after elves and fairies, is that it?"

"No! I just want you to look at this from all angles. To consider all the possibilities."

"I've considered, and I've come to the conclusion that your little visit is over." Melvin stood.

I stood as well. Normally I would have made him physically eject me from his office, but I had a ton of errands to run.

"Melvin, dear, once again you're handling your job all wrong." I sighed. "This time, when you get in over your head, don't come running to me."

He had the temerity to laugh. "That will be the day! Yoder, if I'm wrong about this guy being an Amish man, I'll dance naked in the street."

I shook my head, to clear it of the that awful vision. "If the bank robber turns out to be a genuine Amish man," I said, "*I'll* dance naked in the streets of Hernia."

Since I come from a tradition that eschews sex in a vertical position, lest it lead to dancing, I had no intention of being proven wrong.

My inn, the PennDutch, was closed for the Christmas holidays. I was taking a much needed rest, with a good book in one hand and a plate of fudge in my lap, when the doorbell rang.

"Go away!" I called pleasantly.

The bell rang again.

I looked at the fudge, then at the door. When opportunity knocks—in this case, rings the bell—a good businesswoman will answer. Unfortunately, opportunity generally waits to identify itself after the door has been opened.

With a sigh, I put the book down, popped the last two squares of fudge into my mouth, and padded to the door in my plaid cotton housecoat and pink bunny slippers.

"Yeth?" I said to the man standing on the porch.

The man smiled. I smiled back and, remembering the fudge, swallowed hastily and licked my teeth. The visitor was, in the words of my strumpet sister Susannah, "a hunk." Objectively, he was tall, with shoulders broader than mine, and had hips so narrow he could sit in a child's booster seat. A once beautiful face had been given character by years of sun, and his curly chestnut hair was just beginning to gray at the temples. But it was the piercing blue eyes that made me shudder.

"Cold morning, isn't it?" he said.

I nodded, unwilling to open my mug until I was sure the last of the fudge had dissolved.

"Say," he said, "you wouldn't happen to know if there's a covered bridge nearby. I think it's called the Slave Creek Bridge."

I gave my chompers a final sweep. "As a matter of fact, there is—on the far end of Dinkler Lane. But it's closed. Blocked off on one end by a mud slide. Happened almost a year ago, but it doesn't matter. Nobody used that stretch anymore, not since the state put a new highway in to the east."

"Is the bridge hard to find?"

"I'll say."

"How hard?"

"Well, there are no road signs, for one thing. Haven't been since the Neubrander boys hit their teens. And anyway, it's just a dirt road with more twists and turns than a politician's tongue. That's why the state built the highway."

He laughed. "Is the bridge fully enclosed, or open on the sides?"

"Enclosed—well, it's open on the ends, of course—uh, make that one end. The mud slide took care of the other."

"What color is the bridge?"

"Gray, I think. I haven't been by there since the day after the slide. We all went to look."

"Do you think you could show me the way?"

I stared at him. "Surely you jest."

"I'm quite serious. I'd be happy to pay you for your time."

I closed the door halfway. "I'm a wealthy woman, dear. I don't need your money."

The blue eyes danced. "Then how about taking me there for free?"

I gave him my best menacing scowl. "Who are you, mister? And what are you up to? I have the police on speed dial, you know."

He took a step back and spread strong brown hands. "Sorry, I should have introduced myself. Name's Harry Westerman. I'm a photographer for *American Bridges Magazine*. I'm working on a spread, which we've tentatively titled 'The Bridges of Bedford County.'"

I nodded. Bedford County, Pennsylvania, where I live, boasts many beautiful bridges. And the Slave Creek Bridge, as I remembered it, was one of the best—the mud slide notwithstanding.

"Show me your credentials," I said.

He showed me his driver's license, his American Express card, and his BlueCross BlueShield. Then he showed me a book of stunning photographs he'd taken in nearby Maryland.

"I'll give you credit," he said. "I'll list you in the acknowledgments."

"Just give me a minute to throw on some clothes," I said. I've always wanted to have my name appear in print. *Anywhere* in print.

Harry grinned. "Terrific. Hey, I don't suppose you have anything we could take with as a picnic?"

"You mean food?"

The grin widened. "That's what one generally eats on a picnic, right?"

I blushed to the tips of my toes. "My cook is off this week. All I have is cold cereal, potato salad, and fudge."

"Potato salad and fudge sound good. Anything to drink?"

"Milk and water."

"No wine or beer?"

"This is a Christian establishment," I snapped.

"What brand is the bottled water?"

"God's brand. Comes straight from the spring out back."

He nodded. "I guess that will do."

I scurried off to change into clothes.

We rode in Harry's truck. It was a monstrosity he said he picked up for a song after the war. He didn't say which war, but I guessed Vietnam. He was too old to have served in the Gulf and had abs too tight to make it the Korean.

At any rate, it was a good thing we took his truck, because my Buick wouldn't have been able to handle the ruts on Dinkler Lane. There were plenty of tracks, however, which led me to conclude that some of the more liberal Mennonite kids in the area had used the bridge for necking. If they were Presbyterian or Methodist—well, it might have been used for worse.

Harry stopped the truck about a hundred yards from the bridge. The road had one more sharp turn, and we were looking at the old structure almost broadside. Melting snow had raised the creek level, giving it respectable rapids. The bridge, gray like I remembered, seemed to straddle the current with confidence. The crumpled corner of the mountain to one side somehow added to the charm.

As we gazed at the picture-postcard scene, a red-tailed hawk flew into the open mouth of the bridge. At least that's how it appeared. Given the angle of the bridge, the bird may have flown off to the side.

"Damn," Harry said. "That's the most beautiful thing I've ever seen."

"The bridge or the hawk?" I asked.

"The bridge!"

It wasn't the most beautiful sight I'd seen, but I didn't bother to tell him. "So, when do you start shooting?"

He cocked his head. "What do you mean by that?"

"I mean, when are you going to start taking pictures?"

His laugh sounded remarkably like the creek. "In a minute. To tell you the truth, I'm starving. How about some of that potato salad?"

"It isn't even eleven o'clock, dear. That was supposed to be our lunch."

"Then how about some fudge?"

I sighed. "Okay, but just one. And mind the nuts. My sister Susannah shelled them, and she's as lazy as any three teenagers combined. You might find bits of shell in there, and I'm not responsible if your break your teeth."

"Yes, ma'am," he said with just a trace of sarcasm.

Wouldn't you know, he picked the largest piece of fudge? But he looked so happy eating it, I relented and let him have another.

While he ate, I gazed idly at the bridge. The hawk still hadn't come out—if indeed he'd gone in. Wait a minute, it hadn't gone in! A feral pigeon had just flown out of the bridge and onto the roof, where it was strutting around like the proud new father of twin boys. Since hawks like nothing better than a plump pigeon for lunch, it was a safe bet the bird of prey had indeed flown right on by.

"How interesting," I said, forgetting for a moment that I was alone.

Harry licked the last of the fudge crumbs from his lips. "You mind sharing what's so fascinating?"

"Not at all. See that pigeon there?"

"Where? I don't see anything."

I must admit, I have good eyes. "That white spot on the roof of the bridge. That's a pigeon. It's mostly gray, so it tends to blend in. See it now?"

"Yeah, I think so. What's so interesting about it?"

"Well, it's not so much that it's interesting—it's what I thought I saw that's interesting."

Even handsome, craggy men can get irritated, but Harry was merely amused. "Can you please just tell me what you thought you saw?"

"I thought I saw the hawk fly into the bridge, only it had to be an illusion, because that pigeon flew calmly out and started prancing on the roof. If there was still a hawk in the bridge, that winged rat wouldn't be there."

"That's it?" He sounded almost as disappointed as my thirty-six-year-old sister did last year when she learned there was no Santa.

"I don't expect you to understand, dear, but it reminds me of a case I'm working on."

"Are you a lawyer, as well as an innkeeper?"

I shivered at the mere suggestion. "Heavens, no. I do police work—unofficially, of course. Anyway, I'm working on the case of an Amish bank robber."

He laughed. "You're not serious!"

"I'm as serious as a barnful of revival preachers."

"Now this sounds interesting. Please, tell me more."

"Well, revival preachers generally go in for the full fire-and-brimstone treatment. Not that there's anything wrong with that, mind you, although we Mennonites generally don't take to that sort of thing. But that church down by the interstate, the First and Only True Church of the One and Only Living God of the Tabernacle of Supreme Holiness and Healing and Keeper of the Consecrated Righteousness of the Eternal Flame of Jehovah—" I paused to catch my breath.

"Miss Yoder, you're such a tease. I want to know more about this Amish renegade."

"Oh, that. Well, it's a long story, best told over lunch."

Harry patted a stomach even flatter than my bosom. "Then how about it? I know it's early, but shouldn't we eat when we're hungry? I mean, there aren't any hard and fast rules, are there?"

If he had known Mama, he wouldn't have asked such a silly question. According to my particular and pugnacious progenitress, now passed away, breakfast was meant to be served at six, lunch at noon, and supper at six in the evening. Otherwise the Good Lord wouldn't have created those times six hours apart. Besides, Harry had already broken the rules by eating his dessert before the main course.

I looked around for a suitable spot to spread a blanket. "I suppose we could eat lunch now, but as you know, it's only potato salad—albeit a very good one."

Believe it or not, he took my hand and led me to a flat rock that overlooked Slave Creek and the bridge. We were at least a hundred feet above the streambed, and the view was spectacular, but I couldn't have cared less about scenery. Harry's strong fingers were burning into my flesh, and I will confess to feeling weak-kneed. I may even have stumbled a few times, although I won't admit to doing it just to feel his free hand on my back or shoulders.

When we reached the rock, he helped me spread the blanket, and it was all I could do to keep my mind on lunch. If you ask me, picnics are a sin that should rank right up there next to dancing.

After we were seated—there is no way to get comfortable on a rock—I dished the potato salad out onto paper plates and poured spring water into genuine plastic tumblers. If pressed, I may confess that I fantasized Harry Westerman was my husband. A good husband. Not one like the bigamist I inadvertently married several years back. But, of course, that's another story.

I pretended that Harry and I had been married five years and had come to celebrate our anniversary on the spot where he'd proposed. "Here you go," I said cheerily and handed him a plate.

He took a bite of the salad. "This is really good, Miss Yoder. I mean really good. You should publish a cookbook or something."

I patted my bun, which was covered by a white organza prayer cap. It's a gesture I often do when I'm embarrassed. And as embarrassed as I was, I had to tell him the truth.

"It was my mama's recipe. And please, Mr. Westerman, you must call me Magdalena."

"Then you must call me Harry."

I giggled foolishly. "Harry," I said, feeling like I'd repeated a dirty word.

"Magdalena," Harry said, "tell me more about this Amish bank robber. That's a little unusual, isn't it?"

"You better believe it, buster—I mean, Harry. An Amish person would never rob a bank, and even if he or she did, there would be no gun. The person I'm after is English."

He swallowed a mouthful of salad. "You know this person's nationality?"

I nodded. "He sounded as American as shoofly pie—oops, maybe that's a bad example. But you see, Harry, the Amish refer to anyone not of their faith as 'English.' What I meant was, this person is not of the faith."

"How can you be so sure? I mean, there are exceptions to every rule. People always express surprise when the quiet boy living next door turns out to have a collection of body parts buried in his backyard."

"Maybe so, but this man has a mustache."

"A mustache?"

I filled Harry in on the Amish ban on upper-lip hair. "Of course, he could be an ex-Amish man," I conceded. "He does know his way around with a horse and buggy."

Harry laughed. "No kidding? That's how he makes his getaway?"

"It's absolutely mystifying, Harry. I wouldn't believe it if I hadn't seen it myself. That horse and buggy just disappeared."

He snapped his fingers. "Just like that? Poof?"

"Well, not exactly. I chased him around a corner, down a street, and around another corner. But, of course, the horse was faster than I, so by the time I got there . . . well, there was no place for him to go."

"Fascinating. Absolutely fascinating."

I wondered how long I could keep Harry fascinated by my tales of sleuthing. If we were to be married, I mean. My brief union with the bigamist had left me no delusions of my proficiency when it came to doing the horizontal hootchie-kootchie.

"What's even more fascinating," I said, "is that I know for a fact that this guy pulled the same stunt in Bedford, and again over in Somerset."

"Is that so?"

I nodded vigorously. "The Disappearing Buggy Bandit. That's what we in the biz call him."

"The biz?"

"Law enforcement. Like I told you, I'm an unofficial deputy."

Harry grinned and took a large bite of potato salad. Unfortunately, he began to speak before he swallowed. Once we were married I would have to work on that, or he might pass that habit on to our children. True, I am beyond my childbearing years and shall forever remain as barren as the Gobi Desert, but there is always adoption. I was thinking six children would be a nice even number and would fill the empty spaces around my massive dining room table, the one made by my ancestor Jacob the Strong in the eighteenth century.

"Yeah, you told me," he said. "So, no one has the slightest idea how he does it, eh?"

"Not the slightest. It's like the hawk and the covered bridge. I mean, if the hawk really had entered the bridge . . . now, wait a minute!"

He put his plate on the blanket beside him. I, by the way, was holding mine, and it was shaking like the paint mixer at Home Depot.

"Magdalena, you sound excited."

"I am excited! I just remembered there was a moving van on the street."

"What street?"

"Elm. Near the bank. I distinctly remember having to dodge around that monster to get a view down the street."

"And?"

"Don't you see? That's what happened to the horse and buggy! They disappeared into the moving van."

He laughed. "Magdalena, you seem to have quite an imagination."

Cute and craggy didn't cut it right then. This man was about as bright as Melvin Stoltzfus. Thank heavens it was only our first date—and strictly speaking, not even that.

"Look at that bridge," I cried. "Imagine it on wheels. Imagine a buggy being driven into it, and then the bridge drives away. Presto, the Amish man has disappeared."

He laughed harder. "You're really funny, you know that? Bridges that drive away!"

I wanted to hurl my potato salad at him. "That was an illustration, dear," I said through clenched teeth. "It was the moving van that drove away."

"But you mentioned two other towns where banks had been robbed by this Amish man. Wouldn't a moving van have shown up in their reports?"

"So what if it did? The police weren't looking for a moving van, they were looking for a buggy. But now"—I smiled with satisfaction—"the Buggy Bandit's days are over. We may not ever catch him, but his MO is kaput." I scrambled to my feet, still clutching my plate of potato salad.

"Where are you going?"

"We're going back to my house, of course. I need to make a few calls—or do you have a cell phone?" I don't believe in cell phones, unless they belong to someone else. It's not a religious conviction, mind you. Just fiscal responsibility.

Harry seemed to have become part of the rock. "No, I don't have a cell phone," he said, his voice flat.

And to think I almost married this moody man and raised his passel of kids. "Well, then," I said, "I'll just have to wait until I get home."

"But you haven't had your lunch, and I haven't had a chance to take any pictures."

"Lunch smunch," I said. "I just solved the biggest mystery this county's ever had. Come on, I'll race you to the truck."

"Magdalena, I'm not ready to leave yet."

There was an edge to his voice that made me search his face. That's when I noticed that the area between his nose and lips was paler than the rest of his face. A full shade, in fact. I clutched my plate of salad tighter than ever.

"Whatever you say, dear," I said agreeably. "That idiot pretending to be an Amish man won't be robbing any banks this morning, that's for sure."

Harry blinked. "What makes you say that?"

"Oh, it's just a hunch of mine."

"What makes you so damn sure he's an idiot?"

"Did I say idiot? I meant to say that he's even more stupid than that. Imagine trying to impersonate an Amish man by growing a mustache, while all the time this person was surrounded by real Amish men who didn't have any."

"How do you know he was surrounded by Amish men?"

"Most folks don't realize that there are a variety of Amish styles, depending on the area. The nincompoop had to have spent some time in this area, because his clothes were—"

"Magdalena, you talk too much."

"I beg your pardon?"

"Shut up."

"Why, I never!"

He took a step in my direction. "This idiot," he said, tapping his chest, "was smart enough to find out you'd been assigned to the case, and was able to get you out here alone to see just how much you knew."

"Which wasn't very much. Not at the beginning." I took a step back, in the direction of the truck. If I remembered correctly, he'd left his keys in the ignition—we were alone in the middle of nowhere, after all—and even though I wasn't much of a runner, I could outrun the Taliban if my life depended on it. Odds were, I'd beat him to the truck.

He took a step forward. "But now you know too much. Which is a shame, because I was getting to like you."

"Really?" I considered, just for a second, the prospect of life on the lam. Harry and I would undoubtedly have to take a pass on the six kids, but with me as his cultural guide, any part of the country with a visible Amish presence would be our oyster. Alas, even though Harry gave me the hots, robbing banks did not fall into my moral framework.

I knew he meant me harm, so I had to make a decision. That's when Harry met salad—my salad, along with the plate. Throwing it at him was meant as a diversion to give me enough time to reach the truck. I didn't expect to have such a good aim and get the better portion of it smack dab in his eyes. I certainly didn't expect him to teeter in a circle like a kid on stilts, before falling off the rock altogether.

Fortunately for him, he didn't make it all the way down to Slave Creek. A sycamore sapling growing on a ledge about ten feet down broke his fall. Harry was unscathed, but his jacket caught on a supple branch, and he dangled over the creek bed, unable to free himself.

While he twisted and turned and shouted invectives no proper Mennonite woman should ever have to hear, I fixed myself a fresh plate of potato salad. When I was through with that, I had four pieces of fudge, and this time I didn't even bother to lick my teeth. It was the tastiest lunch I'd had in a long time.

And for the record, I didn't hold Melvin Stoltzfus to his promise to dance naked in the street.

BAKED POTATO SALAD

8-10 small cooked red potatoes
   (jackets on)
½ pound cheese, cubed or shredded
   (I use sharp cheddar)
1 cup mayonnaise
½ cup chopped onion

salt and pepper to taste
¼ pound bacon, cooked and
   crumbled (I use turkey
   bacon cooked in the
   microwave—less fat)
½ cup sliced green olives

Combine potatoes (peeled and diced), cheese, mayonnaise, onions, salt and pepper, and some of the crumbled bacon. Put mixture into a buttered baking dish, top with bacon and olives. Bake at 325F for 40-45 minutes. 8-10 servings.

Culpeper County Library
271 Southgate Shopping Cent
Culpeper Virginia 22701
825-8691

YES, WE HAVE NO BANANAS
by Denise Dietz

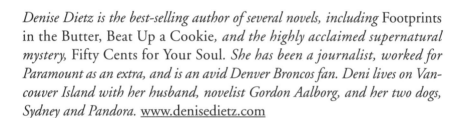

Denise Dietz is the best-selling author of several novels, including Footprints in the Butter, Beat Up a Cookie, *and the highly acclaimed supernatural mystery,* Fifty Cents for Your Soul. *She has been a journalist, worked for Paramount as an extra, and is an avid Denver Broncos fan. Deni lives on Vancouver Island with her husband, novelist Gordon Aalborg, and her two dogs, Sydney and Pandora.* www.denisedietz.com

I looked up at Billy's shoes.

Threadbare jeans sheathed both my rump and Billy's, as he sat in his toddler-sized plastic chair, while my fingers capped a bottle of white shoe polish. The polish didn't hide every scuff mark, but there was no money for new shoes. While I knew that Billy preferred sneakers or cowboy boots, the "slightly used" Buster Browns at the thrift shop had cost a mere two dollars.

"Are you done yet, Mommy?"

Once again, I focused on my three-year-old son. He stood atop the kitchen counter, and from his unaccustomed vantage point he could see that no homemade soup embellished my two-burner stove, no marked-down-for-quick-sale chicken legs defrosted in the sink, and our cupboard was as bare as Mother Hubbard's.

"Yes, Billy Boy," I replied. "I'm done." I bit my lower lip to keep from saying *done in.*

"Sing our song."

"Can she bake a banana pie, Billy Boy, Billy Boy, can she bake a banana pie, charming Billy?"

"Sing the part about his mommy."

"He's a young boy and cannot leave his mother."

Rising from the stool, I lifted Billy down so he could try out his newly polished brown-and-white shoes on the chipped linoleum floor. Watching him examine his left shoe, then his right, I sighed and wished I were newly polished, too.

Until recently I had worked as a waitress at a Mexican restaurant in Manitou Springs, Colorado. Then, wealthy dowager Charlene Grayson called the owner and complained about my service, and the owner fired me. I tried to explain that Miss Grayson was looking for personal revenge, not fine service. That didn't work, so I lost it and said, "She's never even been here. She'd never patronize a greasy-food restaurant with a filthy kitchen and an even dirtier bathroom." Which kind of sealed my fate. An employee should not, under any circumstances, tell the owner that his restaurant is greasy and dirty, even if it is.

To be perfectly honest, waiting tables wasn't cutting it. After rent, baby-sitters, and groceries, I had very little money left. In fact, I'd used the last of my tips for my son's birthday present—a jack-in-the-box. Jack, who possessed an albino face with painted eyes and grin, thrust his head out during the *pop* portion of goes-the-weasel.

Billy said, "Can Jack and me play in the yard, Mommy?"

Yard, I thought, *hah!* What a misnomer! Our pint-sized rental was fronted by one small patch of weeds and one skinny, vertically-challenged tree—nude.

As a kid, I had worn an ankle-length coat, stitched together from irregular scraps of material. My mother called it "Katie's biblical coat of many colors." I loved that coat, even wore it through two years of college. Then I met Billy's father, quit school, and donned a more conventional windbreaker.

Gaudy autumn coats of many colors graced other neighborhood trees, and I had christened ours "Joseph" in a futile attempt to generate some leaves. I guess I believed our tree would try to live up to its biblical name, but Billy began calling Joseph "Mister Banana Tree" after I'd painstakingly tied bananas to its scrawny branches. Now a weekly tradition, Billy would "pick" bananas, commemorating the start of each football game, whereupon I'd bake a banana pie. Then we'd watch the Denver Broncos on our teensy garage-sale TV, punctuating our "Go Broncos" with shouts of "Yum!"

Suddenly, I realized I hadn't given Joseph his coat of many bananas yet, even though it was Saturday. Too many other things had occupied what was left of my mind.

When a potential employer had called my number, a recording rudely stated that my phone was disconnected. My rent was overdue, my car was patched with spit and a prayer, and I kept remembering an anonymous aphorism: *"Cheer up," they said, "things could be worse." So I did and they were.*

"Please, can Jack and me play in the yard?" Billy pleaded, glancing toward the sliver of sunshine that filtered through our one and only window.

"Okay," I replied, "but be careful. If you get mussed, Charlene will have a hissy fit."

"Charlene?" Billy's freckles merged. "Daddy's mommy?"

"No, honey, Daddy's mommy is. . . ." *In the ground with Daddy and Daddy's daddy.* "Remember that funny baseball movie with angels?"

"Angels in the Outhouse?"

"Outfield. I'll bet your daddy and his mommy are helping the Broncos win another Super Bowl. Charlene is. . . ." Once again I hesitated. "Charlene is your great-aunt, and the matriarch of the Grayson family."

"What's a may-tree-ark?"

I wanted to reply that, in this case, it meant bitch. Instead, I hugged my son and said, "Never mind, William Grayson the Third. Today we're gonna have a wonderful time at your birthday party. There'll be cake and ice cream and—"

"Banana pie?"

"Well, maybe not banana pie. But I'd bet my last dollar, if I had one to spare, that there'll be some surprises."

He's a young boy and cannot leave his mother echoed inside my head like bats in a belfry.

Dozens of bats, roused by a bell's frantic clamor.

Bats with fangs.

A uniformed guard stood at Charlene's front gate. He scowled at my 1985 VW and checked my ID twice.

Meanwhile, Billy fidgeted. I knew why. He could smell the barbecue. There's no smell that spawns tummy-growls like barbecue, except maybe the greasy fajitas served by the restaurant where I used to work.

Charlene's estate included tennis courts, a maze of hedges, and a swimming pool. The house, Grayson Manor, wasn't too shabby either. In fact,

I half expected Scarlett O'Hara to burst onto its veranda and circumvent the white columns. She'd be screaming, "The Yankees are comin', the Yankees are comin'."

Which is exactly what I had done three and a half years ago, only I screamed inside my head.

I'd begun my introductory visit to Grayson Manor by sipping tea in its lordly library. Charlene's nephew, William, with whom I was madly in love, kept stuffing his mouth with those silly sandwiches: white bread, no filling, no crust. His stepbrother, Matthew, fingered a brandy snifter. Just your average, everyday Woody Allen movie, except I should have played the maid who served the tea, sandwiches, and brandy.

Crossing and uncrossing my legs, I had controlled my bladder as long as I could, wondering why wealthy dowagers never excuse themselves to pee. Finally, I couldn't wait any longer. On my return from the opulent powder room, I stopped just outside the half-open library door and peeked inside. William had managed to escape, but Matthew was still trapped.

"Katherine is not for William," Charlene was saying, her voice sounding snide and arrogant—even a bit sinister. "She's so common! Did you hear her refer to my Renoir as a pretty picture?"

"It *is* a pretty picture," Matthew replied. "Katie's pretty, too," he added, his Elvis lips issuing forth a theatrical sigh.

"Can't she afford a hairbrush?" Charlene asked with an impacted sniff.

Even though I couldn't be seen, I self-consciously finger-combed my Julia Roberts-*Pretty Woman* mane.

"Katie looks like she could pose for the cover of Ireland's travel brochure," Matthew stated, ducking out of sight to refill his brandy snifter from the crystal bottle at the other end of the room.

"Ireland is where she belongs," Charlene said with another constipated sniff. "Not inside my house—and certainly not engaged to my nephew."

If William had been there, he would have protested. His stepbrother, supposedly the black sheep of the family, had defended me . . . sort of . . . because he thought me pretty. And yet it was Charlene's next words that launched my Scarlett O'Hara veranda run.

"Perhaps I should hire an assassin," she said. "How about you, Matthew? You'd do anything for money."

That night, when I told William, he laughed and said, "Let's elope." Sinking to his knees, he kissed my stomach. "Once our son is born, Charlene will change her tune."

William and I flew to Vegas and recited our vows in a chapel that boasted neon wedding bells; the bats in the belfry came later. After the ceremony, my new husband lost five thousand dollars at the dice tables.

"Plenty more where this comes from," he'd said, handing me slot-machine money before dropping another three thousand at the blackjack tables. The hungry slots ate my quarters, adding layers of guilt to a brain already overburdened with anxiety.

Upon our return to Colorado, William soothed my financial fears beneath the satin sheets that feathered our love nest. Caressing the opulent curve of my belly, he whispered that his son would be William the Third, having previously stated that a daughter would be a breach of etiquette, a social blunder . . . or, in my wrong-side-of-the-tracks phraseology, a screwup.

William was twenty then. He was to get control of his trust fund when he turned twenty-one. But he wrapped his Corvette around an oak exactly one week before his twenty-first birthday, on the same night I gave birth to William the Third.

Funny how the young, especially the rich-young, believe they'll live forever. William and I never discussed death or the disposition of property.

Charlene refused to acknowledge my marriage. William's trust fund reverted back to Charlene's estate, under the terms of the trust. As his widow, my only inheritance was his worldly goods—the wrecked-beyond-repair Corvette, a broken watch, and a pair of gold-plated cuff links. Matthew might have offered moral support, but he must have committed some black-sheep blunder, because it was as if he'd disappeared from the face of the earth.

All I had left was Billy, and unless Charlene willed her fortune to charity—a preposterous premise—my son and I were her only blood heirs. It sounds awful, but I knew the old bat's demise wouldn't effectuate one genuine tear. I also knew she'd defy death until the last possible moment, refusing to believe she couldn't live forever.

Now, after ignoring Billy's existence for three years, she wanted to adopt him and mold him into a "proper Grayson." She had money, power, and attorneys. Where did I fit into this Renoir . . . this pretty picture? I didn't.

Well, in a way I did. If I capitulated, she'd pay me a huge settlement . . . a cool million.

Leading Billy toward the Manor, I glimpsed pony rides. Charlene's perfectly groomed front lawn was decorated with colorful balloons. The food table seemed to stretch for miles. She'd even hired circus performers: an organ-grinder and a mime.

Billy joined the kids around the organ-grinder's monkey, while I walked toward Charlene. Up close, she looked like Bette Davis as Queen Elizabeth . . . and Baby Jane. Her face was as white as Billy's jack-in-the-box. Miniature stoplights ornamented her cheeks. The emerald necklace that circled her chalky throat would have fed and clothed Colorado's homeless for months, if not years. I felt her gaze bore holes through my flimsy, out-of-style party "frock." Thank God I had flung my orange-and-blue Denver Broncos jacket—with its broken zipper—over my arm.

Be cordial, I told myself. *She hasn't got long to live.*

I needn't have conjured up "congenial justifications." Charlene brushed me off as if I were a pesky mosquito. So I handed my jacket to the butler, wandered outside, gulped down some mint-sprigged iced tea, and sat beneath a weeping willow near the organ-grinder.

Then, just like my first visit, I had to pee.

Cursing under my breath, I reentered "Tara." On my way back from the powder room, the desire to resurrect—and correct—the previous scenario overwhelmed me. Peeking into the library, I could see half the room.

A lumpy triangular shape stained the pristine white carpet: sunlight, diffused by the one wedge of wall window not encompassed by green velvet drapes. There was no teacart. No Charlene. No William and Matthew. But I didn't give a rat's spit.

"Who are you to tell William he mustn't marry me?" I said, paraphrasing Scarlett O'Hara's admonition to Ashley. "I'll hate you till you die . . . which might be sooner than you think, you highborn, lowdown. . . ." I knew the word I wanted, the C-word, but I couldn't bring myself to say it. "And you'd better drop your sneaky schemes to adopt Billy," I added, "or I'll commit a breach of etiquette and strangle you with my bare hands."

Feeling vindicated, I returned to the willow, sank onto the ground, and heard the organ-grinder playing something that sounded like the theme from *Friendly Persuasion.* I pictured a young Gary Cooper, whom my deceased husband had resembled. I must have dozed, because I was rudely awakened by a series of strident screams.

Running toward the source of those screams, I found that the Mistress of the Manor had been discovered by a young servant, clothed as if she'd been hired for a *Gaslight* remake. The girl even bobbed a curtsy at me, just before her face liquefied into "Cry Me a River" tears.

Charlene lay on the library floor, a velvet tie-cord knotted around a throat that had once sported an emerald necklace. She looked very, very dead.

Her necklace was missing. So was Billy. I left the room to search for him, but when the homicide detective, Lieutenant Peter Miller, arrived five minutes later, I was told to return.

"My son," I protested. "I've got to find Billy."

"There's a little boy in the library, ma'am," said Miller's subordinate, who could have doubled for Charles Boyer.

Sure enough, Billy sat cross-legged on a cushioned window seat. He was feeding banana bread to the organ-grinder's monkey.

Apparently, Billy had entered the library, stepped over Charlene's dead body, then hidden behind the drapes, now minus one of its tie-cords.

"The may-tree-ark was napping," he told me, "and I wanted to hide Monkey. Can I have him for my birthday?"

"Did you see anyone leave the room, Billy Boy?" I asked, trying not to scare him. A wasted effort. Billy, like the Little Engine That Could, possessed a one-track mind.

"Monkey could stay in our bedroom, Mommy," he pleaded. "I'll give all my other presents back, except Jack. Jack is real, like Pinocchio."

I was about to repeat my question, perhaps in a different context, when Charles Boyer appeared with my Broncos jacket in his hands. I wished him well. There was nothing in its pockets except my driver's license, my car keys, and some quarters I was hoarding for the Laundromat.

Boyer the Cop beckoned to Lieutenant Miller. They talked in hushed tones, then nodded at me. I pointed toward Billy and held up two fingers, signifying give me two minutes, and it was only later that I realized my gesture must have looked like V-for-victory.

Escorting Billy away from the smell of death, into the hallway, I saw that the *Gaslight* servant's tears had been dammed, so I left my son and the stupid monkey in her care. Then I reentered Charlene's pretentious, PBS-decorated library.

"We found Ms. Grayson's missing necklace in your jacket pocket," Miller said, his fingernails negligently picking at the coat's embroidered horse logo, already frayed.

"Are you a Broncos fan, Lieutenant?"

"No, a Raiders fan," he replied, as if somebody always asked that particular question at a Colorado murder scene.

My body shook and my heart raced, but I kept my expression impassive. "I don't have a clue how the emeralds ended up in my jacket," I said carefully, "but I couldn't have killed Charlene. I was outside the whole time. The organ-grinder saw me. He can verify—"

"No, ma'am. The organ-grinder went inside to find his lost monkey."

"But someone else must have seen me."

"Yes, ma'am." Miller looked distressed, as if he'd agreed to sing "The Star-Spangled Banner" at a World Series game and suddenly realized he couldn't reach the "rocket's red glare" high notes. "A servant saw you at the library door. You were angry and shouted—"

"Some lines from G.W.T.W."

"Excuse me?"

"Gone With The Wind, Lieutenant. I paraphrased some lines from . . . you see, Charlene once pissed me off, and at the time, I was much too timid to respond. So today I decided to . . . to. . . ."

"Kill her?"

I had always wondered what quicksand felt like. Now I knew. Even without my verbal blunders, my hatred for Charlene was common knowledge. So were my poverty and my refusal to accept her adoption bribe. I stood alone up to my knees in quicksand, on the deck of a rapidly sinking *Titanic.*

"Where's Leo when you really need him?" I muttered.

"Leo who?" asked Miller. Then, instead of waiting for my answer, he read me my rights.

When I walked into the hallway, Billy clung to me, his legs wrapped around mine. Prying his legs free, I pressed my palms against the soles of his Buster Browns, hoisted his scrunched-up body until his head was level with mine, and felt his shoe polish rub off on my hands. Cheap stuff, I thought. After all this time it hadn't completely dried.

Cradling Billy's rump with my arm, I hugged him good-bye and promised I'd be back soon.

My dream as a kid had always been to ride in a police car, its sirens blaring like one of Frank Zappa's jazz compositions. Funny how reality shatters illusions. For one thing, the sirens didn't blare. They didn't even snore. And Miller was apparently in no great hurry, because his siren-less car stopped at every red light, giving me time to think.

Who would have wanted Charlene dead? Her whole staff, probably. During my first visit, she'd treated them like dirt.

Could the butler have done it?

A long shot at best, I thought, stifling the absurd urge to giggle.

How the hell could I prove my innocence? The monkey! Could the organ-grinder be a suspect? Motive: money. But why hide the emerald necklace inside my jacket pocket?

What a marvelous frame. I had a viable theory—actually more than a theory—but I couldn't identify Charlene's killer without incriminating myself. I had seen enough TV shows to know that if I pointed a finger, the cops would say I was involved.

Whoa! What had Billy said? "I'll give all my other presents back, except Jack. Jack is real, like Pinocchio."

But Jack wasn't real, and Billy knew the difference between "the puppet book" and a jack-in-the-box . . . although I suppose one could call Pinocchio real.

Focus, Katie! A puppet who turns into a live boy, a puppet who turns into a live boy, a puppet who. . . .

I pressed my hands together, forming a prayer wedge. My fingers felt greasy. I shouted for Miller to stop the car.

"So you see, Lieutenant, it isn't Billy's shoe polish at all." I held up my fingers. "It's that makeup that mimes use." I waved my fingers in Miller's face. "The killer must have smeared some on his gloves, then touched the floor when he checked out Charlene's neck for a pulse. Her face was as white as the carpet, so naturally you guys assumed. . . ."

I swallowed. Had the police even noticed the makeup stain? *Let's not go there,* I told myself.

"Billy stepped in the goop," I continued. "The mime never saw Billy, hidden behind the drapes. Maybe he was pouring himself some brandy . . . the brandy bottle is on the other side of the library, away from the windows. Billy saw the mime leave the room . . . saw a white face and a painted smile . . . and thought his new toy had come to life."

Miller scratched at his thatch of dark hair. "Okay, but why frame you? Why not grab the necklace and run?"

"Surely you jest. The emeralds are nothing, compared to Charlene's fortune. If I'm proven guilty of murder, there's no one else to inherit."

They captured Matthew at the airport. He'd wiped his face clean, of course, but left a wee bit of mime-goop behind his ears. He was arrested, tried, and convicted.

Matthew had been sloppy and stupid. The party was a perfect opportunity, the mime costume a perfect disguise. A mime's gloves even voided fingerprints. But he had ignored two traces of white makeup . . . dumb! De-dum-dum. Just the facts, ma'am.

The facts were, Matthew had come to me a month earlier and asked me to help him kill Charlene. I didn't say yes and I didn't say no. I told him I wanted to ponder it. I'd like to think I would have said no.

The facts were, I didn't realize Matthew was the mime. I should have—and would have, had I gotten closer to him. A painted grin could never hide that Elvis sneer.

The facts were, Matthew tried to take out some extra insurance for himself by hiding the emerald necklace in my jacket. He must have heard my fanciful threats to Charlene, then spied me alone, dozing. My only alibi, the organ-grinder, had left to search for his missing monkey.

For what it's worth, that was Matthew's biggest mistake. I might not kill to keep my son, but I'd definitely tattle.

Matthew swore I was his accomplice and offered to testify against me, hoping to accrue a lighter sentence. But no one believed him, especially when I inherited Charlene's fortune, immediately turned Grayson Manor over to an organization devoted to the care of abused women, and provided enough money for years of maintenance. I added a small brass plaque, discreetly screwed to one of the white columns. Underneath Charlene's name it says CONCORDIA DISCORS, Latin for "discordant harmony."

Then I bought the Mexican restaurant where I used to work, gutted its filthy interior, changed its name to Café Utopia, and hired a gourmet chef. But I still use my own recipe for "Charming Billy's Banana Pie."

CHARMING BILLY'S BANANA PIE

Plain Pastry (Single Pie Shell)

1½ cups sifted all-purpose flour   ½ cup shortening
½ teaspoon salt   4 to 5 tablespoons cold water

Preheat oven to 450F. In a bowl, mix flour and salt. Cut in shortening with pastry-blender or blending fork. Sprinkle 1 tablespoon water over part of the flour-shortening mixture. Gently toss with fork; push to one side of bowl. Repeat till all is moistened. Form into a ball. On lightly floured surface, flatten ball slightly and roll ¼ inch thick. (Always roll spoke fashion.) If edges split, pinch together. Transfer pastry to pie pan, trim and crimp edges, prick bottom and sides with a fork, and bake 10 to 12 minutes. Let pie shell cool completely before filling.

Banana Filling

½ cup flour   1 cup half-and-half
½ cup sugar   3 egg yolks
½ teaspoon salt   4 bananas, sliced
1 cup milk

Line pie shell with banana slices, reserving remaining bananas. Sift flour, sugar, and salt into a pan. Add milk and half-and-half. In a separate bowl, beat egg yolks, then add remaining bananas. Heat slowly, stirring with a whisk, until thick. Let cool before pouring into pie shell.

Have fun with whipped-cream topping.

BLOOD TIES
by Camilla T. Crespi

Camilla Crespi has been writing the Simona Griffo series for over a decade now under Trella Crespi and Camilla Crespi. Her short fiction has appeared in the Malice Domestic anthologies, among others.

Henry Cleaver looked like a corpse. Emaciated. Gray. Speechless. Half his face pulled back in a grimace right out of a Stephen King novel. It was really too awful, Margaret decided, as she sat down on the bed.

She touched his good arm. "Dear Henry, what a fix you're in." There was no point in pretending. "You look a fright."

He began to cry without making a sound. Margaret had read that stroke victims often cried at the least provocation. "Now, now, dear, be patient. You're bound to get better."

A groan came out of his throat, and he pushed her hand away, reaching for the chalk resting on the small blackboard next to his hip. She watched as he struggled to write with his left hand. The stroke had paralyzed his entire right side. Margaret leaned closer to try to make out the handwriting. It was very shaky. He smelled of sandalwood, an overwhelming odor. How like her sister to lather a sick man with scent.

"'Help me,'" she read. "How can I help you, Henry? Are you hungry? You always did like my cooking."

He grunted, which she took for a no.

"Do you want your pillows fluffed?"

Another grunt. Louder, more like a bark really. He never had been a patient man.

"Well, be specific. I can't read your mind." If the bedpan was what he was after, she'd call Edith right away.

Henry scratched the chalk on the blackboard, then stared at her with pale blue eyes that looked as if they had turned to glass. All the warmth, the passion for life was gone. Margaret felt a small spasm of regret as she squinted to make out what he had written: "Please, Maggie. Help me die."

It took her more than a minute to respond. "Help you die? Don't be absurd, Henry. Why should I do you any favors?"

Margaret carefully closed the bedroom door. Her hands were shaking with anger. Excitement too, she couldn't deny it. Handsome, rich, and smug Henry wanted her help to die. Who would have ever thought he would come to this?

"Oh, Edith, I can't bear to see him suffer so," she said in what she thought was a suitably sorrowful tone.

"It's not about you, dear." Edith clasped up Margaret's suitcase and strode with it down the wide hall, her footsteps muffled by the small Persian rugs that overlapped each other in a long, straight row. "Henry is my husband. I'm the one who can't bear it. He doesn't like it much, either."

"Yes, of course. I didn't mean. . . ." Margaret scuffled after her sister, her shoes catching on the overlapping rugs that reminded her of the cards she laid out neatly each night for her game of solitaire. She wished herself back in the quiet of her small apartment in Baltimore. No good would come of this visit. Too many emotions and memories rearing up their ugly heads. Besides, her sister was always misunderstanding her best intentions.

"I meant poor, poor Henry," Margaret said. "It's terrible for you too, of course. But you can walk and speak, while Henry. . . . What caused the stroke?"

Edith shook her well-coiffed head. "I don't know. I left him in the library one night and went to take a bath. Just as I was soaping up, the housekeeper ran into the bathroom, screaming that Henry was dead. Thank God, he wasn't."

"Nothing happens out of the blue, Edith. There are always clues. Chronic indigestion, heartburn, an ignored pain that festers, I don't know what else. Well, don't look at me like that. Henry must have had high cholesterol, high blood pressure, something to be reduced to this state!" Margaret knew she was speaking rubbish. She, of all people, knew what surprises life could bring.

"Edith, please!" Margaret stretched out her arm. She hated it that her sister always took charge. "I'm perfectly capable of wheeling my own suitcase!"

Edith swung away from her reach. "You must be tired from your trip. I hope you won't mind, but we'll be taking care of Henry alone. He doesn't require much." They had entered a corridor painted a deep red and covered in photographs of Henry and Edith's busy social life. "I've fired the nurses. Terribly incompetent. I couldn't leave the house for fear they'd steal something, and I was afraid the housekeeper would quit on me if I didn't give her two weeks off."

So! Margaret thought. On one hand she'd been summoned to be a murderer, on the other to play nurse. Edith always did try to manipulate her, and now Henry was getting into the act. *Let's call on dear, dumpy Maggie to get us out of trouble. She's got nothing better to do!*

Margaret decided she would do as she pleased. That meant cooking. The kitchen was the only place she felt at ease, the one place she outshone her sister. She'd make Henry all her best dishes. She would concentrate on soups, to make eating easy for him. There was plenty of nutrition in soups. Split pea soup, potato and leek, corn and clam bisque. And, of course, for dessert, Mother's fruit pudding, which went down with barely a swallow. Berries were plentiful in July. She'd take charge for a change. Maybe the visit wasn't going to be so bad, after all.

"Henry is very fond of you, Maggie. He asked for you to come." Edith stopped in front of the guest-room door.

She was still model-thin, Margaret noticed, and was wearing one of those severe, colorless Italian suits that were all the vogue now and probably cost two years' worth of social security. Her hair was carefully combed in a short bob, the light from the wall sconces giving it a faux-gold glow. Edith had been dying her hair since the age of fifteen. It nearly killed Mother. Her face was tauter than Margaret's, even though Edith was three years older, but then Margaret didn't have the money or the desire to be "surgically enhanced," as Edith liked to put it.

"Henry kept writing your name over and over again on that little blackboard I bought for him," Edith said. "I have no idea why."

Margaret smiled. How like her sister to be jealous, even though she was the pretty one, the smart one. "He wants some good cooking."

"He's on a strict diet." Edith opened the door. "You'll sleep here again. I hope you find it comfortable."

The room was still lovely, but Margaret noticed that the three-tiered chandelier was missing. The double gilt-framed mirrors, the large painting of a summer meadow on the opposite wall also gone. The heavy silk, thyme-green drapes were still in place, as was the four-poster bed steeped in lace frills. Stripped down, the room looked forlorn.

The last time Margaret had seen the house was three years ago, when Henry invited her to attend Edith's surprise seventieth birthday party. He sent the airline ticket, offered money for a special dress—which she didn't accept, of course. She wore her old black velvet—even though she'd gained some weight—and Mother's second set of pearls—the yellow ones that Edith didn't want. Henry danced with her, and for those few minutes before Edith took him away, she twirled back to that June night, when she was a girl of seventeen and Henry an officer in the 8th Cavalry, home from the war in Korea. They danced a fox-trot, and she was sure he could hear the pounding of her heart and think her a silly goose of a girl.

"Are you redecorating again?" she asked her sister.

Edith seemed surprised by the question. "Yes, I suppose I am." She placed Margaret's suitcase on the tooled-leather luggage rack at the foot of the bed and dropped down on the brocade armchair next to it.

"I didn't send for you right away because I was afraid a visit would be too upsetting for you," Edith said, watching her closely, "but Henry has been insisting ever since he's come home from the rehabilitation center." Edith shuddered. "Horrifying experience. I do hope you'll be all right."

"I'm stronger than you think. I'll be fine." Margaret sat down on the bed. The mattress was as hard as rock. She was going to have a bad night's sleep, for sure. "I'm here to help you in whatever way I can, dear."

"Thank you, Maggie. I knew I could count on you. Now, I'll leave you to unpack and rest."

Margaret folded the white lace cover of the bed and lay down on top of the sheet. She closed her eyes and counted to a hundred to bring on sleep, but too many thoughts of the past crowded her head, giving her a headache.

That June night came into focus sharply. The night of the dance, the night she had been sure that happiness was finally hers.

"I want to speak to your father tomorrow," he'd said, walking her home.

Her heart stopped still. He was going to propose. They'd known each other only a month, but they'd been together almost every day.

"What about?" Margaret asked, hoping the croaking of the tree frogs would mask the tremor in her voice.

"You'll find out, but first I need to speak to your father."

"No, no, now," she pleaded. "Tell me now."

He laughed, kissed her lightly on her forehead. When she hugged his neck for a real kiss, he pulled her arms away and a drop of blood fell on her blue tulle skirt. The pin of her corsage had scratched his palm. She quickly pricked herself too. A drop of blood bloomed on the tip of her finger. Carefully she pressed her finger on his scratch—her blood mixing with his.

"You're home now." She had never been happier in her life.

How dare Henry ask her to kill him, to risk jail, after the way he'd treated her. The day after the dance, Edith had come home from college and little Maggie was as good as forgotten. She tried to get him back by pleading with Edith to rebuff him, telling her how much she loved him, how he was going to talk to Dad and then propose to her. Edith laughed and claimed she was imagining it all.

"He just wanted to borrow Dad's car to go on a picnic. He doesn't love you. Whatever gave you that idea?"

Edith was lying, Margaret was sure of it. She always lied. Lied about the money that kept disappearing from Mother's purse, lied about the diaphragm hidden under the mattress, blaming all the bad things she did on someone else. How dumb of her to think Edith would help. Greedy Edith was only too happy to steal Henry from her.

Six months later, Edith married him and Margaret felt as though the sun had been eclipsed. Her seizures started shortly afterward. They made her feel crippled. She stopped trusting anyone, man or woman. Not that many tried to win her friendship. Not a single man. Mother said it was her fault. She left the house only to go food shopping or to the library.

Mother found her a job proofreading for the local paper. Margaret started to feel better after that. She liked spotting errors; it made her feel righteous. Then Mother got sick. With Edith in Chicago, it was up to her to play nurse, cook, and maid. What Edith wanted of her now.

Margaret got up from the bed and crossed to open the window. She gulped the cool late afternoon air coming from the lake. She could taste bitter anger rising to her throat. She unwrapped a caramel she took from her pocket and sucked hard. How many times had she dreamed of Henry's death? Now that it was at her fingertips, she couldn't face that possibility. How would she do it? No, the idea was preposterous.

Margaret picked at her food with a fork. The housekeeper's meat loaf tasted like wet cardboard. They were eating dinner in the spacious, aqua-colored kitchen. The dining room was being redone, Edith said. Margaret had taken a peek. The antique furniture was gone. Thank goodness the squiggly paintings that Edith insisted were great art were gone too. Margaret thought it was an odd time to redecorate the house, with Henry so sick, but Edith did love to spend his money.

Margaret supposed it was a kind of therapy. She told Edith she was much happier in the kitchen. She thought the dining room was too formal and forbidding, too reminiscent of the dining room of their childhood, where they had to eat in silence, their backs rigid while Mother and Father covered their disappointment in each other and their lack of funds behind fraying, lace-edged napkins.

"Good food will perk Henry right up," Margaret said. "I'll have to see what the green market offers tomorrow morning." She noticed her sister drink half a glass of red wine in one gulp. This was something new. In the past Edith had indulged only in bubbly water with a twist of lime. It was unlike Edith to let emotions get in the way of her life.

"Did Henry write anything while you were with him?" Edith asked suddenly. "You'd tell me wouldn't you, Maggie, if he asked you for anything?"

Margaret got up to slice some of that good Amish cheddar she had brought from home. She had also brought country bread she'd baked fresh that morning. "Ask me for what? What would your husband want from me? Chocolate chip cookies?"

"I don't know. He specifically asked to see you alone. He's been so depressed, and I know he worries about me. I was afraid . . . oh, never mind. I'm getting morbid."

"At the sight of me, all Henry did was drool. I felt quite flattered."

"Maggie!"

"Sorry, Edith. I thought a little humor might help."

Edith looked at her as if she'd taken leave of her senses. "You're sure helping me with Henry won't put too much stress on you?"

Suave, graceful Henry never waltzing around a dance floor again, never taking his beloved wife into his arms again? "No stress whatsoever," Margaret said, squaring her shoulders, "and I haven't had a seizure in years!"

"I don't want you to be hurt too. I couldn't stand it."

"If you must know, I brought my medicine. I take good care of myself, so stop worrying. You sound exactly like Mother."

"Sorry about that. Want some wine?"

"I don't drink, Edith."

Edith pushed her plate away, refilled her wineglass. "Well, I'm going to end up an alcoholic before too long."

"You'll lose your figure." Margaret placed a thick slice of cheese on her bread and started eating carefully, pinching her mouth shut after each bite to make sure no crumbs fell on the table.

"Who cares, with my husband in this state?" Edith listened for a moment to the intercom. The only sound from Henry's room was white noise. "He's not going to get better, you know."

"Of course he will."

"After six months of rehabilitation, all he can do is write with his left hand."

Edith's eyes looked up, searching her sister's face. *For what?* Margaret wondered. *Comfort? Reassurance? That would be a first.*

"He's so depressed. The doctors told him he could live for years. He can't stand the humiliation of being an invalid."

Edith was the one being humiliated, Margaret had no doubt about that! No fancy rich husband to escort her to the best restaurants, the Philharmonic, all the society parties. Her fancy friends feeling sorry for her at first, then abandoning her. Margaret could see it the way she saw all the mistakes in the copy she'd pored over for years. It gave her the same satisfaction.

"Maggie, if anything should happen to me, you'll take care of Henry, won't you?"

Half-dead Henry? No, thank you very much. The Henry she wanted was long gone. "Nothing's going to happen to you."

"You wouldn't have to worry about money. Our lawyer has a power of attorney that I've signed over to you in case. You must promise me, Maggie, that you won't send him to a hospice. It would kill him. Promise!"

Margaret took her sister's hand and searched her face. It was colorless, even her lips had grown white. She looked suddenly ugly. "Edith, you're not having foolish thoughts, are you? That would be of no use to Henry. You must stop brooding. Remember what Mother used to say? 'Take a deep breath and tighten your corset.' Be grateful Henry's still alive."

"Oh, Maggie, what would I do without you?" Edith threw her arms around her sister. "I'm so happy you're here. With you, everything's going to be all right."

Margaret's heart thawed at those words. Finally a little appreciation.

"I couldn't live without him."

Margaret pulled away. "I think you read too much Danielle Steel.

Women survive the men they love very nicely." Margaret considered herself a prime example.

"I wouldn't survive. Since the first day I met him, I cannot bear to be without him."

A bell rang. Edith scrambled out of her chair. "I'm coming, sweetheart," she called out as she ran out of the room.

Edith in love with Henry? Margaret found it hard to believe. Her sister was a user, not a giver, no matter what anyone else thought. Margaret knew. And yet she looked desperate. She really did need someone strong to help her. It was a nice change.

Margaret started clearing the table, stopped when she heard Edith's voice on the intercom.

"Hello, dearest. Shall I give you a massage?" Then a few grunts and white noise, then silence. How like Edith to cut her off and leave her with the dirty dishes!

Margaret quickly finished clearing the table and washing the dishes. Her curiosity had been roused. She set off for the hall, where the overlapping rugs lay in wait, ready to trip her, but she stepped over them carefully. When she reached Henry's door, she found she was sweating. Edith's voice was quite loud.

"No, Henry, I will never do that. How could you even think it?" She was crying. "And I refuse to put you in a hospice. They're too horrible! I love you, Henry. If we have to, we'll sell the house and find a small apartment to live in, just the two of us. I'm perfectly capable of taking care of you. Please, Henry, don't worry about the money. As long as we're together, we'll be fine."

Margaret wiped her face with the dish towel that was still in her hand. Sell the house? Worry about money? Didn't they have tons of it? She turned away, dumbfounded, and crept back to her room to think.

In the middle of the night, Margaret tiptoed out of her bedroom, listened in the corridor to make sure Edith was asleep, and slowly made her way to the study. *Thank God for those stupid carpets*, she thought, as they muffled the creaking floor. Once in the study, she closed the door, drew the drapes, and turned on the desk lamp. The desk was covered in Edith's usual disorder. So much the better, she would never notice that anyone had rifled through her papers. Margaret leafed through bill after bill, bank statements, medical reports, and letters from the insurance company, even a folder of X rays. It was going to take half the night to sort it all out.

By the time dawn came, Margaret made her silent way back to bed with a feeling of immense satisfaction. The situation of the Cleaver household was now clear. The medical reports confirmed that Henry could live for years, but he'd been stingy with his health insurance plan, and now coverage was about to run out. Medicare wasn't going to cover him for much longer either. He had too much money for Medicaid, but if he lived for years, not enough to keep the lifestyle with which he had spoiled Edith.

That explained the missing furniture, the fired nurses. Probably the housekeeper had been let go too; she cost $24,000 a year. Twenty-four-hour care cost $7,000 a month. Redecorating the house three years ago had gone way over budget, and then Henry invested in some dot-coms and lost money.

That's what brought the stroke on, Margaret was sure of it. For the first time in her life, Edith couldn't get what she wanted. Henry was not going to get well, and money wasn't going to keep pouring in for her to spend. Well, it served her right for stealing Henry away from her. It served them both right.

Margaret lay down on the too-hard bed and waited for the spasm in her heart to die down. *Please let it not be a seizure.* She reached for her epilepsy medicine just in case. She had to be careful not to take too much, or else she would sedate herself to death. It was all in the dosage.

"Sleep well?" Margaret asked in a cheery voice a few hours later when Edith finally walked into the kitchen. "How is Henry this morning?" She brushed the brioche with melted butter.

"You look like you haven't slept all night," Edith said, pouring herself some orange juice. "Are you all right?"

"The bed was harder than I'm used to, but I don't think I'm the one we should worry about. How is Henry? I've prepared a tray for him with fresh bread and homemade apple butter I brought with me. I'll warm up the milk in the microwave to soften the bread as soon as I put these slices in the oven."

"I can't get him to eat anything. It's as if. . . ."

"As if what?"

Edith dropped down in the chair in front of the kitchen table. She looked haggard this morning, every bit her age and then some, Margaret noticed with some satisfaction.

"What were you going to say, Edith?"

"Nothing. I'm tired and sick with worry over Henry, and I don't always make much sense."

Worried about Henry's dwindling money was more like it. "Cheer up," Margaret said. "I know just how to get his appetite going again. Mother's summer pudding. I went out shopping early this morning and found the most wonderful berries and a brioche that is almost as good as the one I make. I'm taking shortcuts because we're in a hurry to cheer Henry up, aren't we?"

"Henry can't eat eggs, butter, and cream. He'll have another stroke!"

"Oh, Edith, you're exaggerating, as usual. 'Everything in moderation,' Mother used to say, and she was right. We do need to perk him up—and quickly. Remember how he gobbled up my pudding at your surprise birthday party?"

"You insisted on making it even though he had hired the best caterers in Chicago. Yes, I remember."

Margaret didn't hear her sister. She had stopped whisking the sugar and egg yolks to look out of the bay window. In the distance she could see a patch of Lake Michigan, the same gray blue of the dress she had worn at the June dance, so many years ago. They had eaten dinner with her parents before going. Mother had made the pudding especially for Henry.

"Why, Mrs. Hollings, this dish is almost as good and as sweet as Maggie," he'd said after the first bite. Mother had beamed, while her own cheeks burned at the compliment.

"Henry just loves that pudding," Margaret said now as she resumed whisking. "I'll serve it at lunch. It's guaranteed to lift his spirits to the sky."

Edith looked pleased. "Thank you, Maggie, you're a lifesaver. But don't let him eat too much. That stuff is positively addictive."

Margaret walked over to where her sister was sitting. She had come to a decision that filled her with a sense of happiness she hadn't felt in far too many years. She stroked Edith's hair the way she had done as a child when she had marveled at its thickness, its natural wave. "Does that mean I can tempt you into having some too?"

"Oh, Maggie, now *you're* the one who sounds like Mother. Did she ever let us say no to her pudding?" Edith squeezed Margaret's hand. "Of course I'll have some."

Margaret smiled.

* * *

At the funeral home, Margaret had stopped smiling. The visitors surrounding her stared at her with curiosity, some with genuine grief on their faces. She wasn't well-known in the Cleavers' circle of friends. Those who had attended Edith's surprise birthday party barely remembered her. She was dressed in one of Edith's Armani suits. The skirt had been let out and the jacket was too tight to button, but nonetheless, it gave Margaret an air of elegance she had always lacked. She even wore lipstick for the occasion.

Ruth, Edith's best friend, crossed herself as she walked past Henry, keeping her gaze averted from the open coffin. "I still can't believe," she whispered, "that your sister killed Henry and then committed suicide. Why would she do something so crazy? How did she do it?"

"An overdose of epilepsy medicine in Mother's summer pudding." It had been simple really. At lunch she'd dropped Henry's glass. The diversion allowed her to quickly switch plates.

"You mustn't blame my sister. Henry wanted to die. He wrote it on the blackboard and she repeated it out loud. I heard her on the intercom. I gave the blackboard to the police so they would understand. It was euthanasia, not murder. She loved him very much, you see. From the first day she met him, she wanted to be with him always. So you see, if Henry died, she wanted to die too."

Ruth sniffled into her handkerchief. "How tragic. But she does look nice lying in her coffin. It's as if your sister is at peace."

She was the one at peace now. There was plenty of money left to keep her happy. "Wearing one of my Armani suits makes her look so much better." Edith dabbed at her dry eyes. "Poor Maggie never did know how to dress."

MOTHER'S SUMMER PUDDING

10 ¼" slices of brioche

3 tablespoons butter, melted

1 cup raspberries (fresh or
   frozen)

1 cup blueberries

½ cup sugar

3 egg yolks

1 cup buttermilk

1 cup half-and-half

1 teaspoon vanilla extract

Preheat oven to 450F. Brush brioche slices with melted butter, and toast in the oven until golden. In a casserole, layer toasted slices buttered side down, topping each layer with berries. Beat sugar and egg yolks in a large bowl until well blended. Heat buttermilk and cream almost to a boil and add vanilla extract. Slowly whisk scalded cream and buttermilk into egg and sugar mixture. Mix well and pour over the bread. Place a smaller pan on top of the casserole dish, adding weights if necessary, to make sure bread is submerged in liquid. Let stand for half an hour.

Place casserole in a pan of hot water and bake in a preheated oven at 375F for one hour or until a knife inserted in the center comes out clean. Serve warm, topped with ice cream.

Serves 4-6.

No-Star Murder
by Kris Neri

Kris Neri is the much-nominated author of the Tracy Eaton mystery series. Besides her novels, Kris is a successful short-story author and one-third of the delightful Redheaded League, when not mentoring other mystery authors in the craft of writing. www.krisneri.com

Nicky Sarkowski often thought his mother must have slipped on a banana peel on her way to the hospital to deliver him—his luck wasn't just bad, it was a joke. Deals not only didn't work out for Nicky, they crashed and burned without a shred of dignity.

Like that time he decided to cash in on the Beanie Baby craze and hired some ditzy broad to make knock-offs for him. Naturally, with Nicky's luck, she neglected to mention she didn't own a sewing machine. But still, wouldn't you think the hand-stitched, indistinguishable little lumps would appeal to someone?

Even worse, disasters in Nicky's life always came with a one-two punch. Never in threes, like celebrity deaths. And not individually, as isolated bumps on an otherwise even road. But always in twos, like unsynchronized blasts from a double-barrel shotgun. Nicky had spent his entire life waiting for the other shoe to drop—and lately he didn't have to wait long.

The phone on the restaurant's front desk rang. As Nicky reached for it, he noticed a smear of egg on the soft gold tie he'd bought to smarten up his seedy taupe suit. He picked at the egg with his fingernail. Only he'd forgotten that a ballpoint pen had left a glop of ink there earlier in the morning. Now his tie not only sported the remnants of his breakfast, but a sticky black stain. See, a one-two punch.

Nicky finally grabbed the relentlessly ringing phone. "Chez Nicholas," he said in an accent that fell somewhere between bad French and fractured Italian. "How may I help you?"

"You can start by remembering to pay me my dough," a cocky voice answered.

Lucky Duran. Nicky should have known if he received any call, it would be his loan shark. Fortunately, Lucky was just yanking his chain this time. The money wasn't due for two weeks yet, and Nicky was going to need every bit of that time to gather it together.

When Nicky first latched onto this restaurant gig, he'd thought it would be his ticket to Easy Street. Everyone was a foodie today. Who knew they expected the food to be good? Still, Chez Nicholas could have kept limping along as it had been since it opened its doors, were it not for the shaft directed Nicky's way by his old boyhood pal, Red Rinaldi.

Lucky broke into Nicky's troubled reverie with, "You hear me, Nicky boy?"

Nicky could visualize Lucky in his mind: gray silk suit and cocky strut, incongruously coupled with a baby face that looked like it had yet to see a razor, a wiseguy wannabe. Lucky wasn't even a real loan shark. Well, not an established one. Nicky had heard that Lucky even had some civilian day job which kept him going till he made it to the big time in the bad-guy biz.

Still, Nicky would never have crossed the young thug. Lucky was tougher than he looked. He'd put his fair share of saps in the hospital. Even jail provided no escape. Lucky knew guys to do his bidding there. And despite the fact that they worked for him, Lucky still collected every dime those guys owed him. From jail pay, yet!

Sweat beaded on Nicky's brow, and his phony accent vanished. "I ain't outta time yet, Lucky. But I'll have your money by the due date, I swear."

"Make sure you do," Lucky said with clipped dismissal. "I'd hate to hurt you, Nicky boy. But I will."

Nicky couldn't help but sigh when he hung up. He had a plan to get the money, but he'd need a week to carry it out, plus another week with sufficient scratch flowing in to gather together what he owed Lucky. That was cutting it awfully fine. With his ludicrous luck, Nicky couldn't afford to let one single thing go wrong. Not to mention two things.

The door to Chez Nicholas flew open, admitting a young couple who wanted a table for lunch. The girl was a pretty little thing with spiky blonde hair and a colorful sundress. She hung on the arm of a muscular young man in a tight black T-shirt and jeans.

For a moment, in a rare burst of honesty, Nicky considered saying, "Eat here? Are you nuts? Run for your lives!" But what the heck. They were young—their immune systems had to be strong.

With a jaunty little hop, Nicky came around the desk, only to discover the heel of his shoe had fallen off. Well, he refused to fix it in front of the only suckers to grace Chez Nicholas in days. With the menus hiding the mess on his tie and a limp in his step—another one-two punch— he led them on a circuitous route around the empty restaurant, skillfully avoiding the spot where the threadbare paisley carpet was held together by silver duct tape. He deposited them in a booth that looked out on the last of the flower boxes whose plants still had a whisper of life.

Nicky beamed fondly at the young couple. "Not from around here, are you?" he asked in his phony Continental accent.

"You can hear that in our Midwestern speech, huh?" the girl asked with a laugh.

Nicky smiled noncommittally. The truth was, no one who lived in Atlanta would set foot in Chez Nicholas—thanks to the shaft dealt him by Red Rinaldi.

To look at snooty, sophisticated Red, you'd never guess he'd grown up back in the old neighborhood with Nicky. But he was always a funny kid. A little red-haired dandy with a dickey, who would use words like *cacophony* when what he meant was noise.

Red had been just a lowly food writer when he moved up to New York. Over time he became the most revered, and feared, restaurant critic in the Northeast. But Red developed health problems, a heart condition and an ulcer. He returned home and worked only part-time, writing restaurant reviews for *The Atlanta Sun* and various local magazines. But even if his hours and working conditions were restricted, Red still carried enough power to make restaurateurs pray that he'd review their establishments—nearly as often as they prayed he wouldn't!

Nicky had recognized Red instantly when he came to Chez Nicholas. His carroty hair had given way to silver, but his slim build and stuffy sense of style remained. Naturally, Nicky didn't let on. But he assigned his best waiter and most accomplished cook to that table. Red had ordered a variety of dishes, though he only nibbled at them. And he really loaded up on antacids afterward. Nicky didn't take that personally; news of Red's ulcer had swiftly become local lore. But who ever heard of a restaurant critic with indigestion?

Nicky could barely contain his excitement. All the effort he and his staff had poured into Red's dining experience had to result in one of his rare five-star reviews, Nicky felt sure. His hands shook as he turned the newspaper pages on the day Red's column appeared, and he nearly choked when he read it, though hardly from delight. Red had given Chez Nicholas a crummy one-star rating. One star! The review upset Nicky too much to read it all, but phrases like, "Tureen of Ptomaine" and "Sludge du Jour" jumped out at him.

Naturally, business came to an abrupt halt. Which necessitated a loan from Lucky just to keep the doors open. It was then that Nicky devised a plan that would simultaneously allow him to reverse his fortunes, even as it made Red pay for what he did.

Nicky hobbled back to the captain's desk, where he found a bottle of glue and squeezed a glop onto the heel of his shoe. Unfortunately, a drop also landed on his poor tie. By rights, something else had to happen to that tie now, he thought. One-two, remember?

But he didn't have time to worry about his tie. Another phase of his plan had to be set in motion. Nicky scurried to the kitchen door. But just as he was about to push it open, he heard a loud crash on the other side. Heck, everyone in a six-mile radius must have heard it. Nicky turned back to the young couple, who were starting to look a touch wary. He tossed off a carefree laugh, as if to say these things happen all the time. At Chez Nicholas, they did.

Finally, he pushed through the door to where he found his entire staff huddled around a pile of broken crockery. Of course, only two employees remained after the rest of those rats deserted the ship sunk by Red's review. Jorge was a wiry man who penciled a thin moustache on his upper lip, where he was apparently incapable of growing one. Formerly a dishwasher, Jorge was now the executive chef. Annie, a nearsighted woman in thick glasses—Nicky's bookkeeper when there had been a few pennies to count—doubled as a pastry chef. Nicky was betting it had been Annie who plowed into the stack of dishes; he thought he saw some burned cake layers mixed into the broken china.

"Jorge, I gotta go out," Nicky said. "Serve the lunches when they're ready."

Jorge returned to stirring a pot of soup, slowly scratching his hair over the pot. "I don't know, Mr. S. How am I gonna cook and serve?"

It was only one table, Nicky thought. How hard could it be?

"Why you gotta go out at this time everyday?" Jorge asked in a whine. "Right during the lunchtime rush?"

"Never mind. Who's the boss?" Nicky growled. "Get Annie to serve," he added, before remembering that would inevitably result in a huge dry-cleaning bill. Didn't matter. Once Nicky was through with Red, the money was going to flow through the door like water through a faucet.

Nicky scooted out of his restaurant's front door, catching his beleaguered tie on a nail before he left. Disaster in twos, naturally. He hopped around the block to where he left his car. He never parked his rusted-out wreck in the Chez Nicholas parking lot—might scare away the customers. All two of them.

He drove to the gas station he used for these outings. Once in the station's rest room, he changed into the nondescript brown pants and shirt he'd bought at a uniform store. The waistband of the pants was starting to pinch, Nicky noticed. How could a guy so down on his luck gain weight? He was obviously the only one who liked the food at Chez Nicholas.

Before leaving, Nicky remembered to attach to the car door the magnet-backed sign for a nonexistent messenger service. Then Nicky drove to the neighborhood of neat, upscale homes where Red had relocated. He brought the beater to a stop along a curb and waited.

Nicky always parked well away from the nosy old biddy who lived across the street from Red. He'd spotted her the first time he'd come— tight gray curls too rigid to wilt, mean grooves cut between her thick eyebrows, and a pair of binoculars she kept trained on the street. Nothing happened on her turf that she didn't know about. After his first visit, Nicky made sure he didn't arouse her suspicions.

It helped that Red was such a creature of habit and that, as a local celebrity, his practices were well documented in the articles written about him since his return. He refused to work at the offices of *The Sun* or the few magazines he reviewed for. He worked out of his house, typing his reviews on an old manual typewriter he'd used throughout his career, which the publications sent messengers to pick up. The only times Red left his house were to visit the restaurants he reviewed and for the walk his doctor made him take each day.

Like clockwork, Red's front door opened precisely at 1:15 P.M. He stepped out, a thin, ashen-colored man dressed to the nines even to take a stroll in his own neighborhood. Nicky watched as Red pulled the door shut behind him. What was not written in those articles on Red Rinaldi, but which Nicky had discovered from watching him, was that Red never locked his door. If one of the various messengers assigned to Red came by for whichever column was due that day, he let himself into the house and picked up the article left out for him. Well, why should Red worry about leaving his house unlocked, with ol' Eagle Eyes pressing her binoculars to the window across the street?

Once Nicky saw Red turn the corner, he went into action. He drove his car right up to Red's curb and parked it so the sign faced the nosy old biddy. Just another messenger.

Nicky meandered up the path, at the same relaxed pace as the other messengers. But the instant he stepped into the house, he rushed to the bathroom medicine cabinet, where Red stored his heart medicine. Nicky yanked an old jelly jar from his shirt pocket, whose bottom held some fine white powder. One by one, Nicky opened a few of Red's dioxin capsules and dumped half of their contents into his jar. Then he took from his pocket an envelope filled with confectioners' sugar and carefully made up the loss in those capsules with another white powder.

Nicky hadn't skimmed quite so much medicine at first. But then he noticed Red's doctor had increased his dosage. Obviously, Red wasn't doing well on the medication with Nicky cutting it down. Once the dosage was upped, Nicky had increased his take. Red's ticker had to be just hanging on by now.

Though he'd been skimming Red's dioxin for weeks, it was still a struggle to keep his hands from shaking. He had to be so careful, yet he didn't have much time. With the old broad watching, he couldn't stay much longer than the other messengers. And Red's walks were awfully short.

He returned Red's prescription to the medicine chest. Then he held up his own jar of powder. Had he accumulated enough dioxin? He wished he could be sure. He'd gone to the library to see how much it would take to do Red in, but the article he found made his head spin. Indications and contraindications—what did all that mean? Well, there was one point that had jumped out at him, but he couldn't remember it now. Anyway, how important could it be?

Nicky slipped his jar of purloined dioxin back into his uniform shirt pocket and gave it a pat for luck. Ready or not, it was time for Red Rinaldi to pay the piper.

Nicky was jazzed by the time he arrived back at Chez Nicholas, knowing that after weeks of planning and stealing medicine, he was finally ready to put his idea in motion. What he hadn't counted on was the wrench Red would throw in the works.

"Nicholas, surely you can't imagine that because we shared boyhood proximity thirty years ago, I'll overturn my review for you," Red drawled in the preppie accent he'd cultivated even before his time in New York. "My readers count on my integrity."

Integrity? Was that what he called the shaft he gave an old buddy? "Red, I'm not asking you to write something you don't mean, I'm just begging you, pal, to give me another chance."

Nicky kept wheedling, but Red resisted.

"I swore to myself I'd never again set foot in the abomination that is Chez Nicholas," Red said. "No offense intended, of course."

"None taken," Nicky said through clenched teeth. "But that's the beauty of my idea, Red. You won't have to. I'll prepare my famous tomato-basil pesto lasagna with four cheeses right in your own house." Famous? Hah! It happened to be the only thing Nicky could actually make. Some ex-girlfriend had left the recipe behind when she stopped seeing him. It was sheer luck that the dish would serve his purpose.

Then, without any warning, but with a curious little laugh in his voice, Red said, "Oh, very well. You're on, my old friend."

Nicky tried not to heave a sigh of relief into the phone, but he couldn't help it. He did wonder about that odd little laugh of Red's, but he dismissed it as unimportant. Finally, the breaks were coming his way.

He showed up at Red's door the next night, laden down with grocery bags. It hadn't been easy buying that stuff, either. He'd counted on using the bucks the young couple left for lunch the previous day. But according to Jorge, after one bite of their entrées, they ran from the place, threatening to sue. Nicky had to hock some of Annie's jewelry, which he swiped from her locker, to get enough dough. He'd get her stuff back when the bucks started rolling in, he assured himself. In the meantime, she was too blind to know the pieces were gone.

He was still feeling bad about what he did to Annie, when Red yanked the door open. The smirk Nicky had heard in Red's voice the day before was now plastered across his face. It gave Nicky an uneasy feeling.

Nicky started to carry his bags to the kitchen, when he remembered to act like he'd never been there before. He stopped and asked Red for directions, and was even savvy enough to throw in some praise for Red's snooty decor.

Once in the kitchen, Nicky made the pesto really strong, lots of basil leaves and plenty of garlic. That would mask the taste of the dioxin. And he made the filling really creamy, comfort food to lull Red into a false sense of security.

While the lasagna was bubbling in the oven, Nicky opened the wine he'd brought and carried it to where Red sat at the dining table. Red took a sip of the juice that should have been liquid gold, for all it had set Nicky back. Red wiggled his lips like a rabbit munching a carrot as he sucked the sip down his throat.

"A haughty little wench," Red finally proclaimed, "but ultimately, one living above her station."

Huh? Nicky thought. *Is he talking about the wine or some broad?*

Then Nicky served a premixed salad he'd picked up at the supermarket with some froufrou bottled dressing.

"Acidic," Red proclaimed, wrinkling his nose. "You could find better on the supermarket shelves."

Don't bet the farm on that, Nicky thought. But he was getting nervous. If Red really hated the first courses, would he hang in there long enough to eat the lasagna? He was so distracted by that idea that, when Red asked for some antacids, Nicky absently gave him the large bottle he found in the kitchen. Though Red made no move to leave his place at the table, he did keep the antacids next to his place setting and nibbled at them while waiting for the next course.

Nicky served the soup he'd gotten as a takeout from another restaurant.

"The broth is too weak, and the vegetables are soft," Red decided.

Who knew? Nicky thought. If he had any idea the other guys were as bad as Chez Nicholas, he'd have brought along some of that crap Jorge made up.

Finally, it was time for the main event. Nicky cut a big slice of the lasagna and topped it with extra pesto to increase the dioxin dose. He wished again that he'd studied that dioxin article better. And he wished he could remember the point he'd considered significant at the time. But he convinced himself he'd thrown enough medication in the sauce to fell a rhino, not to mention a guy with Red's tricky ticker. Then, remembering the way those TV chefs always dust the plate with so much stuff they look like they'd been caught in a confetti storm, Nicky grabbed a handful of dried oregano from a jar he found in Red's cabinet and pitched fistfuls of it at the unused parts of the plate.

While Red finished chewing the handful of antacids he'd shaken from the bottle moments before, he took the plate and turned it around. "Now this looks interesting," he said, crunching. He took a moment to blow the excess oregano off the plate before placing it on the table.

Red cut a big forkful of lasagna and slipped it into his mouth. He chewed in silence. When he finished it, he paused and took another big bite.

That's the ticket, Nicky thought. *Keep 'em coming.*

And Red did. Bite after bite he ate, without saying a word.

Only when the lasagna was nearly finished, did Red push himself away from the table. "Not bad, Nicholas," he muttered with a surprised smirk shaping his lips. "Truly not bad." He wolfed down a few handfuls of antacids before he rose from the table, a trifle unsteadily. "I'm feeling tired, though. If you permit me to lie down for a while, I'll inform you later what changes, if any, I intend to make to my earlier review."

"Sure thing, Red. Get your rest."

That curious smile returned for a moment as Red paused before heading to the bedroom. "Nicholas, if the messenger service from the paper comes, you'll be sure to give him the column in the envelope next to the typewriter, won't you? There's a good man."

Yeah, yeah, Nicky thought. *Just go to bed, Red. Let the dioxin do its job.*

Nicky gave Red enough time to fall asleep. Then he crept into the bedroom and sat by Red's bed. Through the long hours of the night he watched the slowing rise of Red's chest as he slept—until the point when it didn't seem to be rising at all.

Yes! Nicky thought.

Red was a goner. The first part of the plan had worked. Now to put the second part in motion. For once, a one-two punch was going to benefit Nicky.

With the sun bright in the sky now, Nicky rushed to the living room to where Red kept his famous manual typewriter, on a desk positioned before the large picture window. He planned to write his own glowing review of Chez Nicholas, which he'd leave for the paper's messenger to find. With as low-key a life as Red had lived, it would be days before anyone inquired about him. Plenty of time for Nicky's own review to appear in the paper.

Nicky fed a sheet of paper into the typewriter. But before starting his opus, he took a moment to take Red's column from the manila envelope next to the typewriter. He couldn't believe what he saw on that sheet of paper. Red had already written his revised review of Chez Nicholas—and he'd changed his rating from one star to none.

No stars. None. Zip.

That rat. He'd formed his conclusion about the meal Nicky promised to make for him before he ever tasted it. And even though Red liked the lasagna Nicky prepared for him, he told Nicky to give that review to the messenger from the paper. Anger blinded Nicky. If Red wasn't already dead—well, he'd be a dead man, that much was sure.

Nicky had showed him, though. He committed a five-star murder on Red. And now he'd write his own five-star review of Chez Nicholas. Nicky put his fingers to the keys, and the praise for his own restaurant flowed through his fingertips. He felt like he was dancing on Red's grave.

Once he finished, he crumpled Red's old review and tossed it into the trash can under the desk. He slipped his own five-star review of Chez Nicholas into Red's envelope and returned it to the desk where Red had left his.

It really had all come together. Once that glowing review appeared in the newspaper a couple of days later, business would boom at Chez Nicholas. The bucks would flow through the door along with the diners. Plenty of time to build up enough cash to pay off Lucky.

Nothing—absolutely nothing—could hold Nicky back now.

He thought he heard a sound from another part of the house. How was that possible? He was the only guy there. The only live guy, that is. Just his imagination, Nicky decided.

But suddenly, Red stumbled into the room. "Nicholas, my good man, can you help me? I feel woozy."

If Nicky hadn't been sitting at Red's desk, he would have collapsed. Red was alive! Not just alive, but getting around pretty good for a guy who took in a truckload of dioxin. All at once the information from that article he'd read came flooding back to Nicky. Antacids impede the absorption of dioxin, the article had warned. The richness of Nicky's meal, which he needed to hide the dioxin—was the very element that necessitated all those antacids, and they negated the dioxin. Talk about a vicious circle!

Red seemed to become more alert, as a frown creased his forehead. "Nicholas, what are you doing at my desk?"

No, Nicky thought. The one-two punch was not going to knock him out again. Not this time. When Red staggered toward him, Nicky jumped to his feet. He grabbed the heavy manual typewriter and swung it at Red's head. Blood shot out in every direction, and Red fell dead at Nicky's feet.

Not a pretty murder, Nicky thought. But it got the job done. He could still pull this off. He'd just have to hide Red's body until—

Without warning, the front door opened and a man in the uniform of a messenger service, with a cap pulled low over his face, blew into the room. "LD messenger service, Mr. Rinaldi," a voice oddly familiar to Nicky rang out. "Here to pick up your column."

The messenger automatically headed in the direction of the desk, where Red had always left his column for pickup. But he stopped a few feet into the room and stared at Nicky, still clutching the bloody typewriter. And then at the body at his feet.

"Is he . . . dead?" the messenger asked. "Nicky boy, you done a bad thing."

Nicky boy, Nicky thought. How did this messenger know him? But there was only one person who called him Nicky boy.

Nicky peered below the bill of the messenger's cap. "Lucky?" So this was Lucky's day job.

"In living color," Lucky said in his cocky way. "Which is more than I can say for this poor slob." He gestured to where Red's body lay on the floor.

"Lucky, you gotta help me," Nicky cried, still unconsciously gesturing with the heavy typewriter.

With a impudent grin, Lucky said, "Me, Nicky boy—I'd be glad to. But you killed him before an audience." He gestured to the big picture window. "I guarantee you the old lady with the binoculars has already—"

Even before Lucky could finish that thought, the sound of approaching police sirens could be heard.

"But look at it this way, Nicky boy. You and me are gonna get really close, since you'll be my collection man in the joint—till you pay off every last cent you owe me."

As the patrol cars screeched to a halt outside the open front door, Nicky thought he could hear the double blast of a shotgun going off inside his head.

The one-two punch had done him again.

TOMATO-BASIL PESTO AND FOUR-CHEESE LASAGNA

2 cups tightly packed basil leaves	½ cup olive oil
½ cup grated Romano cheese	¼ cup pine nuts
3 cloves garlic	2 cups canned tomatoes

To make the sauce, combine basil leaves, cheese, garlic, and olive oil together in a food processor. Process well, scraping mixture off the sides of the bowl as needed. Add nuts and process until nuts are chopped into small pieces. Do not over-process; the nuts should be visible. Chop drained canned tomatoes into small pieces. Reserve the can with juice until the end. Stir tomato pieces into the pesto.

To make the filling, mix together in a large mixing bowl:

1 cup soft ricotta cheese	2 extra-large eggs, beaten well
½ cup grated mozzarella cheese	2 tablespoons chopped fresh
½ cup grated Romano cheese	parsley
½ cup grated asiago cheese	salt & pepper to taste

To assemble, spread a little of the pesto on the bottom of a square or rectangular baking dish. Cover the bottom of the pan with a layer of no-bake lasagna noodles. Spread ¼ of the cheese mixture evenly over the noodles. Dribble a small amount of pesto evenly over the cheese. Repeat until all the cheese mixture has been spread between lasagna noodle layers, and about ⅔-¾ of the pesto has been used. Cover final cheese layer with lasagna noodles. Pour the remaining pesto over the top lasagna noodles, covering completely. If you haven't reserved enough pesto, you can thin the sauce with a little of the juice you reserved from the canned tomatoes.

Cover with aluminum foil and bake for half an hour at 350F. Remove foil and sprinkle ¼ cup grated mozzarella over the top. Bake for an additional half hour, or until the center is hot and bubbly. Remove from oven and wait at least 5 minutes to let cheese set before cutting.

BEST SERVED CHILLED
by Robert Perry

Robert Perry is happily married to a wife with shellfish allergies. He would never ever mistakenly steam shrimp in the house or otherwise endanger her life. He currently works for a marketing agency. He has been published in numerous small-press magazines and anthologies, including Canine Christmas, *by the editor of this fine anthology. He and his wife are also amateur chefs, own a Doberman, and are terrorized by a four-year-old who channels Clarence Darrow to get out of whatever current situation he was tangentially involved in but not directly responsible for.*

It would have been easy to play off of her food allergy, slipping delicate flakes of tender crab into the gruyère, wine, and garlic sauce lightly drizzled over the al dente penne, watching her face turn red then blue as her trachea closed off. Her visage would complement the fresh steamed green of the asparagus spears and the garnish of red and yellow pepper strips, assuming her frantic clawing did not dislodge her plate from the table. The warm glow of the scene playing out in my mind quickly chilled at the thought of the police interrogation that would follow. I doubted anyone would believe that I did not know of her deadly shellfish allergy, nor would they believe I had mistakenly switched real crab for the redfish substitute that could only be called "faux crab" by people who would call Velveeta "cheese" without breaking into derisive snorts.

Veronica had not driven me to this. Few things in life were so simple that one cause could be singled out. A long litany of slights and abuses, imagined and real, had been accumulated on both sides, as with any relationship where people are intimately kept in close proximity. Divorce was an option of last resort, somewhere below Walter Mitty-ish fantasies of

painful convulsions and twisted sheet metal sprinkled with shattered glass
and bodies on asphalt. I was not privy to her thoughts, though I imagined they, too, involved stray sniper shots and flesh roasted in a smoke-
filled building, if only to assuage my guilt over my own fantasies.

Divorce was the ultimate confession of failure, a dish neither of us
would eat, no matter how well seasoned with the statistics of others
brought down. To divorce would be to lose. Living in hate, in a pact of
mutually assured destruction, was less a failure than a norm. And murder—an untraceable murder—would be the ultimate victory. Even an
accident would not be as sweet, a deus ex machina that took no skill and
somehow lessened the feeling of victory that pulling off a murder would
bring.

"The garlic is just a hair singed, honey." Veronica smiled, a languid
contempt hidden beneath a pleasant gesture. "Gives the sauce a slightly
bitter taste. Perhaps thirty seconds less in the olive oil would have served
you better. This would be a perfect dish to serve tomorrow, with strips of
grilled chicken."

"I concur. Perhaps with the chocolate almond soufflé you made several weeks ago," I said, mentioning a soufflé she had baked that had caught
an unfortunate blast of cool air when I opened the window near the oven.
The guests had all assured her that it was delectable, but both of us could
read the schadenfreude dripping from their eyes, none happier than I to
drink deeply of her aesthetic failure.

Hardness crept behind her frozen smile. Point scored. Game even
again. I watched a meteorite crash through our roof and plow into her
skull, leaving her headless corpse holding a fork in her right hand, poised
just above her plate. Shrugging off the smile that started to play across
my face and a momentary discomfort that ran through my shoulder, I
cleared my eyes to see her whole again.

I stood and carried my plate to the main sink, my back to her, and
wondered at the target I presented. But subtlety was her game as much as
mine; a gun or knife would be déclassé and vulgar. I had suspected her of
using poisons several months ago when she started cutting into my meal-
preparation days, making dinner for us five days a week rather than three,
but my continued good health and a quick chemical analysis by a friend at
the local university belied the guess.

Oddly, the sauce was inflicting major heartburn upon me, a curse I had
not suffered until recently. I refused to give in, however, and take an

antacid. Instead, I fetched a glass of Evian and some wheat wafers in hopes they would give a better base for absorption.

"Heartburn again, dear?" Veronica inquired.

I quietly cursed her perceptiveness and sat back across from her. "A touch of discomfort, nothing more."

She studied my face as I studied hers.

"I must run to Kera's," she said. "Do you need help cleaning before I go visit her?"

I shook my head. In times past, before the blooming hatred, we had always reciprocated on chores; a dinner fixed by one was a dinner cleaned up by the other. Recently, though, it had been me cleaning no matter who cooked, as she always had appointments to attend, friends to meet, or commitments to honor. As it served only to seal my feelings on the cross I bear, I rather relished the self-elected martyrdom even as I grew to despise her even more.

Another man might have suspected an affair. I was indifferent. If she was frequenting some sordid love nest with a paramour, the behavior was no better than I expected. At least she was not bowling or performing step aerobics at some social salon bedecked with Nautilus equipment. As much as the thought of Ver on an exercise bike amused me, chances were better that she was at *La Boheme*—or at least in the lobby, so as to be seen without having to endure the actual spectacle—rather than deigning to perspire at a gym. And both were unlikely, given her desire to save face, pretending her facade of a marriage was no more taut and strained than the skin on a face-lift's countenance.

She paused to pull on my leather jacket, from the coat rack. Hers was, no doubt, at the cleaner again for its monthly treatment of water repellent. She also grabbed a baseball cap, stenciled with some museum fund-raiser she had attended, its pedigree her ironic nod to the vox populi and necessary for keeping her hair from looking too windblown after exiting her convertible.

For a moment, the sound of car doors and the garage door interrupted the pleasant thoughts, directing my attention to her place setting. Her wineglass was drained, a small drop pooled on the bottom. Her dinner looked stirred around the plate, the finicky machinations of a child attempting to seem sated before running off to indulge in Twinkies or Ben & Jerry's Chocolate Chip Cookie Dough Ice Cream.

When she was gone, I stood again, feeling a gas bubble expand and push inside my chest. Noted and catalogued, I let it slide to the back of my consciousness and studied the two plates, two forks, two knives, two glasses—hers wine, mine water—and three pots with accompanying utensils that made up the skeleton of our dinner. She was gone again, a minor death, not in the French sense, but in the real sense of absence, of fear and loneliness and anger. It was worse when she was here—I experienced all of the same emotions, except her corpse was animated.

I thought again of shrimp, of scallops, crab, and oysters. I wondered how much allergen it takes to produce anaphylactic shock, and if it would kill or simply disable. The thought slipped away as the difficulty of introducing the substance while feigning ignorance rose once again to the forefront. I wondered if the allergen proteins were excreted in any of my bodily fluids. Since Ver had shown an unexpected predilection lately for my bodily fluids, perhaps I could consume a massive amount of buttered crustaceans and deliver death with my own petit mort. A new take on the lethal injection.

I rinsed the dirty dishes, listening to the water rush from the faucet and cascade over stainless steel, copper, and Pfaltzgraff plates in the Midnight Sun pattern, and feeling the hot embrace of liquid over my fingers. Something was wrong.

Opening my eyes, placing the plate into the sink, and shutting off the water, I listened and looked around. A spot in our knife rack caught my attention, an empty spot where a ten-inch chef's knife should have resided. The knife was not in the sink, nor, when I opened the door where it should not be, in the dishwasher. Although Veronica still occasionally deposited a knife inside the verboten hallows of the dishwasher, I had exploded enough times that she did not usually place the Wüsthof-Trident cutlery inside. Which only added to my current confusion, since knives that large and heavy did not easily disappear.

My at-first-casual rifling through drawers and cabinetry turned more frenzied with each successive failure until I found myself looking in such odd locations as the ice-maker unit inside the freezer, the wine cabinet, and the recycling bin. When I observed all signs of logic slipping away from my search locations list, I paused. There was no reason to be upset, other than my own guilt for dreaming of her death and the unproven suspicion she wished me dead.

I sat down again. If I were a knife, where would I be? Veronica's neck. A quick slice, 180 degrees, spurting arteries, her head almost ripped off by the savagery of the attack. Then washed and dropped into the river or a Dumpster on the opposite side of town. Ah, to be a knife.

The kitchen straightened, the dishes placed in receptive racks, I walked into the front room. *Her* front room, I thought, with no traces of my tastes apparent behind the deep blue leather sofa, above the golden hardwood floor, or in the forced casual scattering of *Condé Nast Travelers* and *Robb Reports* upon the glass-topped antique coffee table. The room felt wrong, but only in its phony pretensions to a social class we were not part of, certainly not in its aesthetics.

A recalled comment from dinner forced me back into the kitchen to start preparation of dishes for the next day's fete. The menu was carefully arranged in a binder, along with the appropriate recipes. I looked it over, then placed water on to boil. I pulled out ingredients I would need, then wandered, in need of some respite before tackling the thought of Ver's friends ruminating in our dining room.

I walked into my room, my office and den. Still tasteful but obviously used, with discarded paper stacked in trays by the printer for recycling when printing drafts. My desk was a valueless antique, dark cherry wood in vivid contrast to the golden floor beneath. Scratches and drips of paint marred its sides and surface from years of use, first in my parents' basement, then in my first apartment, and finally in my suburban gulag, where it seemed a part of me but not the surroundings. A brown leather office chair held dictionaries and thesauri and a scattering of other reference books, while *my* chair—one I had chosen rather than the gift foisted upon me as a suggestion of appropriateness—invited me to sit, lean back, and read or write.

A Mac sat in its box, unopened and unwanted in its designer blueberry hue and feeble functionality, while two simple gray boxes hummed between the printer desk and my writing desk. One box was loaded with Linux and served as a teaching tool and firewall, where I could play at being a programmer while avoiding social interactions with my spouse; the other was game box and production machine, from where I could send my thoughts, carefully considered and revised until they seemed more profound than they were, out to a hostile audience. Veronica never entered the room, a maintained pout since I had rejected her Apple gift (a word whose German definition, "poison," was more correct when dealing with Ver than its English connotations), opting for my beige and gray machines that did not complement the curtains, the lamp shade (since stuck on a shelf, replaced by a sleek black-and-chrome lamp), nor the pretentious faux avant-garde posters now partially covered with a Jackie Chan poster and Big Bad Voodoo Daddy show card.

I sat and touched the mouse as I listened to distant sirens screaming to answer the calls for help from spouses who'd survived another round of physical abuse, or bicyclists mowed down by idiots in SUVs discussing movie times on their phones with dates they would see in person mere minutes later. A sudden impulse to use the phone hit me, though I had no one to call. I toyed with the silver handpiece a moment before turning it on, to hear nothing.

It took only moments to determine it was unplugged, from both the electric and the phone jack, and to rectify both. Plugged in, however, it produced the fast-busy tone of a phone off the hook. Still with no one to call, but greatly intrigued as to why anyone would go to all the trouble to make sure I could not use the phone, I walked to Ver's makeup room, off of our master bedroom, and found her sleek black phone ever so casually fallen into her hamper, covered in Victoria's Secret underwear and Hilfiger T-shirts.

Without really thinking, I called my parents. Their machine picked up, so I left a message, then dropped the phone onto the sofa. A quick pop into the kitchen to start the bisque for the next day, then I decided to walk next door to borrow a cup of Kahlúa, nominally for pots de crème but also to fill an irrational need for validation, for acknowledgement.

Fortunately, Sonya didn't even question the need for Kahlúa. I waited on the porch while she fetched it, looking back at our house for figures concealed in the shadows. I was so intent on searching for potential assassins hidden behind the magnolia bush and clutching my missing chef knife that Sonya nearly killed me by touching my shoulder.

"Did you see something?" she asked.

"No. I was just . . . looking at . . . nothing. . . ." I trailed away, sounding lame even to my own ears. Oddly enough, I was not looking at nothing but rather at Ver's car, her custom-painted S2000 outside of its warm nest of the heated garage. Just washed and gleaming, as it was every other day, its vanity plates proclaimed VERISCUTE, her attempt at a dual language pun, to the dusk.

I once explained that a true pun functioning in two languages should have full meaning in both languages; whereas "cute" in Latin was etymologically closest to "cutus" meaning "corner," so her attempt at "truly cute" was sorely lacking. "Veriscute" worked as a pun for me because I under-stood "true corner" as "truly cornered." Plus, some knowledge of "cute" being a root in "persecute" and "prosecute," as in "first corner" and "asking corner" respectively, led me down a merry path when I had been able to feel merry.

"Well, try not to down it all in one swoop." Sonya smiled, with a questioning look.

I thanked her and walked cautiously back across our yards. Ver's car had not disappeared, yet I knew she was not home. She'd probably found my keys in my coat pocket and simply took my car rather than come back in and engage me in conversation. Although that would not explain why hers was out of the garage. My Sentra was gone, another mystery to induce worry.

Inside, I wondered if this was the way escaped prisoners felt. Or maybe kings, whose heads uneasily wore their crowns. Did Ver hate me enough to kill me? No doubt she fantasized the same as I, of some fresh start. Only hers would involve some compliant trophy husband who could produce symphony tickets or opening-night seats to any gala with a quick call, but would never force her to go. He could drop names and terms au courant then fade to the background, as friends and acquaintances admired his Adonis-like form and Solomonic mind. For Ver's friends, it would probably be Brad Pitt's looks and Alex Trebek's mind.

I sleepwalked into the kitchen and started a lazy preparation of pots de crème. I had all the ingredients, and both the preparation and the con-suming seemed like comforting actions. I melted Merckens dark chocolate in heavy cream and added a touch of Kahlúa, as well as some powdered espresso. As the ganache cooled, I cracked six eggs, separating the white into a glass bowl I could store away for later, adding the yolks directly to the chocolate and stirring each one quickly in.

Cooking was peaceful. A combination of art and science, of chemistry and sculpture, of substance and style. Yet I would not have been doing it now if I had not been nervous. I would have been in front of my moni-tor, immersed in an imaginary landscape far removed from my too-real kitchen and failing—or failed—relationship.

Staring at the empty quart container of cream, I reflected. We had been going through cream and butter quickly. Perhaps Veronica had been try-ing to poison me in a different way. Dinners had been heavy on the sauces recently, and she always seemed to have an inner shine at my discomfort, almost a self-congratulatory glee whenever she asked about heartburn. A slow death by cholesterol poisoning, looking self-inflicted or at least self-chosen. Clever, but so long-term. It would explain why she was eating less of her dinners lately. Especially if she were spiking it with vitamin A or some other fat-soluble potential toxin.

Sirens again whined in the distance, growing closer, then retreating off to rescue some newly distressed damsel or punish some malefactor. I checked the temperature of the rich chocolate mixture, which appeared to need another five minutes before transfer to individual demitasses and refrigeration. So I sat.

Although I'm not a big fan of mystery stories, it occurred to me that a missing knife, a missing jacket, a missing car, and a disconnected phone could add up to some master sleuth's expository salon meeting where she indicates the ex-brother-in-law who was an amateur ethnobotanophar-macologist who spent time in Madagascar and therefore had access to a little-known species of euphorbia and had administered enough of its convulsive toxin to the maid to cause her to slip, shooting too much insulin into the lone heir to the Bulslip fortune. . . .

My coat. My knife, arguably. My car. Me without alibi for a certain length of time in which my car would be seen near or at the scene of a crime.

I was not a target for assassination, which gave me several microseconds of relief. I must have intuited that, thus my desperate desire to establish a visual contact and recorded message. Which meant I was probably safe. Unless Veronica—or, more likely, her hired killer—killed Sonya. Kera was a better target than Sonya, since I had indulged in a momentary indiscretion with her, which somehow tainted her with guilt in the imagined rules for the game, but she seemed much more difficult to work a frame around. Granted, with my car parked at her house, my jacket observed walking in, and my knife to be found buried between her ribs, not much more evidence would be needed, but I could think of no motive for me.

I looked out the window to Sonya's house, wishing this were chess rather than a potentially deadly game, with my life or freedom as the stake. I certainly could not call the police with a suspicion, founded or not, that my wife was trying to kill me or set me up as a patsy in some heinous crime. What passed as evidence in the fanciful imaginings of literary sleuths was sure to not do a whit to convince their real counterparts.

The real mysteries in life are often explained by vanity. Though deathly allergic to shellfish, Veronica insisted that our dinner parties be able to offer shrimp, lobster, crab, or crayfish as a sign of prosperity. I would cook them when she was out and wash the dishes and utensils carefully, and she would simply avoid shrimp cocktail, crayfish étouffé, lobster bisque, or king crab legs, as others marveled at her exquisite delicacies. I ran a spatula around the pan where lobster continued on its way to bisque-dom, and looked at it.

I debated walking to Sonya's again, on the pretense of offering her some of the pots de crème. The thought of proffering an unfinished dessert, not fully set and missing its garnish of a whipped cream floret, was too much, though. Instead, I poured the mixture into eight demitasses, scraping down the bowl with a spatula to fill the last cup, and placed them on a tray in the refrigerator. The stress seemed to collect in my chest and push outward with a painful throb, but I fought it down.

It wouldn't make sense for me to park at Sonya's, walk in, and kill her, since I lived next door. So why my car? Sitting down again, I ran through several scenarios. Veronica could claim I told her to take my car, with the implication being I was trying to establish an alibi. She could have given the car and jacket to her hired killer and had him kill somebody else, leaving my knife, with my fingerprints, buried in the victim. Dressed as me, she could have killed somebody, though it seemed remote, given her preoccupation with cleanliness and not touching "icky" things. I was sure a dying human fell under the "icky" category. Or, it could all be a misunderstanding, engendered by my own hatred and the ensuing guilty paranoia.

I turned on our Barista, thinking that a large cappuccino, if not calming, might be comforting. Next to the espresso-roasted beans in the freezer was a carton of chocolate peppermint ice cream from a local dairy, a carton I remembered emptying four days earlier. It seemed unlikely I had placed it back in some forgetful moment, so I lifted it, finding it heavier than an empty carton should be.

Inside were three plastic bags, each containing what resembled frozen milky spit. My wife had obviously read, or watched, *Presumed Innocent*, and mistaken it for a how-to primer. Or she had just decided to try artificial insemination without telling me. I found the latter unlikely. Not that she wouldn't tell me—just that she wasn't likely to want my progeny. My DNA at the scene of a rape/murder would be even more difficult to explain than my knife.

I felt an intense pain in my left shoulder, something that felt like a masseuse would need to knead it for weeks.

Sirens again wailed, this time increasing in volume until they seemed right outside my door. I could see the red lights flashing through the glass semicircle of the front door, as well as reflecting on the kitchen windowsill. What had she done?

A determined knock sounded from the door. I wiped my hands absently on a towel, throwing it onto my shoulder as I walked to the front door. The expected police officer stood there, but only one. An ambulance and several squad cars decorated the street, but an indefinable serenity settled over me. There was no way to have done fingerprinting or DNA testing in the small amount of time she had been gone. Blackness engulfed me.

A committee of visually-impaired and mentally-impaired patients had decorated the hospital room. I considered other explanations, but none were as simple. Two dull aches inside my chest took my mind off of the interiors by Bellevue. One was physical. The other, harder to define, had arrived after piecing together stories from the police, the news, and friends the morning after my cardio incident.

Veronica had failed. She had actually done worse than failed; she had been the cause of the ambulance awaiting me as I suffered a small cardiac arrest. Heartburn and stress had combined with a very minor heart attack to make me pass out, but her carefully plotted scheme had too many variables. Assuming me bright enough to follow her clues, she had fostered my arterial clogging with rich dinners and set my stress levels on high. But heart attacks are impossible to predict, even when the patient was being primed. Not that my self-elected fat intake levels needed much supplementing, but it had apparently worked to her advantage.

It was wishful thinking that the sirens responding to her phoned-in, false-alarm rape of Sonya would kill me quickly enough to negate the proximity of the ambulance. Or maybe she was hoping that even if I lived I'd see how desperately she wanted to get rid of me and I would instigate divorce proceedings, making it my failure. She was wrong in so many ways.

I would even get to go home that evening, in time to meet a dinner party where my condition would be the cause célèbre until attention could be diverted to some fad artist or social injustice that had surfaced to their collective consciousness long enough to elicit a benefit, a check, and a quick farewell. Perhaps heart disease would fill that plate. Or perhaps something else. Whatever the topic, I was sure my knife would be comfortably inserted back into its waiting slot and my jacket would be hung on the valet. The iced cream treat would be flushed, and life would seem so normal.

Of course, Ver would never go to trial for her non-crime. I suspected I would not either, for forgetting to wash the spatula before lovingly filling her demitasse with an extra-rich chocolate confection. Pots de crème was a treat, like so many, best served chilled.

POTS DE CRÈME

½ cup + 3 tablespoons of
  Kahlúa or other coffee
  liqueur
1 cup whole milk
1½ cups heavy cream
4 teaspoons instant coffee

16 oz. semisweet or bittersweet
  chocolate, finely chopped—
  Merckens monopol (bittersweet) or Callebaut semisweet recommended
6 egg yolks

Add ½ cup of Kahlúa to ½ cup of milk in a glass. Add ice cubes. Drink leisurely while making the pots de crème.

Heat cream and remaining milk combined in saucepan over medium heat until it just starts to bubble. Take off heat and add instant coffee. Pour over chocolate and stir until all chocolate is melted. Let cool for several minutes, stirring to aid cooling. Whisk in egg yolks. Make sure they are blended thoroughly, then heat again to about 160F, whisking constantly. Remove from heat and pour into a steel bowl. Add remaining Kahlúa and whisk. Quickly cool in an ice-water bath, then pour into 8 demitasses or custard cups. Refrigerate. Make sure cups are covered with plastic wrap. Ready after 2-3 hours. Serve within a day or so.

Garnish with homemade whipped cream flavored with a hint of chocolate liqueur, Godiva or other. Add a few white, milk, and dark chocolate curls, preferably Nestlé's (Peter's) Snowcap or Guittard for the white, not some pasty shortening bark purchased at a local purveyor of low-class confectionaries. For the milk chocolate, again, look for something a cut above the usual dross foisted on the undeveloped palate of street urchins: Merckens or Callebaut or Guittard. For the dark, the ones recommended for the recipe are quite good, as are Merckens Yucatan buttons, though those will need to be melted and rehardened into a shape easier to make curls from. Make the curls with a vegetable peeler dragged along the chocolate. I prefer at room temperature, though some think working with cold chocolate is easier. I refer to them as philistines.

UNDERCOOKED
by Jeffrey Marks

Jeffrey Marks is the author of the U. S. Grant mystery series, which includes The Ambush of My Name *and* A Good Soldier. *He also writes mystery non-fiction, most recently* Atomic Renaissance. *He has been nominated for every major mystery award. Marks lives in Cincinnati with his family and his Scottish terrier, Ellery.* www.jeffreymarks.com

The aromas of warm bread and fresh fruit filled the room. Ulysses Grant had experienced similar domestic scenes during peacetime. However, at the close of 1863, he'd taken to cutting his supply lines, leaving his men to scavenge any fare they could carry. The agrarian South offered an amazing buffet, but dessert was a luxury in foraging. No one grew pies and chocolate cake for the men.

This home had a dozen pies, by Grant's count. A sink and plain metal counter marked the center of the kitchen, with a large pie cabinet to the left of the sink. A rolling pin lay crossways on the floor, and flour dusted the counter. An icebox and a china chest stood on the far side of the sink. The scene was cluttered further by the prostrate figure of a woman. She had fallen onto her dough, bleeding crimson into the beige paste.

Grant looked around the room, trying not to touch anything, but sorely tempted by the feast. He'd been summoned to Lookout Mountain on the heels of his victory at Vicksburg. Southern forces had overwhelmed the larger Federal troops and pushed them to a point where winding mountain trails were the only means of egress. Grant knew of their rugged nature only too well. He'd traversed Mississippi and Tennessee with an injured leg, arriving here a few days ago.

Still, their headquarters had seemed far enough from the vortex of the battles—so much so that civilians had been allowed to stay in their homes. Grant thought of the headlines—a woman shot by marauding Federals. Killed by her own country.

The general had opted to stay in the largest and nicest home on the mountainside. The stately house, serving as Grant's headquarters, looked down on a handful of modest dwellings—much the way that the gangly Lincoln in his stovepipe hat gazed down on the men around him.

The woman had lived in one of those little homes and died from what looked like a bullet from one of Grant's men.

Some of the men had been practicing drills outside the manor home. Grant wondered if one of their guns could have accidentally discharged into the dwelling. Despite the improvements made in firearms during the course of the war, many of the weapons were the same ones used in the Revolutionary War eighty years earlier. Guns fired without warning. Worse yet, rifles and muskets jammed, leaving soldiers to skewering the enemies with bayonets in order to save their own lives.

Thick clouds of acrid gun smoke accompanied drills. The men were lucky not to shoot each other in the pseudo-fog that erupted from the gun barrels. Stray bullets destroyed livestock, crops, and trees. Why would civilians be immune? Grant thought about Manassas, where spectators had watched the battle as they would a concert. A symphony in carnage. It was only when the Federals had started to retreat that the onlookers decided that newspaper accounts of the battle would suffice.

Even so, these young'uns thought themselves impervious to war—until they saw death up close. Jenny Rowe had seen it a tad too close for comfort. A bullet had punctured her kitchen window, scattering shards of glass to the left of the victim. She'd been baking pies for the troops, filling her cabinet with treats for the Federals. This part of East Tennessee was known for its Union leanings, making the killing all that much more senseless.

Jenny had definitely made a name for herself both in looks and cuisine. Grant had heard of the desserts at headquarters. Even beyond death, the general could sense her allure. Her figure was shown to an advantage in the dress stained red. Her blonde hair, no longer up in a bun, fell across the counter. Her cornflower blue eyes stared blindly away, and trickles of blood dripped from her pug nose.

Captain Ferguson held out a sheet of paper for him to see. "Sir, we issued an order for all civilians to take cover when the drills were executed this morning. Notices were posted." The page looked like many others Grant had seen in his day, a summary notice to evacuate or take cover until the drills ceased. Bullets didn't discern between innocent and guilty, civilian and soldier. Both justice and artillery were blind. Many of the troops were fresh off the farm and needed all the training they could get.

The general had not met Captain Ferguson until arriving at the skirts of Chattanooga. The man seemed efficient enough but was a bit lax with the recruits. Grant had made his name at the beginning of the war by shaping men up for battle. Ferguson, with his pleasing manners and quiet tone, didn't look like a fighting man. More like a nursemaid for green troops. His uniform hung off his lanky frame. Grant looked up to watch the captain's expression. The trimmed whiskers and weak chin made Ferguson look like a man out for sparking, rather than leading troops.

Grant took a bit of dough and rolled it in his fingers. The enlisted men on both sides would love some home-baked victuals, but not until this matter was solved. He pinched the dough flat. The mix was still spongy; it hadn't been long since the woman had been shot.

"Who found the body?" he asked.

A young man with blond hair that fell over his eyes stepped forward. "I did, sir."

From what Grant could see of his eyes, they were red-rimmed. He looked a farmer with his dark tan and bare feet, dressed in a brown cotton shirt and dungarees frayed in a few places. He seemed out of place in the tidy kitchen, rubbing the soles of his feet on the legs of his denim pants. The man's hands seemed to clench an unseen object as he stood there.

Grant studied the man for a second. "And you are?"

"Zechariah Rowe, Jenny's husband. I heard a shot and came in here. Found her body just like this." He pulled a red bandanna from his back pocket and blew his nose with a snort. His pinched fingers shook his whole head. "We'd only been married a few months."

Grant grasped the man's hand and placed the other on the widower's shoulder. "I'm sorry about your loss. Did you see the notice about taking cover during the marching drills?"

Rowe sniffed again while nodding. "Yeah, but Jenny said she wanted to finish up the pies. She didn't think no harm would come to her in her own house."

Grant could hear the sounds of troops outside. The air stunk of acrid smoke from cannons and rifles. The Rowes' windows had been closed, but the smashed glass panes let in reminders of war. The odors battled the aromas of home baking. The pies smelled so delicious that Grant was tempted to take one to camp with him. He'd been without home-baked sustenance for so long that he couldn't remember the taste of a fluffy crust or fresh fruit.

He and Ferguson took their leave and walked around the perimeter of the Rowe home. The wood structure had been built a few years back, a two-story house whitewashed in more peaceful times. The windows showed the accumulation of gun smoke and mud from the fall rains. A sturdy porch jutted out almost to the dirt road that led to Grant's residence. He made his way around the small veranda, looking for signs of who might have shot the woman. An investigation of the shooting would be required so the locals would feel safe in knowing their lives were not in danger. The fear of looting in a war zone caused near vigilantism in some towns.

Ferguson stepped across some cut blossoms in the front path and made his way to the lane. A woman in a plain peach cotton dress shuffled across the rutted path to approach him. She stopped to say something inaudible to Ferguson, and Grant swore that she passed him something. Grant made his way over to the pair as she started to talk more loudly.

"General, this is Mrs. Butler. She claims to have heard the shooting."

The woman wore dirt-smudged rouge, and dark circles as eyeliner, with hanks of hair that had come down from her coiffure. She showed the signs of battle as much as any of Grant's men. With her broad figure, she would have made an easy target. Grant could see that the dress seams had been let out at least twice. Perhaps she was a frequent visitor to the Rowes' home and their pie festival.

"The men was close, sir," she said. "I could hear the sounds of gunfire from the cellar."

Grant nodded and turned his head to look at the Rowes' window. Any gunman would have a fairly straight shot into their kitchen, but the angle looked wrong. The woman would've had to have been standing in the pie cabinet for the bullet to have penetrated her from this line of fire. "How did you know that Mrs. Rowe had been injured?"

The woman raised her head and looked into the general's eyes. The pale green hue of the orbs was almost overcome by her pupils. "Well, sir, I heard the tinkle of glass breaking, you know like someone had dropped the good china. I couldn't tell if it was from a gunshot, because there were so much noise all around us. They seemed to be in the cellar with me, if you know what I mean."

Grant knew the sounds of battle and gunfire all too well. This was his second excursion into warfare, having spent years south of the Rio Grande battling Santa Anna in the Mexican War. He'd managed to come through that war unscathed, but he'd lost too many good friends to take a battle lightly.

"Did you hear anything else? Was that the only sound you heard?" Grant eyed Ferguson, wondering if the man had brought witnesses who had heard gunfire during the morning. There'd be a line up the road if that was the case.

Mrs. Butler gave a small smile to Captain Ferguson. She licked her lips and continued. "After a minute or so, I heard the worst noise. A woman screaming and screaming. Then it stopped, and that was worse yet. I just knowed someone was dead."

A burly man with thick arms and big hands stepped from the Butler house and approached the trio. He came with a quick step that belied his size. He wore the overalls and striped shirt of a farmer. Towering over Grant's 5'8", he said, "Excuse me, sir, but my wife's a bit out of sorts because of all the gunfire. You'll have to excuse her. She's a mite delicate."

Grant would never have characterized the woman as anything other than a sturdy farm woman, but he knew that some men protected their wives fiercely. Grant was more likely to be protected from his wife, Julia, than to protect her.

Ferguson cleared his throat. "I presume you're Mr. Butler. Your wife heard the killing of a civilian, sir. She's been a big help."

Butler looked askance at his wife, who now rested under his shoulder. "You shouldn't listen too much to her stories," he said. "Martha likes a bit of gossip here and again. Pay her no nevermind. She's been a tad over-wrought by all this, Captain Ferguson."

Grant took a step back from the couple. Ferguson certainly seemed to be popular with the locals. "Did you know Mrs. Rowe, Mr. Butler?"

"Not like all them other men, sir. She was a bit of a handful for her groom, that's for sure." Butler squeezed his wife closer to his big frame.

She squirmed, and Grant wondered if she bristled under his watch. Did she have more to share about her neighbor—things she couldn't say in front of her husband?

"What other men?" Grant put a finger under his collar. Fraternizing with the troops was frowned upon, especially by married womenfolk. This was not going to be a tidy end to a difficult situation. The general had no desire to turn the sympathizers against the Federal cause. He'd counted on their support to turn the tide in this battle.

"Well, sir, I'm not one to talk," Butler began, "but Mrs. Rowe was known to entertain some of the troops here while her husband was plowing the fields. She was known for more than them pies, for sure."

Mrs. Butler had puckered her lips into a thin pink line of disapproval. The general couldn't tell if she was more perturbed about her husband's telling the news or her not having a chance to relate the story first. Grant was surprised at the man's willingness to indulge in neighborhood gossip. Most men didn't go in for such things.

Grant muttered under his breath. He had warned the men about mingling with the civilians. No quicker way to set off the populace than to run rampant through a village. Still, women who had lost their way or been reduced to poverty often flocked to the camps for food and a bit of coin. Some of the officers, like old Joe Hooker, allowed it to transpire without comment. Other, more God-fearing officers tried to put a stop to the outrage.

Grant stole a glance at Ferguson as the Butlers walked away. "Captain, care to tell me how that man knew your name?"

Ferguson hung his head as the pair walked back to the Rowe home. "Well, sir, I've visited Mrs. Rowe here to help her with—"

"Was this a common occurrence around Chattanooga—Mrs. Rowe and her pies? Did all the men know about this?"

Ferguson and Grant passed by the porch. Grant looked down at the cut blossoms again and wondered if the flowers had been used for wooing the young beauty. Not much call for flowers during a military occupation. Had she been entertaining earlier in the morning?

Ferguson cleared his throat and spit on the side of the road. "I'm afraid so. She's been coming around the division's camp for the past few weeks. She used the pies as a diversion. The men would pay a high price for a pie, and Miss Jenny would stay with them for a while. If you get my meaning, sir."

The captain's face turned a bright crimson in the midday sun. Grant hoped that he had the good graces to be embarrassed by the admission.

"And no one reported this woman to their commanders?" Grant knew the answer even though he wanted an explanation from Ferguson. No one had mentioned the woman to him during his briefings. Possible embarrassment from down the lane would have been reported.

"Well, sir. I wouldn't know. She was an awfully pretty woman, and you got home-cooking to boot." Ferguson tried a weak smile, but it fit as poorly as his jacket.

"Captain, this is not a joking matter. A woman is dead. Now how does that man know your name?"

Ferguson cleared his throat again. "Sir, it seems that Private Jenkins came down with a rather awkward ailment. I had to pay a call on Mrs. Rowe about it and encourage her on behalf of the camp doctor to seek some treatment. She wasn't home when I came by. Her neighbor there came out, and we chatted for a few minutes."

Grant looked into the captain's eyes for signs of mendacity. "And that's all that happened? You didn't have relations with the woman?"

"No, sir. Not with what I knew about her at that point."

"Have you had any reports of stray gunfire here? Sporadic shots in the area?"

"No one admits to coming near to the house. We can't find any troop activity near here."

"And what of Private Jenkins? Is he still here?" Grant eyed the divisions of men who had set up camp down the hill from them. He wondered if any of the new recruits had the aim to fire at a window from that distance.

"No, sir. Jenkins was mortally wounded in battle two weeks ago. It couldn't have been him, for sure."

Grant and Ferguson came to the Rowe house and knocked. No one answered. Grant pushed the door open and stepped into the kitchen area. The glass crunched under his feet as he walked around the room. He opened the door of the pie cabinet. It looked like a hutch, except that the panels had been replaced by perforated metal sheets to let the air flow through to cool the baked goods.

He hunkered down to look inside at the shelves of pastries. A small hole pierced its back panel. He pushed his finger through the hole and felt the intact wall behind the cabinet. He scanned the rest of the wood, but it was pristine. Mrs. Rowe took care of the pie cabinet. It was the source of family funds in uncertain times, not to mention a never-ending excuse to visit the soldiers as well. Grant inspected the door of the cabinet, but it was in good shape, moving quietly on its hinges.

He looked up to see Rowe standing in the doorway. "What, pray tell, are you doing in my kitchen?" the man said. "This is not a field of battle. You don't have any right to be in here."

Grant took a hunting knife from his belt and held it over the decimated form of the woman. "I need to get some evidence from your wife. I'll need to make an incision on her."

Rowe screamed and threw himself at the general. "Not my Jenny." The two struggled as Ferguson looked on. The knife clattered to the floor and Ferguson snatched it up.

Grant subdued the man without much trouble, pinning an arm behind Rowe's back. "Why don't you tell the truth, Mr. Rowe? It would save us all a lot of trouble."

The man's body shook with sobbing. "I killed her. I couldn't stand it anymore. I knew what she was doing, but I couldn't stop her. Then yesterday she told me that she was pregnant. Had no idea who the baby belonged to, but that I was to raise it as my own. I was stunned. I couldn't believe she was asking this of me."

Grant kept his grip on the man. "Then what happened today?"

"I was in the next room, trying to stay clear of the noise. Jenny was in the kitchen cooking, despite the threat of gunfire. I showed her the notices, but she just laughed. I heard a shot. Someone had shot out the window. I came out to the kitchen, carrying a rifle. One of your men must have left it here when they were paying a visit to my Jenny. She told me about the shot and laughed. She said that none of her men would hurt her. I seen the bullet hadn't left a mark on the walls. I went to the window, raised my gun, and fired. She screamed and fell down dead."

"And you hid the gun and went to the neighbors."

Rowe nodded. "I put it in the cellar behind some bags of feed. No one would have thought to look for it there."

Grant pushed the man toward Ferguson. "Captain, make sure this man gets to the authorities."

Ferguson saluted. "Yes, sir. My pleasure. How did you know it wasn't an accident?"

Grant tugged on his beard. "I found it hard to believe that a single bullet in all this shooting went astray and killed someone. When I started looking around the room, I found another bullet hole besides the one in Mrs. Rowe. That made two shots fired. I remembered Mrs. Butler's words about the scream coming after the shot and started to wonder if another inhabitant of the house might have done her in. That's the reason for all my questions."

Ferguson nodded. "Very good, sir. I'm on my way."

GREEN APPLE PIE

6 green apples	2 tablespoons brandy
1 cup sugar	dried currants
3 tablespoons melted butter	cinnamon, cloves, or other
4 eggs, beaten	spice to taste
1 teaspoon lemon juice	1 layer pie crust

Grate raw six good apples, add a cup of sugar, three tablespoonfuls of melted butter, four eggs, a little lemon juice, two tablespoonfuls of brandy, a few dried currants, and a little spice. Line plates [pie pan(s)] with a paste [layer of pie crust], fill, and bake [375F for 50 minutes] without an upper crust.

From *Civil War Recipes: Receipts from the Pages of Godey's Lady's Book*, Lily May Spaulding and John Spaulding, editors. This 1862 recipe originally appeared in *Godey's Lady's Book*, a leading women's magazine of the nineteenth century.

MURDER, THE MISSING HEIR AND THE BOILED EGG

by Amy Myers

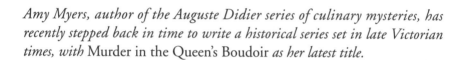

Amy Myers, author of the Auguste Didier series of culinary mysteries, has recently stepped back in time to write a historical series set in late Victorian times, with Murder in the Queen's Boudoir *as her latest title.*

Auguste Didier stared gloomily at the eggs for boiling, awaiting his pleasure. He had none to offer, although he admitted that his ill humour had nothing to do with them. Still in its shell, one egg looked much like another, but today they provided an unfortunate reminder that he must choose which of two young gentlemen was the bad egg. They could not both be the missing heir to Lord Luckens.

Not that his lordship was dead. On the contrary, when last week he had brazenly staggered into the kitchens of Plum's Club for Gentlemen, over which Auguste presided as maître chef, he was very much alive. His stagger had not been so much due to age or the club's excellent wine cellars; rather, his gait suggested a life spent perpetually astride a horse, and his feet a mere aberration of nature to be ignored.

"Ha!" The grey moustache had bristled, and keen eyes shot a triumphant look, as though Auguste were a fox planning a speedy exit from this world. "You the detective fellow?"

"The chef fellow, your lordship," Auguste murmured patiently, casting a despairing glance at his hollandaise sauce, which had been delighted at this opportunity to curdle. His detective work had come about by chance and was not an art in which he could lay claim to perfection, as were his culinary skills.

Lord Luckens ignored his remark. "Splendid. Here's what I need you to do. I want you to cook a dinner for me at Luckens Place. Know the old ruin, do you? You can cook what you like."

Auguste relaxed. He must have misheard mention of detection work, for this assignment presented no such problem. Indeed, the idea was an attractive one, for he had heard that Luckens Place in Sussex, far from being an old ruin, was a magnificent Elizabethan mansion with its own ornate banqueting house in the grounds, and a splendid towered gatehouse with a bedroom where Good Queen Bess herself was said to have slept. He might even cook an Elizabethan dinner and suggest they follow the old custom of walking to the banqueting house for sweetmeats and desserts. He warmed to Lord Luckens immediately.

"You cook it," Lord Luckens boomed on, "and then supervise the dinner in the Great Chamber, where it's to be served."

"You wish me to act as butler too?" Professional etiquette rose up in protest.

"No, no." An impatient hand flailed at this stupidity. "Just stand there like a blasted maître d'."

Auguste gaped at him, wondering just what his lordship's butler would have to say about this irregular suggestion.

"It's like this. I'm getting on in life. Time to think of wills," Lord Luckens trumpeted. "Only had one son, George, and he flounced out in 1867, thirty years ago, when he was twenty-one. Never bothered to keep in touch, never made the fortune he reckoned on. I had one of those Pinkerton detective fellows track him down a few years back, and they told me George died in Leadville, Colorado, in '79."

"I'm sorry to hear that, sir."

Auguste received a glare in thanks for his concern.

"Never understood the fellow. Took after his mother. Bookish. Not the sort to marry. Understand me?"

"Yes, sir."

"Seems I was wrong." Apparently this did not often occur, since Lord Luckens admitted it with great reluctance. "Pinkerton found out he left a widow, but she moved away and vanished. I'd no interest in her, so I called off the hounds. My solicitor fellow in London, Jenkins, said where there were widows there might also be sons, so he advertised. Every good-for-nothing in the States claimed to be George's son, but old Jenkins is a wily old bird, and he's whittled them down to two. He's crawled over the evidence and is convinced it's one of them, but he can't blasted well decide which. One's a silver miner in Leadville, the other's a New York business-man, and both are flourishing birth certificates saying their father's George Luckens. They can't be brothers. Born within four months of each other, and even George with his saintly ideas couldn't achieve that. Thought you might like a crack at it, eh?"

"Me?" Auguste's heart sank, even as his mind began to fill with the delights of experimenting with suckets, leaches, possets, and marigold tarts. He had not surrendered easily, however. "Who would inherit, sir, if no claimant can be found to satisfy you and your solicitors?"

"Knew you'd ask that," Lord Luckens replied darkly. "I had a brother once, Horatio. Couldn't stand the fellow. He couldn't stand me either. Died years ago, but he left a blasted son, as priggish and self-righteous as his blasted father. *And* a bachelor in his fifties. Another of those blasted nancies. Sort of fellow who, given his way, would see this country go to the dogs. Not content with sitting in the Commons, he's all for sitting in the Lords and putting a spoke in the wheel there too. With *my* title. He's got wind of this dinner and is insisting on his right to attend. Lady Luckens said it's fair enough and will save trouble later. Suppose she's right, damn it. His name's Jonathan Luckens—heard of him?"

Auguste most certainly had. You could hardly live in England and not have heard of him. A member of Keir Hardie's burgeoning Labour party, he seemed unlikely to be enthusiastic about inheriting a title, yet Auguste could well understand why he and Lord Luckens did not see eye to eye. He was, if Auguste remembered correctly, a vehement supporter of the rights of women to vote, which was not a policy Lord Luckens would be likely to endorse.

Despite his reluctance, the case began to intrigue him—and besides, he'd always wanted to cook an Elizabethan banquet. . . .

Auguste fidgeted nervously in the Great Chamber, under the frosty eye of the butler, who obviously suspected Auguste's presence as chef was a ruse to disguise the fact he was being assessed to replace him. He must be nearly eighty, so this would not be surprising, but Auguste could do with-out heavy disapproval at his elbow this evening.

At any moment, the double doors would be thrown open by the foot-men, and the guests would enter. Auguste glanced round at the awaiting banquet, or such of it as had already made its appearance. The spit-roasted carp stuffed with dried fruit and spices would appear shortly, the goose and sorrel sauce, a pie of Paris, two large chickens to masquerade as peacocks, complete with fanned-out tail feathers, the samphire salad, lemon salad—his mind flitted over merely some of the wonders he had prepared—all for the sake of a handful of diners whose concentration would be on fraud, not food.

The doors opened at last to reveal the six diners. On Lord Luckens's arm was a severe-looking lady in her middle years, dressed in grey, with only a cameo brooch as adornment. She, Auguste had gathered from the butler, was Miss Twistleden, Lady Luckens's companion. At the rear of the short procession of six was Lady Luckens, a sweet-faced, grey-haired old lady. She was clinging to the arm of Jonathan Luckens, whom Auguste recognised from sketches in the *Illustrated London News*. Gimlet-eyed and thin, his immaculately trimmed beard quivering at the ready for any chance to demolish his rivals, he looked to Auguste a formidable opponent. He wouldn't care to be in the false claimant's shoes (or boots), or, come to that, in the true claimant's either. Sandwiched between these two couples must be the two claimants, Red and William, both allegedly surnamed Luckens. They were *not* arm in arm. Far from it.

"Pa!"

There was an immediate and simultaneous howl from both of them as their eyes fell on the portrait of George Luckens, age twenty-one, which hung on the far wall facing them as they entered the Great Chamber.

"Gee, that's how I remember the old son of a gun," one of them shouted.

No doubt who he was, Auguste decided: the Colorado claimant. Red Luckens, towering over his companion, was dressed more like one of Buffalo Bill's cowboy riders than an English dinner guest. But the hat was missing to complete his ensemble of high boots, sturdy brown trousers and jacket, yellow shirt, and huge buckle belt. The holster slung at his side was empty, to Auguste's relief.

Auguste had met many Americans in the course of his employment, Americans in Paris, Americans in London, Americans in the depth of the English countryside, rich Americans and poor Americans, and they had ranged, as do most nations, from the highly civilised, down through the ranks of the vulgar wealthy and back up again to the straightforwardly unassuming. Never, however, had he seen (or heard) two American gentlemen of such disparity as these two.

Red's rival claimant, William Luckens, was hardly less ostentatious than Red, in that, although clad in conventional evening dress, he wore the new tuxedo dinner jacket so popular in the United States and still so incorrect here. He might be shorter than Red, but his pugnacious chin and sturdy build suggested he would meet punch for punch.

Red, seated at the table, gazed in rapt devotion at the portrait. "That's how Red Luckens remembers the old guy," he said. "Like me, he was a humble but happy silver miner. Yes sirree, Grandpappy."

Auguste shuddered. Such an endearment was hardly furthering Claimant Number One's cause with Lord Luckens.

"That's *my* pa." William had a New York accent and a quieter voice. "It sure chokes me up seeing the old fellow up there." His unctuous, soulful glance at Lord Luckens was even harder to stomach than Red's brashness.

"What splendid memories both you gentlemen have," Jonathan sneered, "considering you were only seven when my cousin George died."

"Sure do, Cousin Jonathan," Red replied cheerfully. "Why, I remember him kissing my ma as though it were yesterday."

"Tell me about her," Lord Luckens said grimly.

"Why, she was the purtiest little thing, a dancer she was—"

William interrupted angrily. "My mother—your daughter-in-law, sir—was a lady. Pa met her in Colorado. A schoolteacher. Dancer, my foot. Whoever your parents were, cowboy, your ma most likely came from the whorehouse."

"Say that again!" Red leapt up from the table, overturning his chair in the process and towering over William, who continued eating his carp imperturbably, to Auguste's full approval.

"You don't look like George," Lady Luckens observed plaintively to both of them. She had the vacant stare of the elderly who have chosen to let the world pass by them, but this might be deceptive, Auguste thought.

"No," barked Miss Twistleden, defensive of her mistress.

"I agree, Aunt Viola," Jonathan said superciliously. "Nor like Uncle Alfred here. But then that's hardly surprising," he added, turning toward the claimants, "since it's quite clear neither of you is my esteemed uncle's grandson."

"Quite clear, eh, blast your eyes, Jonathan?" Lord Luckens growled. "Not to me. Any proof of that statement, have you?"

"No, but it will emerge soon enough."

"I take after Ma, ma'am." Red casually threw a chicken bone over his shoulder, to the horror of the butler and Auguste alike. *What would the courteous host do in such circumstances,* he wondered. *Proceed to throw his own over his shoulder, or ignore the faux pas?*

Lord Luckens didn't appear to notice, and it was left to William to place his delicately and with much show on the dish provided for the purpose.

"See here, mister," Red continued earnestly to Jonathan, "I've a photograph here of my old man not long before he died. We moved to Leadville, Colorado, in '77 from California, and here's the proof of *that*." He produced a dog-eared, faded photograph of a group of miners outside Billy Nye's Saloon. "I was just five years old when this was taken."

"Why, that's no proof at all. You can't tell one face from another," William cried in triumph, seizing it from him. "Now, just you look at this carte de visite I got here. Signed on the back: 'Your affectionate George.'" He tossed it onto the table, and Jonathan and Red immediately made a grab for it. Red won.

"Mind letting me see a pic of my own son, Red?" Lord Luckens growled.

"That stuffed shirt's not my pa! He was a silver miner," roared Red, reluctantly handing it over.

"Who struck it rich just before he died, enabling my mother to bring me to New York to start a new life," William capped him triumphantly.

"Oh yeah?" Red sneered. "What do you say, Grandpappy?"

Grandpappy wasn't saying anything, but his glare should have been sufficient an answer for most people.

"I know what I say," Jonathan smirked. "If that's all the proof you've got, I rather think I'd win in any contest at law."

"Oh, they've got better proof than this, Jonathan. I explained that to you." Lord Luckens recovered his good humour. "Too much to be faulted. That's why we're here. Two impeccable birth certificates, duly registered in their birth towns, one for a child to Mollie Luckens, née Huggett, dancer, on 20 April '72 in San Francisco, one to Amelia Luckens, née Bruart, schoolteacher, on 13 August '72 in Denver, Colorado."

"I guess that makes me elder brother and the future Lord Luckens, if it comes to our splitting it, Will," Red spluttered into his wine.

"I'll expose you for the bunco artist you are, long before it comes to that," snarled William. "You're no good even as a professional fraud."

"I'll expose the pair of you even sooner," Jonathan sneered. "We in the

Labour Party believe in justice for all. The courts will make short work of both you incompetent bunglers."

"Not me, my friend," William rejoined. "Concentrate on Mr. Wyatt Earp here."

"I prefer to concentrate on this excellent beef. Most interesting flavour to it." Jonathan momentarily won Auguste's approval.

"Call this beef stew?" growled Red, elegantly holding a piece of meat with two fingers.

Auguste in fact called it a beef hare, a dish whose spicings of onion, clove, and nutmeg appealed to him.

"Any Leadville chef would get booted out of town for this," Red continued in disgust.

Auguste made an instant decision never to visit Leadville, but refrained from active interference in the conversation in the interest of earning his fee. So far his betting was even on the two rivals, and if there was any tripping up to be done, Jonathan Luckens was more than capable of doing it.

"In New York, fortunately, we can appreciate the finer blessings of life." One point to William!

"Including money, I've no doubt," Jonathan quipped. "Although both of you have quite an interest in that, don't you?"

"Pa." Red looked soulfully at the painting. "I'm here to get acquainted with my old grandpappy while there's still time." Minus one to him.

Auguste had been so entranced by the battle, he realised he had forgotten to worry about whether the potatoes were cooked as the Elizabethan court would have enjoyed this newly discovered delicacy.

Old Grandpappy growled something Auguste failed to catch, but William and Jonathan both looked pleased. What he did hear was Lord Luckens's next order: "Show them the letters, William."

William needed no urging, and produced a small bundle of letters tied with tape. He extracted one and leaned forward to pass it to Jonathan, but Red was too quick for him and tore it from his hands.

"Can you even read it?" William asked politely.

"Sure can," he snorted. "When old Red smells a rotten fish." He waved it in the air and said, "When was this written—yesterday?"

"Read it out loud, Red," Lord Luckens commanded.

Red obliged, albeit slowly. "My darling Amelia, Denver is just dandy. Wait till you see it. Our claim is sold, and we'll be rich, just like I promised you. You'll be strolling along the New York streets before the fall. I'll be back in Leadville to sort things out, and then we'll be clip-clopping our way to happiness. Your loving George."

"My little George." Lady Luckens looked pleased. "He always had a poetic streak in him. How sad he never reached New York."

"Sad," echoed Miss Twistleden.

"No, ma'am," Red hooted with glee, "but he never reached it because he never intended to go at all. He remained in Leadville, married to my ma, *Mollie,* until he got run down by that darned wagon."

"Then how could he have written this letter?" Miss Twistleden was emboldened to ask.

"Ma'am, he didn't. Our William here wrote it—and the rest."

"For once I agree with you, Red," Jonathan sniggered. "It's a most interesting letter in many ways." He picked it up from the table, where Red had let it fall, and looked at it with an air of faint amusement.

"Forgive me," Lord Luckens said heavily, "but I should, I suppose, recognise my own son's writing."

"You'd be only too eager to do so, I'm sure," Jonathan agreed sweetly.

Lord Luckens looked at him sharply. "My solicitor's checked it out with a handwriting authority."

"Then why this charade?" Jonathan asked politely. "Unless—"

"Yes, mister, I got letters too," Red drawled. "Not so many, 'cause Pa and Ma were never separated more than the once, when he comes to Leadville from San Francisco in '77, and she followed a month later. Pa wasn't one for writing much—guess he'd have written you more, Grandpappy, if he had been. Look at this." He tossed a scrap of yellowing paper onto the table, narrowly avoiding his beer glass (a refinement demanded of the butler, to Auguste's combined horror and amusement).

Jonathan picked it up. "Moll, miss you, sweetheart," he read out. "Come to me March. George."

"How thoughtful." Lady Luckens's eyes filled with tears, at which her husband growled:

"Time to move, Viola."

"What the heck for?" Red demanded. "This your quaint English custom of getting rid of the ladies?"

"No, sir," Jonathan chortled. "An even quainter custom of repairing to the banqueting house for our dessert."

"In Chuck's Diner you get the food brought to you." Red snapped his fingers at Auguste and the butler. "Maybe you fellows could learn a thing or two."

"Perhaps you could learn even more, Red," William said disdainfully. "Good manners, perhaps?"

The banqueting house at Luckens Place was a separate building about two hundred yards from the main house, with one large room, a serving area, and a retiring room. Luckens ancestors stared down in beneficent envy of their descendants' banquets of elaborate sweetmeats and jellies. Auguste had contented himself for this small gathering with orangeflower and rosewater creams, lettuce suckets, two leaches, candied marigolds, and apricots, raspberry cakes, some preserves, and a moulded and iced marchpane centrepiece of the Luckens arms.

He cast an anxious eye over his work. At least here, with a more informal atmosphere, he could pass among the guests and keep an eye both on his culinary work and on the two claimants. He was puzzled about the latter, who at the moment seemed to have forgotten their differences, as they demolished his Elizabethan delights with great gusto. No doubt their animated tête-à-tête was comparing them favourably with home fare.

"Blasted titbits," Lord Luckens commented on a plate of kissing comfits, presented to him by Auguste. "Nothing like a savoury to end a meal."

Auguste agreed. It was revolting, in his view, to kill the pleasant afterglow of a meal with strong anchovies or cooked cheese or kidneys.

"Ever tried hominy grits?" Red asked, strolling up to them, with one hand busy feeding a slice of the Luckens arms into his mouth. "I'll sure miss 'em when I get to come here for good."

"Don't concern yourself, Red." William was following hard on his heels. "You'll be on grits for the rest of your life."

"Don't be too sure of that, pal." Red helped himself to a candied marigold, then elegantly spat it out into his empty glass, which he handed to Auguste.

"I think you *both* can be sure of it," Jonathan remarked complacently. "I shall be the next Lord Luckens."

"How about waiting till I'm dead?" his present lordship shouted furiously at his guests.

Lady Luckens's brow was clouded as she added her own contribution to the conversation. "I am a great admirer of our dear Queen, especially in her Diamond Jubilee year, but I feel she has enough palaces already. And there's Osborne, of course."

Red looked puzzled. "Don't quite follow you, Grandmammy."

"I believe my aunt refers to the fact that I myself have no heirs," Jonathan explained kindly. "And if no others can be traced, the estate is likely to revert to the Crown after my death."

"Over my dead body," William declared.

"Dear Victoria," Lady Luckens said brightly. "How she loves the Isle of Wight. We took our honeymoon there, do you remember, Alfred? We walked to Alum Bay, visited Carisbrooke Castle—ah, the peace. I don't wonder our dear Queen loves it so."

"Grandma, I can assure you the Queen will not be the recipient of this estate *ever*," William said earnestly. "I myself am married, with a son. Little Jefferson is your great-grandson."

"Bunkum!" Red yelled. "*I'm* your grandson, ma'am, and I can tell you, Red Luckens is gonna sire a whole wagonload of kids. No nancies here." He smirked at Jonathan. "No wife, no heirs, eh?"

"But after meeting you two gentlemen this evening," Jonathan retorted quietly, "I am quite sure—forgive me, Uncle—who will be wearing the coronet next. I should like a word with you both later."

"And I'd like a word with you *now*, Didier." Lord Luckens stomped over to a reluctant Auguste and drew him aside from the marvels of his banquet. "That blasted nephew of mine seems to have made his mind up. Have *you* found out which one's my grandson yet?"

Auguste hedged. "I'm still assembling ingredients, sir."

"Eh?" Lord Luckens had no time for metaphor.

"I've told Red and William we'll sleep on it. That all right with you?"

"Yes, sir." Auguste was only too grateful. Such suspicions as he had as to who was the impostor were vague, swimming around like unwelcome lumps in a Béchamel sauce. A night's sleep would smooth out his thinking, leaving the paste smooth.

"I've told Jonathan what you're here for. Know what he replied?" Lord Luckens guffawed. "'I hope his detection is better than his cooking,' he said. The beef was surprisingly good, but he'd seldom tasted a worse pie. Don't worry yourself, Didier. Everyone makes mistakes."

Auguste Didier seethed. *He* never did.

Auguste woke up suddenly to find firstly that it was still the middle of the night and secondly that he would not be able to sleep again without paying attention to the demands of nature. He had been pleasantly surprised to find his room was on the guest floor and not in the servants' quarters, but he was not so impressed with the chamber pot under his bed. Lord Luckens did not go in for modern inventions like bathrooms or, apparently, indoor privies. Somewhere, he decided, one must surely exist, and he went out to prowl in search of it.

So far as Auguste could tell, there had been little opportunity for Jonathan to beard his elected impostor during the remaining time the gathering had stayed in the banqueting house, and he presumed that Jonathan, too, had decided to postpone any confrontation until morning. As he walked along the corridor, Auguste was uncomfortably aware of his squeaking footsteps. The guest rooms were so far from the Queen's Chamber, where Jonathan was sleeping, that Auguste wondered whether Red and William had been assigned these rooms deliberately, so that the floorboards would give warning of visitors. No sound came from either of their rooms, however.

Reaching a closed door across the corridor without succeeding in his quest, Auguste realised he had reached one of the towers flanking the Queen's Chamber. Perhaps even now Jonathan was having his "word." Who could tell behind these thick walls? Between Auguste and the chamber lay a six-foot tower room, and any sound would be muffled.

He took the staircase down to the entrance hall, and at the foot of the tower his search was rewarded. Nevertheless, a vague anxiety hovered inside him, as, primary mission accomplished—in what must surely be the *original* scorned water closet invented by Sir John Harington for Queen Elizabeth—Auguste returned to bed.

He awoke hours later to the sounds of disturbance outside his room; the noise reached a crescendo as pounding footsteps passed his door. *Perhaps*, he told himself hopefully, *the housemaid has dropped the water ewer.* He snuggled down once more under the inviting blankets, for there was no sign of a housemaid's ministrations to light a fire in the grate, where the previous night's ashes still presented a melancholy picture.

Then his door flew open, and his host, fully dressed, stood on the threshold, gibbering, "Didier, blasted man's dead."

"Dead? Who?" Auguste sat up in bed. "How?" Auguste's first thought that adulterated food might well come out of Lord Luckens's kitchen was dismissed. Yesterday it had been supervised by *him*.

"Shot."

Auguste stared at him. "But who?"

"My blasted sodomite nephew—or that's what he calls himself. I told him he was no part of the Luckens family—lets the side down. He can get up to what he likes in his bed, but women with the vote indeed. Next thing we know, there'll be women in parliament."

Lord Luckens brooded on this potential catastrophe for a moment before returning to his present one. "Might have killed himself, of course," he said hopefully. "Just like him, to choose my house." He ruminated, then sighed. "Unlikely, I grant you. Which one of those two did it? Which one's the fraud, Didier? This is going to mean having police barging around, and I want to know what's what before they get here."

Auguste leapt from his bed to find his dressing robe. "Where was Mr. Luckens found?"

"In his bedroom. Where else? If that's your standard of detection—"

Not waiting for him to finish his tirade, Auguste, followed by his lordship, hurried to the Queen's Chamber. News had spread quickly, for William and Red were already there, standing one on each side of the body.

"Move aside, if you please, gentlemen," Auguste said, steeling himself for the ordeal and glad that he had not yet had breakfast.

Jonathan Luckens, still fully dressed in his evening clothes, lay on his back on the rug by his bed, sightless eyes staring upwards, shot through the temple. One hand hung limply down, and on the rug at his side was the gun, a Smith & Wesson. Auguste confirmed the obvious, then turned to his lordship.

"You were right, sir," he said. "It's murder. There are no powder burns round the wound or on the hand, as there would be if he had shot himself. In my opinion, he was shot from some feet away."

"*Murder?*" William squeaked in horror.

Red seemed equally appalled. "See here—" he began.

"Did any of you hear anything?" Auguste asked.

"Thick walls," Lord Luckens said complacently, taking the credit for his ancestors' masonry.

"A risk, though." Auguste frowned. "Suppose someone had heard; there's only one passage, and the murderer would have been trapped."

"Window's open," Lord Luckens snorted. "Plenty of footholds on the ivy."

Auguste went to look. "It is certainly possible, but—" He broke off, collecting his thoughts as he looked round the room. Nothing seemed unusual, until he opened a bedside drawer. Inside was a pistol.

"What the devil's that doing there?" Lord Luckens glared. "I don't leave guns around for my guests to play with. It's mine, all right, but he must have taken it from the gun room. With good reason, I'd say."

Not commenting on the "good reason," Auguste said quietly, "*Messieurs*, I suggest that we all retire from this room and that it is locked until the police arrive."

William and Red were only too happy to agree, and after some demur, Lord Luckens escorted them to the morning room. Heavily paneled in dark wood, with only narrow windows and sombre furnishings, this gloomy chamber did little to dispel their melancholy. Even Red was subdued.

"Who do you reckon did it?" William asked quietly.

"A hobo?" Red offered feebly. "What you folks call a tramp?"

Lord Luckens snorted. "Not blasted likely. Jonathan had discovered which of you is the false claimant to the estate, and he was about to expose you. Took the gun to defend himself when he tackled you. Instead, you walked in and shot him. Quite obvious, isn't it? A child of ten could see that."

"Not so obvious," William retorted, though not so fiercely as usual. "Why should he expose one of us? If one of us is knocked from the running, the other one is thereby proven as the true heir. Of course, my hot-headed friend here could well have lost his temper with Jonathan last night."

Red did not reply immediately, and when he did, like William, his heart did not seem to be in his protestations. "Listen, pal, if I wanted to kill a man, I'd do it honestly, with the fists I was given to fight with, man-to-man. How would I get a firearm in this country anyway? This here holster came over empty and it's stayed empty."

"Smith & Wessons are American," William snapped back.

"Sure, and it's the right of every American citizen—including you, bucko—to carry one."

"In defence of others, I believe," Auguste intervened, "not in defence of his entitlement to a title and money. I have one question to ask both of you before I make my report to the police, and it's this: Which of you did Jonathan Luckens ask to see first last night? There wasn't an opportunity in the banqueting house, so it must have been here, in his room."

"Not me," William came in promptly.

"Nor me," Red said earnestly.

"Suppose they both went," Lord Luckens growled. "Thought of that?"

"We didn't, Grandpappy," Red assured him. "Why, speaking for myself, I slept like a baby all night."

"Says you," William snarled.

Auguste was puzzled. This was all very odd.

After the police were notified, Auguste returned to the kitchen, for he needed room to think—and breakfast. Both were possible since the servants were taking theirs in the servants' hall. What should he have? All he could face was a drink of soothing chocolate. Then his eye fell on the humble egg. An egg!

One could always rely on an egg. Unassuming, nutritious, the self-sacrificing base of the most perfect dishes in the world. Who thought of the egg while a bavarois was in one's mouth? Who thought of the egg while a sauce hollandaise eased itself into one's stomach? Yes, he would boil himself an egg, plain and unadorned, perhaps with soldiers, as in the English fashion, crustless buttered bread cut into strips.

Eagerly, Auguste placed the egg in the boiling water, turned the ornamental egg timer, from Alum Bay no doubt, upside down for the coloured sands to run through, and prepared to watch the cooking of his breakfast.

Coloured sands? Alum Bay? Queen Victoria? *Egg timer?* He stared at it hypnotised, as first the solution of the case of the missing heir and then that of the murder of Jonathan Luckens clarified in his mind like heated butter. It was as plain as a boiled egg.

"Well?" Lord Luckens demanded, after Auguste had requested a private interview. "Which of them did it?"

"I prefer to tell you which is the impostor."

"Same thing."

"Not necessarily."

"Have it your own blasted way then. Just tell me."

"Red Luckens is a fraud. I am convinced he has never been near a silver mine in his life, for hominy grits is a Southern dish and Colorado is not in the South of the United States. Also, he is, like a neatly trimmed poached egg, too good to be naturally true."

"So William's my grandson then," Lord Luckens said glumly. "Pity. Red has more spunk in him. Still, it's better than the estate going to Queen Victoria, God bless her. And Red killed Jonathan. Might have guessed it."

"No, sir."

"So it was William shot him," Lord Luckens said immediately. "He knew Jonathan had got it the wrong way round, and wasn't going to risk his precious inheritance vanishing."

"No, sir. William, as well as Red, is an impostor. That letter must surely have been forged, for he wrote, 'Wait till you see Denver,' as though it would be his wife's first visit. In fact, William purports to have been born there, so that is impossible. I was puzzled by their apparently amicable private conversation at the banquet, and suspect they were discussing their spoils."

"You're raving, Didier. How can both of them be impostors? There'd be no spoils to discuss."

"I refer to the spoils they have or will shortly receive from you, Lord Luckens."

"What the devil do you mean?" he shouted, red in the face with anger.

"I looked at this case the wrong way up. It took an egg timer to understand that I needed to stand it on its head and let the sand trickle through. When I did so, it was quite obvious that neither of these gentlemen could be your missing heir. That, in any case, was always a possibility, but the egg timer caused me to realise that it was you who had planned the whole thing, hired their services, forged the so-called evidence, and falsely claimed to them and probably your solicitor that Pinkertons had checked out the birth certificates in the States."

"Think I'm out of my mind, do you? I'd have to adopt one of them to keep Jonathan out of it. Why the devil should I adopt a stranger?"

"Because you hated your brother and then his son so much."

"Enough to adopt an out-of-work actor and a smooth-talking rogue? That's who they are—and that I can prove. How could I have known one of them was going to shoot the fellow to make sure of his inheritance?"

"You couldn't. You hated your nephew so much, you'd prefer the Queen to have the estate. With Jonathan dead, you would later find proof that neither Red nor William is your missing heir. There is, in fact, no missing heir. It was a plot to rid yourself of Jonathan by murder. You shot him, Lord Luckens, in the expectation one of them would be blamed."

To Auguste's surprise, Lord Luckens did not treat him to an outburst of abuse. Instead, he gave a bark of laughter.

"You're clever for a Frenchie, Didier. Not clever enough, though. If I were a murderer, I'd be unmasked the minute those two rabbits blabbed to the police. No, I'll tell you what really happened. I hired them, all right. The mistake I made was to make it a gamble for them. Whichever you unmasked as the impostor would get nothing but his expenses; the one you decided was my grandson would get £5,000. Tidy sum, eh? Worth killing for. Hadn't foreseen that. Whichever Jonathan picked on as the impostor had good reason to stop him talking. With two such prime suspects, the police aren't going to suspect me just because I didn't like the fellow, no matter what beans they spilled about my hiring them."

"Would the police not believe it a little strange that you were willing to pay so much money merely for the pleasure of seeing your nephew's ambitions temporarily thwarted? You could hardly explain that you knew in advance of hiring Red and William that Jonathan would no longer be alive when you disclosed the truth about them."

Lord Luckens gave a gargoyle grin of pure evil. "They'll understand why I hired them, Didier. I'm a poor old man of eighty and can't hang around forever. Devoted to Lady Luckens, tears in her eyes, not too bright in the head, loving husband wants to make her happy. What better than that her beloved grandson is returned to her? Worth any price, that. Might even adopt one of them—which do you fancy, Didier? Money is no object to make her ladyship happy. They'll believe *me*, not a blasted chef."

"They will when they hear what I have to say."

His lordship snorted. "You stick to cooking, Didier. Blasted sugared lettuce stalks."

With some effort Auguste ignored the insult to his suckets. "I asked myself why Jonathan should have armed himself with a pistol to defend himself and then left it in a drawer when a nighttime visitor arrived. If he were expecting Red or William, or if the visit were unannounced, the pistol would be within easy reach; if he knew the caller was you, however, he would hardly have felt fear for his life. I believe that you told him you were coming, giving the excuse that at such a time and in such a place you could not be overheard if Jonathan were to tell you whom he suspected of being the impostor. Or perhaps he suspected them both. You, Lord Luckens, were the only person who need not fear the gunshot being overheard. What more natural than that the host, who sleeps nearby and who has placed his guests' bedrooms far away from the Queen's Chamber, should be first on the scene to find the cause of the alarm?"

"Poppycock," Lord Luckens snorted, with less conviction.

"I think not. Had you hired only one impostor, you might well have succeeded. Your mistake, Lord Luckens, was to over-egg the pudding by hiring two, to try to make your story more convincing."

Through the window Auguste could see the police arriving. "You were the bad egg," he continued. "Your mistake was that you asked me, a master chef, to cook it."

CAVIAR STUFFED EGGS

After you've inherited the family fortune, here's a recipe that uses boiled eggs.

6 hard-boiled eggs
¼ cup sour cream
3 tablespoons chives, plus
   more for garnish

1 lemon, juiced
½ teaspoon wasabi powder or
   dry mustard
4 ounces salmon caviar

Cut the eggs in half and remove the yolks. Mash the yolks, then mix them with the sour cream, chives, lemon juice, and wasabi. Fill back into the whites. Top with caviar and garnish with chives.

Yield: 4 to 6 servings
Prep Time: 15 minutes
Cook Time: 10 minutes
Difficulty: Easy
Recipe courtesy Wayne Harley Brachman

RECIPE FOR REVENGE
by William Allen Peck

William A. Peck, Creative Director of a Baltimore ad agency, studied creative writing at Johns Hopkins University. A lifelong Francophile, he has written a series of novels starring Chief Inspector Henri Duquesne, the protagonist of "Recipe for Revenge." He owes his culinary leanings—as well as much else—to his beautiful wife, Janis.

The corpse was as cold as the broth that his head unceremoniously displaced from its white china bowl. His blazer-clad torso, sprawled over the linen tablecloth, had knocked over the crystal stemware, and an empty wineglass flirted dangerously with the edge of the table. Chief Inspector Henri Duquesne had seen messy bodies before, but never one dripping—not with blood—but with bouillabaisse.

"Who saw the victim die?" he gruffed to the nervously assembled crowd of customers, waiters and busboys, chefs, and other help who were forced to stay in the restaurant's dining room by uniformed police at the exits.

Maître d'hôtel and owner, Jacques Roget, cleared his throat, his dark goatee bobbing over his bow tie. He towered in height and personality over most of those around him, his head seeming to float above his shoulders. Even without his immaculate tuxedo, his ramrod stance made it obvious he ran the place.

"I was across the room, at my station." He pointed with an aristocratic chin toward the podium by the entrance to one of the Côte d'Azur's most revered dining establishments. Even a recent downgrading by the *Michelin Red Guide* from three stars to two hadn't hurt its popularity. For this Sunday lunch it was particularly crowded with devotees of its fresh seafood, the air heavy with the bouquet of saffron, savory, thyme, rosemary, and other heady Mediterranean herbs and spices.

The decor was an Art Nouveau fantasy of swirling mermaids, fish, and sea flora that could have existed only in the artist's mind. Duquesne always felt out of place here in his rumpled pin-striped suit, but his robust body bore evidence that nothing could deter him from tucking in to the chef's famous fish soups whenever he had the opportunity—i.e. the offer of a free meal. The restaurant was out of the price range of even a senior police official such as himself, but he wasn't above accepting favors. He'd accept them but, people learned to their chagrin, never grant them.

"There was a loud strangling sound," the owner explained, "almost like an animal rutting, followed by a noisy crash, and I just glimpsed Monsieur Lapage's head slam into his plate. Bouillabaisse flew everywhere, as you can see." He flapped his hands in distaste at the splattered waiter and few customers who had been seated nearby. His tone of voice indicated that he would never approve of such behavior, even from a good customer. "I didn't hear a gunshot, but then the lunchtime crowd is a bit noisy, and a shot could sound like a champagne cork popping, couldn't it?"

"Chief Inspector, I was his waiter." A man whose white jacket was covered in soup stepped up to Duquesne. "He always asked for my section when he came in."

"Your name?" The notebook and Bic pen appeared effortlessly from an inside jacket pocket.

"Michel Berrault," the man answered proudly, as if expecting the chief inspector to recognize the name. "I was closest to him when he died, and I saw everything."

Duquesne doubted that. He had spoken to hundreds of witnesses, and they seldom, if ever, saw "everything," but he kept his opinion to himself and listened, pen poised over the page to encourage the man to be precise.

"He had just started on his meal when he seemed to have a seizure and dropped over into his bowl. At first we thought he had a heart attack, but we pulled his head back, fearing he might drown in the liquid, and saw this. . . ." With professional aplomb, as if lifting the cover of a silver chafing dish, Berrault raised the victim's head up by his thinning hair and pointed to a small bullet hole, seeping red, almost dead in the center of the man's forehead.

"I'll miss him," the waiter commented without irony, "he was a good tipper."

Duquesne moved closer and held the man's face between his hands to study the wound, obviously caused by a small-caliber weapon. It was a tough-looking face with a tendency toward jowls. Now dripping with soup and framed by shaggy gray hair, the deeply etched brow was marked by an oozing red spot that gave him an Indian-like appearance. His blood had leaked out into the liquid, which had caught the chief inspector's eye when he first saw the victim. He had never seen such a red bouillabaisse before. Something else was different about it: the ingredients were scattered all about, but there were no shells.

"Aren't there supposed to be mussels, clams, and other shellfish in your bouillabaisse?" he called out to the man wearing the tallest white hat in the place, indicating he was the head chef. "Chef Ballou, isn't it? When I ate here, that seemed to be your signature."

Ballou's large-veined nose almost dipped down to his chin as he expressed his displeasure. "Monsieur Lapage was allergic to mollusks, so I was ordered to remove them from my recipe." He scowled openly at his boss, who was still standing nearby.

Duquesne acknowledged the information with a *tch* of the tongue, then turned his attention back to the corpse. As much as he liked to talk about food, he was here to do a job, and this wasn't going to be an easy one.

Positioning the man's head at the angle at which he most likely held it while eating, Duquesne traced an imaginary line from the bullet hole back to where it must have originated. The line ended at some drapery, covering windows in a far corner of the room. It would have been a perfect place for someone to hide before pulling the trigger, and easy enough to slip away from once the attention of the room was focused on the victim.

"Everybody take a seat," he called out in a commanding voice, to bring some order to the disgruntled crowd. "As you know, there's been a murder. Nobody can leave until I've finished taking statements and we've searched the premises."

He returned the petulant mutterings with the burning eyes of someone used to getting his way. In all likelihood, somebody in the room was the killer, and the weapon was still in his or her possession. The image of a maniac holding all these people hostage was one of the few things that could make him uneasy, and he was relieved when the backup detail of uniformed police that he had called for entered the room.

"We're going to have to search not only the restaurant, but each one of you, for the murder weapon. The better you cooperate, the quicker and easier it will go for all of you." This brought a howl of protest from the movers and shakers who could afford the price of a meal here, but he quieted them by smashing his fist down on a nearby table, noisily scattering silverware and dishes.

Roget, sensing the destruction of his establishment, tried to calm him. "Please be assured, Chief Inspector, that I and my staff will cooperate in every way possible. What can we do?"

Duquesne turned his attention back to the owner, his expression softening slightly. "Just have them stand by and out of the way of the officers. Meanwhile, you can tell me a bit about the victim." He picked up his pen and notebook and nodded for the man to continue.

"He was a *very* good customer, Monsieur le Inspector." The owner seemed pleased to be able to calm the situation so easily and slid into a chair near the kitchen, inviting the inspector to join him. He was back to playing host in his dining room again. "He was a lonely widower, you know. Made a fortune buying and selling high-tech companies in Paris, but retired here to Nice when his wife's health began to fail. For all his tough reputation as a hard-nosed businessman, he was very devoted to her, and he gave everything up to try to help restore her health. They dined here on our seafood often, and ever since she passed away, he's been coming in and sitting at their same table—often ordering her favorite dish."

"The bouillabaisse?"

"*Oui.*"

"How often did he come in?"

"Two, three times a week. We'll miss him."

Duquesne nodded. He understood that what Roget would really miss was the man's wallet. "You say he had a hard-nosed reputation. Did he have enemies?"

The owner shrugged, lips forming the classic French expression for "Who knows?" Aloud he added, "I don't like to speak ill of the dead, monsieur, and he was a good friend of the house, but yes, I would say that many people lost their jobs, and more lost significant sums of money due to his downsizing their companies or eliminating them all together. You couldn't find a hall in all of France that would hold all of them if they were considered suspects."

Duquesne looked around at the roomful of restless customers and employees and wondered how he was going to get through interviewing even a tenth of them before calling it a day.

"The murderer . . . how easy would it have been for him to have left here after pulling the trigger?" he asked Roget.

The man snapped his fingers. "Almost impossible. There are only two ways in and out. I was at the front door. No one got past me after Monsieur Lapage collapsed into his plate. I immediately instructed our kitchen staff to secure the back door, so no one could have left that way either."

"What about those windows over there?" The inspector nodded toward the drapery where the killer might have hidden.

"Sealed. Can't be opened. There are only the two doors."

Duquesne surveyed the motley assembly. Among the customers were some of Nice's most influential high rollers, people who had no trouble throwing their weight around. He had called for Claude Grillot to come assist with the interrogation, but the lieutenant hadn't yet arrived, and he knew he couldn't keep these people penned up long in an increasingly uncomfortable—and probably dangerous—environment.

The pleasant aroma of freshly grilled or sautéed seafood had turned into a stale, musky perfume that stung the nostrils. Somebody out there had the murder weapon and had proven a willingness to use it. It made him nervous, and he scratched his shaggy, black toupee, conscious that sweat was beginning to ooze down his ruddy forehead.

Needing to speed up the process, he whispered, "You know your patrons well, I assume?"

Even seated, Roget drew himself bolt upright. "*Oui.* It is my job to know not only who they are, but where they fit in the social scheme of things."

"Anybody here strike you as being out of place, someone who just doesn't 'fit in,' as you say?"

The man stared out over the throng. "Hmm . . . maybe. There are some people I don't know. People who aren't dressed quite right, that kind of thing."

"Exactly. And anybody who might have had a grudge against Lapage, either because he cost them money or a job—or for any other reason?"

Again Roget swept them with critical eyes. "Yes, some of my patrons were investors in companies that Monsieur Lapage took over. Might be a few former employees, too. He may well have cost them money. They don't share that kind of information with me."

Duquesne handed him his pad and pen. "Would you write down

names of anyone who you know had any kind of relationship with the deceased? Those who might have had it in for him for any reason whatever, or who don't fit in with your usual customer profile. No one will know you gave me their names."

When Roget replied with a look that said he could never do such a thing, Duquesne's voice turned menacing. "Otherwise, I'll have to keep everybody here all day and long into the night. Imagine what that will do for your reputation."

That encouraged the owner-maître d' to change his mind, and after consulting his reservation book, he jotted down nearly a dozen names but looked away as he handed the pad back.

Duquesne noted a few people that he recognized, pillars of the community who were not likely candidates as killers, and he passed over them for the present. The first name that Roget had written down—and therefore must have had some reason to suspect—was one he didn't know and he called it out:

"Guillaume Allard!"

A spindly figure toward the back of the room tentatively raised his hand.

Duquesne arose and nodded toward an alcove. "Let's talk in here." He proceeded toward an unoccupied table without checking to see if he was being followed.

After the two were seated opposite one another in the nook popular with couples who didn't want to be observed—"the room for lovers" as the staff referred to it—Duquesne started without preamble. "Monsieur Allard? You are by yourself today?"

Allard, a slender, gray figure in a tweed jacket, looked confused and glanced toward where he had been sitting. "I'm with my wife and another couple. Should I . . . get them?" A slight stutter betrayed his nervousness.

Duquesne pulled his lower lip, as if in deep thought. "We'll call them over if I think it necessary." He appeared to be studying something in his notebook. "What was your relationship with the deceased, Monsieur Lapage?"

Allard blinked, surprise distorting his features. "Relationship? I had none. Only. . . ."

"Yes?" The inspector's eyes were black darts.

Allard was no match for him and he looked away. "Well, I worked for a software company he bought."

Duquesne's look penetrated the shell of ensuing silence, until the man continued.

"He merged it with one of his other companies," Allard said, "and then fired all the top management, including myself. But I never met the man. Wouldn't have known it was he who was shot here today, if our waiter hadn't told me."

"So Lapage cost you your job?" Duquesne looked the man up and down. "But you can still afford to eat in a classy restaurant like this."

Allard glanced away. He was obviously very uncomfortable with the question. "Well, you see, I had stock in my old company, and when Lapage took it over, we all got shares in the new firm. His cost-cutting was hard on us as far as our careers were concerned, but the stock has soared in value under the new regime."

"So you can afford to eat here, even though you're unemployed." Duquesne completed the thought, not unaware of the sound of envy in his voice.

Refusing to meet his eyes, the man answered with a shrug.

"What about the couple you're with? Another poor slob booted out on his ass by the mean Monsieur Lapage?"

Allard finally faced his inquisitor. "The fact that the stock did well enough for us to afford to eat out once in a while has nothing to do with the fact that I don't have a job anymore. If I could get one, I'd welcome the chance to be productive, but in the software field, I'm considered too old, and that's all I know. Until something comes along, I intend to enjoy perks like dining here at Monsieur Lapage's expense."

"No remorse over the fact that he died today?"

Allard thought about his answer, but now that the dam had broken, he no longer acted shy about facing Duquesne. "Feel bad about it? No, not really. I'd be a hypocrite if I said otherwise. But hate him enough to take his life?" He shook his head and tried to compose his features. "Before he died, I might have said yes, but that would have been big talk. I'd never have the guts to shoot somebody, as much as I'd like to say I could. It's what makes people like me different from people like Lapage. He could kill his enemies, economically or otherwise. I could never do either, much as I might want to."

Duquesne saw that the interview was going nowhere and dismissed Allard before he got maudlin. The inspector noted that the uniformed officers were doing a methodical job of searching each patron and all of the crannies in the restaurant where a small-caliber pistol could be hidden. But he also knew that a determined killer would have thought it out in advance, and if he hadn't already escaped the restaurant, he had faded into the woodwork—he and his weapon. Duquesne tended to think of suspects in the masculine because most of the murderers he had apprehended over a long career were male, although he had enough experience with female crooks not to exclude them from his inquiry. Thinking that, he called for the next pair of names on the list.

"Helene Dublon and Francine Lutece?"

Two tall, attractive, well-dressed women in their early forties stood up and hesitatingly followed him into the alcove.

"You're regulars here?" he asked after establishing which was Helene and which Francine.

"No," Helene, the prettier, blonde half of the pair, replied. "This is our first time here."

"But you knew Monsieur Lapage?"

They looked at one another, eyes locked in uncertainty, it seemed, before Helene finally stammered, "I . . . I did. I used to work for him."

Surprised at their reaction, Duquesne raised his bushy eyebrows and aimed one in her direction.

"We . . . we once were friends."

"Friends?" This was taking a direction the chief inspector hadn't expected.

"I became his executive assistant when he took over Microware."

"They were lovers," Francine broke in, drawing a dirty look from her companion.

"But I thought the deceased and his wife—" Duquesne began.

"Were devoted?" Helene laughed. "It was a game with him. Nothing presents a bigger challenge to a woman than a happily married man. Turned out, I was just one of a long line. Her hold over him was the fact that she controlled fifty percent of the voting shares in his company. It wasn't generally known, but his original stake came from her family."

Duquesne had put down his pad and was watching her with disbelief.

She crossed her legs. "He moved his office down here when she got sick, and I thought he'd send for me—he had promised we'd get married when she passed away. Instead I got the news over the Internet that the company was being downsized. I became one of the casualties. He wouldn't even take my phone calls."

"So you followed him down here with blood in your eye?" Duquesne asked, keeping one eye on the woman's handbag. He didn't know if it had been searched yet, and he didn't want to take any chances.

"Actually, we're down here on our honeymoon," Francine interceded.

Duquesne shifted his look to her, fighting a show of surprise.

"She was so hurt by Lapage, she told me she could never trust men again. Well, of course, I consoled her, and one thing led to another. . . ."

"So the two of you are . . . as they say in the papers . . . an item?" Duquesne asked, hating the term but not knowing how else to phrase the question.

In answer, Helene squeezed her companion's hand as Francine's face lighted up, radiating all the colors of a Mediterranean sunset. "I've never been happier," Helene said. "Actually, Lapage did me the biggest favor of my life. If it hadn't been for him, I'd have never known what real happiness is."

It was nearly dinnertime before Duquesne and his lieutenant, who had arrived just after the inspector finished with the two women, completed their interviews of the dozen customers on Roget's list, plus a few others among the staff. Meanwhile, officers from forensics had removed the body and scoured the place for a weapon, without turning one up.

Duquesne dismissed most of those he interviewed with an admonition to stay in town where they could be reached, but his intuition told him he wouldn't be calling them back. So far, no one had displayed the little verbal and facial tics that the inspector used as a virtual lie detector—and which had made him such an effective interrogator.

He sank down at a table by the kitchen and signaled for the owner. "Monsieur Lapage must have been a very good customer," he mumbled, scribbling a few notes of his observations into his notebook. "What was his allergy?"

"It's not uncommon." Roget deduced immediately that Duquesne was asking about Lapage's inability to eat certain shellfish. "It's not the mollusks per se he was allergic to, but some parasite that sometimes lives inside even the cleanest, freshest of them. Most people are unaffected, but a few, like poor Monsieur Lapage, get severe stomach cramps and worse from eating them."

"But it's not fatal?"

"Rarely. When we learned of Monsieur Lapage's condition, I told Chef Ballou to revise his recipe. He was such a regular customer, and it's not uncommon to serve bouillabaisse without mussels and other shellfish, you know."

"But it was your featured dish. Don't other customers miss it?"

"And the Michelin inspectors." The chef had been standing nearby and aimed his nose dangerously in Roget's direction. "I'm sure that's why they downgraded us from three stars to two."

"You couldn't just take them out of the soup you served to the victim?" Duquesne asked, disappointed that such a thing could happen to such a justifiably famous dish—one that he himself hoped to enjoy again.

The chef shook his head. "Whatever he was allergic to would still be in the soup, which we make ahead. The fish are cooked to order, but the broth with the shellfish must be prepared in advance and simmer so the flavors all mix. Monsieur Lapage dined here often, so. . . ." He raised his meaty hands in frustration and repeated, "I know leaving out the mollusks is what cost us our star."

"Nonsense," the owner barked, "I told you that you needed to be more creative in the kitchen in other ways. Michelin doesn't rank you based on just one dish."

The chef made a guttural sound and turned on his heel toward the kitchen.

Duquesne stopped him. "Not so fast, Chef Ballou. Please come sit down with us and tell me more about what goes into your bouillabaisse."

The chef eased himself down reluctantly beside Duquesne but seemed to direct his words to his boss. "No one but me knows all of the ingredients, what herbs and spices I use. I supervise it myself and let no one else near it. What does my recipe have to do with it, anyway? Monsieur Lapage died with a gunshot wound."

"Just say I'm an admirer. I know your recipe is probably a secret, but as a police inspector, I can assure you it won't go any further than me."

Ballou looked at Roget, who seemed to threaten his chef with eyes that commanded him to answer.

After a short struggle of wills, Ballou turned back to the chief inspector. "Well, it's no secret that I use the freshest fish available each day, so the exact seafood that goes into the pot varies, but generally it's whiting, bass, red snapper, sole, John Dory. And of course, I always include fresh lobster. That's the one irreplaceable ingredient."

"Unlike the shellfish like mussels, clams, and cockles?"

Rather than answer, Ballou shot his boss a sour look before returning to the recipe. "Of course we always make the stock from scratch. I start by sautéing garlic and onions in olive oil. I use more garlic than most. Then I add the bones and heads of the fish to the pot, along with water and dry white wine, a lot of parsley, and lemon juice. Those are the basics. The rest I'm not revealing, even to you."

Duquesne interrupted impatiently. "You used to add the mussels at this point?"

Ballou shook his head, squirting a nasty look at Roget once again. "They come later, otherwise they'd be tough, but I did add some of their 'liquor' to the soup, to give it just the right flavor."

"And you think that eliminating them caused you to be downgraded by the Michelin inspectors?"

"I know it. They even questioned the waiter about it on the two occasions they ate here before the last book came out. They don't give out three stars lightly. Only nineteen chefs in all of France can claim three stars, and I was one of them."

"The stars go to the restaurant, let me remind you," Roget retorted, meeting a hostile glance with one of his own.

"Not exactly true." Ballou rose threateningly. "If I were to quit before the next book comes out, you'd lose yet another star. They clearly belong to the chef."

Duquesne came between the two men before Ballou's upraised fist could find the owner's nose. "And I understand that the more stars you have, the more money you're worth."

"They belong to the restaurant," Roget countered, trying to force himself around Duquesne's bulk. "I invested millions of francs in decor in order to keep that third star, and you lost it by refusing to update your cuisine. The inspectors are looking for fresh innovation, and our menu hasn't changed in years."

"It's the menu we've become famous for," Ballou said. "When we dropped the mussels, clams, and cockles from the bouillabaisse, we upset a lot of customers, as well as the Michelin inspectors. Just ask the waiters. They tell me they hear it every day."

Roget didn't bother to answer this. Instead he tried to grab his chef by the throat, and Duquesne had to wrestle with both men to keep them from choking one another.

"Stop it," he commanded in a stentorian voice. "Or I'll arrest you both."

He managed to get them to sit down on either side of him without calling for reinforcements from the uniformed officers, who were looking at the scuffle with anticipation, after having no luck locating the murder weapon.

He signaled for his lieutenant to come over. "Grillot, have they searched the kitchen yet?"

Younger and taller than the chief inspector by half a head, Grillot pulled at his moustache and nodded in the affirmative. "The men have searched all the customers and staff, too, but it hasn't turned up." He was clearly exasperated after interviewing all afternoon, and undoubtedly wanted to go home as much as any of them. "Any other ideas, Chief Inspector?"

"Go into the kitchen and see if there isn't a big vat on the stove where they prepare the bouillabaisse."

"There sure is. Saw it myself. Makes me salivate just thinking about the aroma."

"Well, I want you to find a big dipper and fish around down at the bottom of the vat. See what you come up with." Duquesne caught the look on Ballou's face.

"I don't think we looked there, Chief," Grillot joked. "The bouillabaisse is kind of sacred around here. Off-limits to us mere mortals."

Ballou wasn't taking it as a joke. "Nobody touches the bouillabaisse but me," he thundered, rising out of his chair despite Duquesne's attempt to stop him.

"Is that where you dropped your gun after you shot Monsieur Lapage?" Duquesne asked, keeping his voice calm.

The chef backed away before Grillot or Duquesne could grab him. As they tried to stop him, he snatched a steak knife off a nearby table.

"That knife won't do you much good against all our firepower," Duquesne said with all the authority his voice could manage, "especially when your gun is in the soup."

"But not for long," Ballou shouted, turning and bolting toward the kitchen before anybody could put a hand on him.

Duquesne, despite his bulk, was only steps behind him. As the inspector rushed through the swinging doors, he saw the chef collide with his stove and plunge his arm, elbow deep, into the hot vat. Ballou, his face distorted by pain, retracted a small-caliber pistol that was likely missing a single bullet from its clip.

"How did you know it was me, Chief Inspector?" he asked, smile now that he had the weapon to defend himself.

"Didn't know. Just a wild guess, a little trick I use when I run out of ideas," Duquesne confessed, smiling back, just to get some reaction out of Ballou. The truth was, it had been apparent that the chef blamed Lapage for his loss of a third Michelin star and all the money and prestige it brought. Shooting Jacques Roget might have given him satisfaction, but it would have spelled the end of the restaurant and thus have been the equivalent of shooting himself.

But the truth was written in Ballou's expressions, especially when it was suggested they search the bouillabaisse for the murder weapon. Duquesne had hoped he would react as he had and wasn't unprepared for Ballou facing him down with the pistol, still dripping with steaming hot broth.

"Hand it over, Ballou. That thing could be more dangerous than mollusks in your bouillabaisse." He held his hand out and approached the chef with the steadfastness of a snail.

Just when he was in point-blank range, Ballou pulled the trigger. Time defied the laws of physics for Duquesne, but the pistol didn't fire.

"I think you cooked it too long," the chief inspector snapped, hurling himself toward Ballou, who dodged just in time, shoving the steaming vat in his direction. The hot liquid exploded over him as if a volcano had erupted on the stovetop.

In his career, Duquesne had been shot, stabbed, and been the victim of a bomb explosion, but he had seldom felt such pain as molten liquid burning into the flesh of his hands and face. Ballou, meanwhile, had found a meat cleaver and wielded it as if he knew what he was doing.

Duquesne didn't have time to think. His hands were numb, and he didn't feel a thing as he grabbed the now half-full bouillabaisse pot and threw the contents right in Ballou's face.

The scream was reputed to have grayed the hair of several customers in the restaurant. Ballou collapsed in a paroxysm of cries just as Grillot and a half dozen uniformed police stormed into the kitchen. They grabbed him, although he was no longer a threat to anybody; and in an act of mercy, Duquesne doused him with a pitcher of cold water to help relieve the burning pain.

"I know how it feels," the inspector muttered as the chef was carried away. He soaked his own hands and face under running cold water for several minutes before returning to the main dining room, where Jacques Roget was nervously waiting for him.

No longer imperious, the maître d' was waiting with a bottle of his best brandy. He poured generous snifters for Duquesne and himself—for "medicinal purposes," he explained—before the chief inspector could decline.

"I knew Ballou was fanatical about his recipes—it's what made him such a great chef—but I never dreamed he would kill someone who caused him to change something," he said, after apologizing that such an incident could happen in his restaurant.

Duquesne raised a reddening hand. "I've seen people do fanatical things over something less consequential than legendary bouillabaisse."

"Speaking of which," Roget added, "I hope that you and your wife will be my guest for dinner some night soon. It would be an honor."

Never one to turn down a dinner invitation, Duquesne nodded with a look of satisfaction. "We'd be delighted. But what are you going to do about a chef? According to Ballou, the stars belong to him."

Roget sounded more relieved than distressed. "To tell you the truth, Ballou was getting to be a giant pain. And people don't come here for the stars. They come for the food. We still have the recipes, the talented staff. And the sous chef is no slouch. I think when you have dinner, you'll be very pleased."

Duquesne looked at the man, whose head was again starting to float above his shoulders, and didn't doubt him for a second. Dinner here was going to be fine. They might even put the mussels back in the bouillabaisse.

JANIS PECK'S BOUILLABAISSE

Fish: You will need a total of 2 pounds of a mixture of miscellaneous firm whitefish such as halibut, grouper, red snapper, mahimahi, sea bass, etc., cut into pieces. Additionally: 1 pound shrimp, 1 pound sea scallops, and 1 small lobster, cooked.

1. Melt together in large soup pot:

   1 cup olive oil   1 tablespoon butter

2. Sauté until very tender (do not brown):

   6 garlic cloves, smashed and minced
   1 medium onion, chopped (about ½ cup)
   1 celery rib, chopped (about ½ cup)
   1 small white potato, chopped (about ¾ cup)
   1 cup chopped sweet peppers (green, yellow, red)
   2 cups chopped fennel (include ribs and bulb)
   1 large or 2 small leeks, white and green parts, chopped (about 2 cups)

3. Add:

   a few grinds black pepper (to taste)
   1 teaspoon salt (or to taste)
   ½ teaspoon red pepper flakes (or to taste)
   ¼ teaspoon celery salt
   1 rounded tablespoon herbs de Provence
   1 rounded teaspoon marjoram
   ½ teaspoon chervil
   1 rounded tablespoon basil
   1 rounded teaspoon turmeric
   1 bay leaf
   half of ¼ cup of chopped, fresh parsley (save the remainder for garnish)
   1 teaspoon (approximately) or 5 grams of saffron threads (or more depending on taste)
   12 (or more) sprigs fresh thyme tied in a bundle

4. Add 32 ounces of fish stock. You can make your own favorite recipe or use the following ingredients. Simmer on lowest setting for 1 hour, taste to correct seasoning.

   3 8-ounce bottles of clam juice
   1 8-ounce container of rich fish stock (in the frozen foods case in specialty markets)
   2 cups dry white wine
   1 15-ounce can vegetable stock (or your own, if you have it)
   2 26-ounce packs Pomi brand chopped or whole tomatoes (if not available, use good Italian canned whole tomatoes; if using whole

tomatoes, mash them into the broth)
juice of 1 lemon
⅓ of the fish (add a few shrimp, shells on)
5. In the blender: puree approximately ⅓ of the broth and return to pot while that simmers.
6. Melt 1 tablespoon butter and 2 tablespoons olive oil in a saucepan. Add the rest of the seafood (shell the shrimp and remove the tough muscle from the sides of the scallops) and sauté until opaque. Salt and pepper to taste.
7. Add the cooked lobster meat and set aside and keep warm.
8. Make your favorite aioli (garlic mayonnaise)—keep cold in refrigerator.
9. Cut a slim baguette into 10 slices, rub olive oil on each piece, and toast in the broiler. When done, rub garlic and sprinkle grated Romano on each piece while still warm. Set aside.
10. Remove the thyme bouquet and the shells from the shrimp in the broth. Pour any liquid in the fish sauté pan into the broth.
11. Distribute the cooked fish among 8-10 bowls, ladle broth over each, place baguette "crouton" on top, drizzle or top with aioli (can also be served on the side), sprinkle with chopped fresh parsley, and serve with crusty French bread and cold Muscadet or other crisp, dry white wine.
P.S. Add mussels, cockles, and clams if you want to live dangerously.

Pierre Franey's Aioli

½ teaspoon finely minced or crushed garlic (or to taste)
1 egg yolk

½ teaspoon white vinegar
salt and fresh ground pepper to taste
¾ cup extra virgin olive oil

Place garlic, egg yolk, vinegar, salt, and pepper in a blender and puree. Add olive oil in a gradual stream until smooth and thickened.

Keep refrigerated.

Yield: ¼ cup (Note: When serving the above Bouillabaisse, double this recipe.)

BLAME IT ON THE BROWNIES
by Toni L. P. Kelner

Toni L. P. Kelner is the author of the Laura Fleming mystery series including the recent Wed and Buried. *The Laura Fleming series is set in Byerly, North Carolina, the imaginary mill town where Laura's large and colorful family lives. Kelner, who was raised in North Carolina like Laura, now lives in Massachusetts. Toni's short fiction was nominated in 2003 for an Anthony.*

The Gang was late, not by much, but just enough to make me wonder if they were really going to show. When the doorbell finally rang, I made myself take a deep breath before opening the door. It wasn't just seeing the Gang again that made me so nervous. My heart was pounding and my mouth was dry because I was desperate to find the truth at last. My sister once said that I crave truth the same way she craved cocaine and that my addiction was as dangerous as hers was. Maybe she was right, but I still had to know why my friend Suzy had died twenty years before.

I made my lips relax into a smile when I saw the two women standing there. Margery's impish grin was the same as ever, even if the face around it was plumper, while Jean looked pale and reserved, but oddly wistful. After a second's hesitation, we burst into a flurry of hugs and air kisses. I was surprised by how good it felt.

"I don't believe it," Margery said. "Dina Willner wearing colors!"

I looked down sheepishly at my turquoise slacks and the matching silk blouse. "I guess I got tired of black." My parents had called me a latter-day beatnik, while the Gang had made jokes about becoming a wannabe Goth, but until recently, I'd stuck with solid black. "But I still don't wear pastels!"

"Thank God for that," Margery said. "Are we the first?" Before I could answer, she said, "See, Jean, I told you we wouldn't be late." Then she turned back to me to add, "Can you believe she's still giving me grief for being late all the time when we were in high school?"

"We're late tonight, too," Jean pointed out. "It's just that Babs is even later."

"She called a few minutes ago," I said. "Something about a meeting running long."

Jean nodded sagely. "Don't they always! I don't know how Father expects me to get my work done when every single meeting goes overtime. I was just telling Margery on the drive over about the last parish building committee meeting. Nobody ever sticks to the agenda. Why do they think I go to the trouble to type it up if we aren't supposed to follow it? If I've told Father once, I've told him a thousand times—"

"Dina, this place is great," Margery interrupted, as she walked around my living room. It was a large room, furnished in gently shaped teak and shades of russet and blue. The oriental carpet and the paintings on the wall were the only touches with patterns—the walls and upholstery were all unbroken solids. "I'd always heard that computer programming paid big, but I didn't know it paid *this* big."

"It's not really programming," I corrected her. "I'm a Web designer."

Margery waved it away. "Web, Internet, information superhighway— it's all the same thing. I can't even e-mail without one of the kids around to walk me through it. God forbid I should ever have to get a real job! I'd never be able to use the technology. Besides which, I'd never have time between all the kids' games and clubs and lessons. The only machine I need to know how to use is a car!"

"I'd be glad to give you computer lessons," Jean said. "I use one to keep track of Father's schedule and the budgets. I even lay out the church bulletin."

"What kind of system do you use?" I asked.

"It's a PC," Jean said proudly.

Thankfully, the doorbell rang again before I had to say anything more, and when I went to answer it, in swept Babs, a cell phone pressed to her ear and one hand raised to forestall our greetings.

"I don't have time for this!" she was saying. "Just do what I told you to do, the way I told you to do it, and have the spreadsheet on my desk when I get there Monday morning." She hung up. "Secretaries!"

Jean's lips tightened.

"Excuse me," Babs said. "Not secretaries—administrative assistants. What I wouldn't give for a real, live secretary who'd do what I want her to do without giving me a list of reasons why she should do something different."

Though I thought that sounded even more insulting, Jean nodded. It was probably one of the few times those two had agreed on anything.

"Well?" Babs said to us. "Isn't anybody going to give me a hug?"

More hugs and air kisses, and the line between the girls we'd been and the women we'd become blurred just for a second. Then we broke apart again and stood there awkwardly.

My therapist says I romanticize the past, at least the good parts. So maybe there had been awkward silences while Suzy was around, but I couldn't remember any, and I'm sure there hadn't been any during the Gang's final sleepover. Suzy was so happy that night, happier than she'd ever been in high school, and it couldn't help but rub off on the rest of us.

Not that she'd been unhappy in high school. She'd made the best grades in our class, dated one of the cutest guys, and was adored by all of us in the Gang. It's just that her mother was so protective of her. In hindsight, I can see that Mrs. Tucker never intended to smother Suzy. She just wanted to keep her safe. We'd all been surprised when she let Suzy go away to school—especially Jean, who'd assumed that she and Suzy would be together like they'd been since elementary school. Suzy confided to me that her mother would never have allowed it if not for the scholarship Suzy had won. Even then, her mother had sworn to bring her right back home if her grades slipped or if she got into any trouble. Of course, Suzy never saw her first report card from college, and the trouble she found was far too close to home.

I realized my guests were looking at me. "Why don't you all have a seat, and I'll get us something to drink." I didn't bother to ask what they wanted. In fact, I already had our drinks waiting in the kitchen, and I brought out a tray with four glasses and two bottles: a two-liter bottle of Coke and a quart of dark rum.

Jean was perched on the end of the armchair, while Margery had shed her shoes and was sprawled across half of the sectional sofa. Babs was prowling through the living room, as if pricing every item, and stopped in front of one of the paintings on the wall. It was my favorite, dark swirls of acrylic that hinted at motion and emotion.

"Is this one of yours?" she asked.

I nodded.

"Have you sold many?"

"Not a single one."

"Aren't they worth anything?"

"Babs, don't be such a bitch," Margery said with fond exasperation.

"I never tried to sell my work. I realized a long time ago that I don't have it in me to be a full-time artist. I only paint when I'm unhappy." I'd painted the one Babs was examining during the long weeks of caring for my sister. "I decided I'd rather be happy than paint, so I switched to Web design."

"A dot-com?" Babs asked.

"Freelance."

"That's the way to go," she said. "You don't have to put up with bean counters watching over your shoulder."

"Babs, I thought you were a bean counter," Margery said.

"I am. Would you want a bitch like me watching your every step?"

We all laughed, and I put the tray down on the coffee table. "Rum and Coke anyone?"

"That takes me back," Margery said. "I wonder if it tastes as good, now that it's legal."

"I can't remember the last time I drank hard liquor," Jean added.

Babs grumbled, "I don't believe I used to drink this crap," but when I fixed hers, she took a healthy swallow.

Once we all had a glass in hand, I pulled a fat cushion from the couch and sank down into it, my legs crossed Indian-style.

"Look at us!" Margery crowed. "Just like old times."

She was right. We'd taken the same positions we always had, as if our places in the circle had been assigned for life. Babs at twelve o'clock, as insistent as ever that she be the focus. Margery to her left, then me, and then Jean.

"Not exactly like old times," Jean pointed out, staring at the gap between Babs and herself. "Suzy isn't here."

I knew the silence must have been painful to my friends, but I was glad that somebody else had broached the subject so I wouldn't have to. I looked at each of them but saw nothing in their faces but sadness.

Then Margery said, "I propose a toast. To Suzy!"

"Here, here," I chimed in, and we stretched out our arms to meet in the middle. "To Suzy!"

We emptied our glasses, and I hastened to fill them again.

"I really shouldn't," Jean said. "Not on an empty stomach."

"Live a little, Jean." Margery took a big gulp. "It's not like you've got to drive home or anything. Personally, I could use a good buzz—especially since I don't have to worry about my rug rats dragging me out of bed first thing in the morning."

"I cannot believe I let you talk us into a slumber party," Babs said.

"Friday nights were always for sleepovers," I reminded her. "It's a tradition."

"It was a tradition twenty years ago. Do you know how hard it was to clear my schedule for this?"

"On Friday night?" Margery objected. "It's not like you have kids to get to soccer practice in the morning."

Babs's eyes glittered, probably because she thought Margery was making a dig about Babs's two failed, childless marriages. "Some of us have other things to do than change diapers and wipe runny noses. My business keeps me busy."

"You don't know what it's like to work 24/7," Margery scoffed, "until you've had kids waking you up with earaches in the middle of the night."

"No, Babs is right," Jean broke in. "We working women have incredible demands on our time. I can't count the number of times Father has called me in on Saturday to handle some crisis for him."

I knew Babs couldn't decide whether to be amused or offended by Jean's comparing her job as church secretary to Babs's own position of chief financial officer, but to my disappointment, she held her tongue.

In fact, everybody stayed on their best behavior for the next few minutes. So I decided that if rum and Coke wasn't going to get them talking, I'd try something else. "Is anybody hungry?"

"Starved," Margery admitted. "What's for dinner?"

"Lasagna, of course."

"With garlic bread?" she asked.

I nodded.

I wasn't sure how lasagna had become the staple for the Gang's sleepovers, though I imagined it had been Suzy's idea. The sleepovers themselves had definitely been at her instigation. Her mother had balked at letting her go out on dates more than one night a week, so this was Suzy's way of getting out of the house as much as possible on the weekend. We'd alternated houses, but some things had never varied: rum and Coke accompanied by lasagna and garlic bread. And of course, the brownies.

"Come on into the kitchen," I said.

We spent the next few minutes putting our meal together while we compared notes about other old friends from high school. The lasagna was already done, and it took no time at all to warm it up and brown the bread I'd already brushed with garlic butter. I poured another round of rum and Coke to relax us further, and we sat down to eat.

I wanted somebody else to mention Suzy again, but it was as if they'd conspired to avoid the subject. Of course, I knew it was nothing more than their reluctance to revisit the pain—I'd spent most of the past twenty years avoiding it myself.

At least we continued to fall into old patterns. Babs would say something outrageous about sex, religion, or politics; Jean would be shocked and start to lecture her; and Margery would try to defuse the situation. My role hadn't changed either. As always, I observed, though I hoped I wasn't as arrogant as I'd been in high school. What we were missing was Suzy's laughter as she gently pointed out all of our failings. It could have been offensive, but not the way Suzy did it.

We made it through dinner, and Margery sighed with satisfaction. "That was wonderful. It's going to be tough to fit in dessert. You do have dessert, don't you?"

"Absolutely. What would a sleepover be without Toklas brownies?"

Somebody gasped, but I'm not sure who. Then Margery said, "You made brownies? Like before? With. . . ."

"With marijuana." I got up from the table. "They wouldn't be Toklas brownies without marijuana."

They weren't actually Toklas brownies, because I used my own recipe instead of the one in the *Alice B. Toklas Cookbook,* but that's how I'd loftily referred to them. It had been during one of those endless games of one-upmanship the Gang had indulged in when I'd announced that my sister had served me marijuana brownies.

In fact, my older sister had merely left a batch unattended long enough for me to filch one, and I'd been so nervous that I wasn't sure if eating it had affected me or not, but I'd assumed an air of worldly sophistication, as if one lousy brownie had permanently raised my consciousness to a higher level.

The Gang had reacted predictably. Jean had been shocked beyond words, and I caught her crossing herself. Babs had pooh-poohed it, but I could tell she was deeply envious, while Margery had wanted to know every detail of the experience. And Suzy, always an adventurer, had asked if I could bring some to the next sleepover.

I'd hemmed and hawed, but in the face of Suzy's persuasiveness and Babs's certainty that I couldn't pull it off, I agreed. It had taken me most of the next week to talk my sister into getting the pot from one of her sources, and I'd had to spend most of my allowance to pay for it. Worst of all had been cooking the brownies, scared to death that one of my parents would wander in while I was baking and want to lick the bowl. But the following Friday night I triumphantly served my first plate of Toklas brownies.

Now in my kitchen, the covered plate I'd hidden in the breadbox looked much the same as the ones from years past, and I lifted off the foil to expose the pile of brownies.

"How could you?" Jean asked indignantly. "After what happened to Suzy!"

"She said it was going to be a traditional sleepover," Babs said. "She had to fix Toklas brownies."

I'd known I could count on Babs to go against whatever Jean said, so I offered them to her first.

She took one and bit into it defiantly.

Next I held the plate out to Margery. Emotions I couldn't track flitted across her face, but she took one and gingerly tasted it.

Next Jean. I held my breath as she hesitated. If this was going to work, we were all going to have to eat the brownies. But she wouldn't even reach her hand out at first. I didn't say anything, just held out the plate while Margery watched and Babs smirked.

Jean said, "They're just like you used to make? Your sister got you the marijuana like before?"

For the first time that night, I lied. "That's right. She still has her sources."

I could only guess at why that had reassured her, but Jean finally took a brownie. Only then did I do the same, and the four of us resolutely chewed.

Margery got punchy first. "Look at us!" she said. "You'd think we were eating fiber biscuits instead of brownies. Come to think of it, I was always regular when I had these things every week."

Babs groaned. "Please, let's not start talking about our plumbing. Then

I'll know we've gotten old."

"I wonder if you could add powdered fiber to brownies," Jean said speculatively. "Father has been having a terrible time with his stool lately."

For some reason, that struck us all as incredibly hilarious, and the giggle fits began. I relaxed, knowing that the barriers were bound to drop.

Though we'd always started our sleepovers with rum and Coke, we'd never been able to get our hands on enough to get really drunk. It was through the brownies that we'd let our hair down. Things we never would have said otherwise had cascaded out. That cannabis-inspired honesty could have broken up the Gang, but Suzy had enacted the rule that prevented it. Anything said was never to be considered the fault of the speaker. "Blame it on the brownies," she'd always said.

Then she'd died, and as hard as I'd tried to blame it on the brownies, I'd ended up blaming myself. No amount of time in therapy had changed that, not even the months as an inpatient.

I let the others enjoy themselves at first, laughing along when Babs told us about idiotic coworkers and Margery matched her with descriptions of soccer moms from hell. Even Jean's tedious tales of herding parishioners made us laugh.

As for me, I recounted some of the lunacies I'd put myself through: gurus and mentors and spiritual guides who found their way through my door and into my pocketbook. Surprisingly, laughing at them with my old friends made me feel better than any session with my current therapist, and I wondered if I should give him up, too.

Another round of brownies later, talk turned toward Suzy, just as I'd known it would. I'd expected Jean to say something, but instead it was Margery who suddenly announced, "I wish Suzy were here!" She turned to the rest of us. "Not that I'm not glad to see all of you, but I really miss Suzy. She was so funny."

Babs nodded. "Probably the toughest of us all."

"And she loved us," Jean put in.

"She understood us," I added, knowing we were remembering in Suzy the traits most important to us. Then I bit the bullet. "I still can't believe she died that way."

Jean took a ragged breath. "It was those brownies. Those damned brownies!" I think all of us were taken aback at her burst of profanity, even Jean herself. "Why in God's name did she eat them while driving?"

The trip to Suzy's school had been a long one, which took her around some steep curves, so at first everybody had assumed she'd just been tired when she lost control of the car and careened off a cliff. Then the coroner's report revealed that the remains of marijuana brownies had been found in Suzy's stomach, and according to the police investigation, Suzy had been driving erratically for miles before she crashed. Witnesses described a fireball that still haunted my dreams.

Ironically, that fireball had kept the rest of us out of trouble. All evidence of the source of the brownies had been destroyed along with our friend. Though the police had questioned each of us, we'd all denied knowing where Suzy could have gotten them. Our parents had been suspicious, too, but never acted on those suspicions. They didn't want to believe that their daughters were involved in drugs. With my sister around, my own parents had already had plenty of practice in denial. Suzy's mother moved away right after the funeral. Nobody knew where she'd ended up.

"Why was Suzy so stupid?" Babs demanded. "She would never even let any of the rest of us climb stairs after we ate brownies. I've never understood how she could have gotten behind the wheel when she was stoned."

"Maybe she didn't start eating them until she was on the road," Margery suggested. "She could have gotten hungry."

"Dina should never have given her the brownies!" Jean said, then turned to me. "Dina, why didn't you mail them to her? She'd still be alive if you'd mailed them to her."

I swallowed hard. If I was after the truth, I was going to have to speak my share, too. "I never even thought of it. When Suzy asked me to make an extra batch for her to take back to school, I figured it would be easier to give them to her when she was here."

She'd been delighted, too, especially when I told her I'd made a triple batch. She had a party planned in her dorm room for the following weekend and wanted the brownies to share with her new friends at school. She'd invited the Gang to come, too, and we'd all been excited by the prospect of a genuine college party. Except Jean. Already miserable because she had to live at home and attend the community college instead of going away like the rest of us had, she'd been devastated when her parents refused to let her spend the weekend with Suzy.

Now that I thought of it, Jean's woes had been why we'd had that final sleepover in the first place. Suzy knew how disappointed she was and had arranged for us all to come back to town as a consolation prize for her oldest friend.

"She said she was saving them all for the party," I went on. "I even double-wrapped them so they'd stay fresh all week. She was going to hide them in her closet so she wouldn't see them and be tempted."

"Don't give Dina a hard time," Babs said. "Suzy was a fool to eat those things. You know it as well as I do. She was a damned fool!"

"I warned her about them that morning after Mass," Jean said sadly. "That was the last time I saw her. God gave me that one last chance." She looked at the rest of us, almost proudly. "I was the last one of the Gang to see her."

"Actually, you weren't," Babs said with studied nonchalance. "Mass ends at noon, right? I saw her later than that."

"She said she was leaving town right after Mass—that's why she couldn't come to my house for Sunday dinner," Jean said, indignant at the twenty-year-old slight.

Babs just shrugged.

"Where did you see her?" Margery asked, sounding suspicious.

"Driving around town somewhere," Babs said vaguely.

"Are you sure it was her?" Jean asked.

"Why would I make that up?"

Of course, we all knew she'd have cheerfully made up all kinds of things to torment Jean, but I didn't think this was one of those times.

"Maybe you saw her on her way to Todd's," Margery suggested. "I didn't want to say anything, because I could tell Jean liked the idea of being the last one of us to have seen Suzy, but she came by my house after Mass, and she was heading to Todd's next."

"Why?" Jean wanted to know.

"She wanted to borrow a sweater. It was her school colors, and it was getting tight on me anyway. I forgot to bring it to the sleepover, so she swung by to pick it up. Only, I could tell something was bothering her, and when I asked her what was wrong, she said she was worried about Todd. She said he'd seemed distant on their last few dates." She looked down at her hands. "I know I shouldn't have, but I told her that I'd heard rumors that Todd was seeing somebody behind her back."

"No! How could Todd do that to her?" Jean asked.

"Some men don't know when they have it good," Margery said with a shrug. "Anyway, I told her to go talk to Todd about it right away, before she left town."

Babs's face turned red. "That's why she showed up. It was your fault!"

"What?" Margery's eyes widened. "It was you? Were you the one seeing Todd?"

"Babs did go to the same college as Todd," I suddenly remembered.

"Lots of people went to that school," Babs said, but for the first time since I'd known her, she looked ashamed. Then she sighed. "I guess there's no reason not to admit it now. Todd and I ran into one another at a frat party and realized we had a lot in common. I felt bad about Suzy, but he swore that he'd been planning to break up with her anyway. He didn't want a long-distance relationship. He was supposed to do it the night after our sleepover, or I never would have gone over to his house that afternoon. He told me he hadn't been able to tell her, but he promised to do it the next week. Then we started . . . necking."

"And Suzy saw you?" Jean said, scandalized.

Babs nodded. "We were sitting in that little park across the street from Todd's house, and suddenly Suzy was there. We tried to explain, but she wouldn't listen. She just ran to her car and drove away." She swallowed visibly. "Todd was the one who told me she was dead—after that, I never wanted to even look at him again. I was. . . ."

I expected her to say she was ashamed, or upset, or guilty. But what she said was, "I was young."

"Phenylethylamine," Margery said.

"What?" I asked.

"It's the chemical that your brain produces when you're in love—it's in chocolate, too. That's why women eat chocolate when they're suffering from a broken heart." She must have seen the blank looks on our faces. "Don't you get it? Chocolate? Brownies? Suzy had just had her heart broken. It wasn't the pot that made Suzy dig into those brownies, it was the chocolate."

Jean said, "How do you know about phenyl-whatever-it-is?"

Margery snapped, "I was a psych major, for heaven's sake, not to mention being number two in our class. And even housewives can read!"

"Sorry," Jean said. "It was just a shock to find out about Babs and Todd." She glared at Babs.

"Jean, it was twenty years ago," Babs said.

"You never forget betrayal!"

"If Suzy were still alive, she wouldn't be holding a grudge. Nobody holds a grudge that long." She cut her eyes toward Margery. "Isn't that right, Margery?"

"What's that supposed to mean?"

"That comment about being number two in our class. You're not still mad at Suzy for beating you out for number one, are you? By what? A tenth of a point?"

"Do you think I still care about that?" Margery demanded.

"You tell me. You'd have gotten that scholarship instead of Suzy if you'd been number one, wouldn't you?"

"Maybe."

"I heard they offered it to you after Suzy died."

"You didn't take it, did you?" Jean asked.

"Of course not," Margery said. "And I never held a grudge against Suzy for winning it, or for having a higher grade point average. I loved her!"

Jean whimpered, "I loved her, too."

"You know damned well I loved her!" Babs said.

I waited, breathless, for more to be said. Suddenly Margery pulled Babs toward her in a fierce hug. The two of them held one another for a minute, then reached for Jean and me, and all four of us embraced, murmuring that we'd all loved Suzy and that we loved each other, too.

But even as I joined in, I cursed inwardly. Though I had a better idea of why Suzy had eaten those brownies, and even knew why my friends might have wanted her dead, I didn't know everything that happened. The only way I could think of to find out more was to tell more of what I knew. So while I hugged my friends, I planned my next steps.

When we broke apart, Jean said, "I'm sorry, Babs. I shouldn't have said those things."

"I shouldn't have, either," Babs replied.

"Blame it on the brownies," Margery said. "We have to blame it on the brownies."

"But we didn't blame the brownies," I said. "We didn't blame the brownies for Suzy's death."

"Of course we did," Margery said. "The brownies got her stoned, and she crashed."

"And who gave her the brownies?" I said. When none of them answered, I did it for them. "I did. You never really blamed the brownies. You blamed me." When they tried to argue, I spoke over them. "I did, too. I knew then that it was my fault that Suzy was dead."

"I never blamed you," Margery said.

"Didn't you? Then why did the Gang break up? Why did we never see each other again after the funeral? Sure, we'd run into one another once in a while, but we were never really friends again. You three couldn't stand to be near me."

"It's not that simple," Babs said. "We were going to different colleges, and after that, living different lives."

"My mother got sick," Jean reminded me, "and I was so busy at the church."

"I got married, and then I had the kids," Margery put in. "None of us blamed you."

"Maybe not, but I blamed myself." I thought about showing them the scars on my wrists, but couldn't do it. "I didn't stop blaming myself until my sister told me what she'd done to me back then.

"You know she was doing drugs in college—that's how she knew where to get the pot for the brownies. Well, she didn't stop with pot—she got into the hard stuff. Then she dropped out of school, hit the streets, and didn't come home for months at a time, even years. When she finally called around the first of the year, she told me she had AIDS."

"Dear Lord," Jean breathed.

"I went and brought her home, but she was too far gone for the doctors to do much. I nursed her as best I could, and mostly we talked, about being kids together and what had happened to the two of us. About Suzy, of course. And about the brownies. She told me about the brownies just a few days before she died."

"Your sister's dead?" Margery said. "I thought you said she got you the marijuana for these brownies."

"I lied," I said. "I bought it from some guy on the street."

Jean's face went white. "From somebody on the street? Not from your sister?"

"What difference does it make?" Babs asked, irritated.

But Jean didn't answer her. She jumped up, looking around wildly for the bathroom. Then she ran into it, slamming the door behind her. Seconds later, we heard the sounds of retching.

"What is she doing?" Babs asked, and Margery went to bang on the door, calling her name.

As for me, I had my answer, but I still wasn't satisfied. I waited patiently till Jean came back out of the bathroom, using one of my guest towels to wipe her mouth and face.

"So it was you," I said to her.

"What's going on?" Babs demanded.

"Shall I tell them," I asked Jean, "or will you?"

Jean just shook her head and sat back down, her eyes blank.

The breath I took was so deep it almost hurt. "My sister told me something before she died, something Jean already knew." I paused to see if Jean would jump in, but when she didn't I continued. "By the time I asked her to help me get pot, she'd already started shoplifting to pay for her habit, and when I offered her enough money to buy more, she jumped at the chance. And she smoked every bit of it herself. Then she put parsley flakes into a plastic bag to give to me, and laughed her ass off while I baked it into brownies."

"It wasn't pot?" Margery said.

"It had to have been pot," Babs said angrily. "We were stoned. I know we were. We got the munchies. We got the giggles. We said things we never would have said if we weren't stoned."

Wearily I said, "Margery, you were the psych major. Explain how people tend to react to drugs the way they expect to. Even if they don't actually take drugs."

Margery said, "What about Suzy? The police said she ate marijuana before she died, not parsley."

"That's right," I said. "She really did eat hash brownies. But I didn't give them to her. You did, didn't you Jean? You switched my brownies with the real thing."

"Oh, please," Babs said. "Where would somebody like Jean get pot?"

"It was easy," Jean said, her voice almost matter-of-fact. "I asked a girl at college who looked like she'd know, and she sent me to a guy who sold it to me. It didn't even cost that much. Then I baked it into brownies, just like Dina thought she had. I didn't have the same recipe, but I hoped nobody would notice. Suzy had said she was leaving town right after Mass, which meant that she had the brownies in her car. So I waited until Father started the homily, and I told Suzy I had to go to the bathroom. Only, I went out to the parking lot instead and found her spare key so I could switch the brownies."

"How could you do that to her?" Margery said. "She was your best friend."

"She said she was going to save them until the party," Jean said. "I told her not to eat them on the way. I told her not to!" She looked at us, seeing the expressions on our faces. "She wasn't supposed to get stoned while driving. I never wanted her to get hurt!"

"Then why in the hell did you switch the brownies?" Babs demanded.

"I loved her," Jean said as if it were the most obvious thing in the world. "I loved her, and I missed her so much. She'd gone away—all of you had gone away—and I was so lonely. I didn't want to hurt her. I just wanted her to come home."

Margery shook her head. "I don't understand."

"I was going to wait until her party, and then call her dorm and tell them Suzy was handing out hash brownies," Jean explained. "I thought sure that would get her thrown out of school, and even if it didn't, her mother would be so upset that she wouldn't let her stay there after that. We would have been together again."

"What a shitty thing to do!" Babs said. "Did you even care about what Suzy wanted? Or the trouble the rest of us would have gotten into?"

"I just wanted Suzy to come home," Jean said.

Jean's breath caught in her throat, and I knew I should stop, but I had to know everything. "But how did you know there wasn't really marijuana in my brownies, when I didn't even know?"

"It was after you brought them the first time. I was so scared of eating them—I didn't want to become a drug addict like your sister."

"Oh, please!" Babs sneered.

Jean ignored her. "I ate one that night, because Suzy wanted me to, but I was afraid. So I went to the library to find out more about marijuana, what it could do to me. That's when I found out that we couldn't have really eaten hash brownies. Do you remember how stoned we got right away? Eating hash brownies doesn't work that fast—it can take an hour or more to affect you. So the next week, I snuck a brownie into my pocketbook and took it to a cop I knew at church. I told him I'd found it, and I was afraid that it had pot in it but I didn't want to get anybody in trouble if it didn't. He had it analyzed for me and told me it was clean. So I knew it was all right to eat them."

"But you let us keep thinking we were really getting stoned?" Babs said.

A tiny smile crossed Jean's lips. "I liked knowing something nobody else did."

"What about tonight?" Margery asked. "Why did you go make yourself throw up?"

"When Dina said her sister hadn't given her the pot, I realized I'd eaten hash for real."

"No you didn't," I said. "I lied about that, too."

At first she looked hurt, but then said, "I should have realized that—I panicked. But it was hash brownies that killed Suzy, and I couldn't bear it." Then she hung her head. "Only it wasn't really the brownies that killed her, was it? It was me."

I closed my eyes for a moment, waiting for the relief I'd been seeking for all those years. Finally I could tell myself with certainty that Suzy hadn't died because of my brownies. I hadn't killed her after all. But did I honestly believe that Jean had?

Then Margery said, "It was as much me as it was you, Jean. Suzy wouldn't have found out about Todd and Babs that way if I hadn't sent her over to his house."

"You didn't know who Todd was seeing," Babs said reluctantly. "Seeing me with him was what pushed her over the edge."

"And Suzy would never have known about hash brownies in the first place if I hadn't bragged about eating one." I ran my fingers through my hair wearily. I'd thought that once I knew the truth, I'd be able to let go of the blame. All I'd done was to stain my friends with guilt, while still feeling guilty myself.

"No!" I said as firmly as I could. "None of us set out to hurt Suzy— she would never have blamed us for what happened." I looked at each of them in turn, willing them to believe it. Willing myself to believe it. "We all know what she'd say if she were with us now, don't we?"

The three women looked at me with nearly identical expressions of mingled despair and hope.

"Blame the brownies," I said. "Blame it on the brownies."

MEXICAN BROWNIES WITH CANELA WHIPPED CREAM

We can't include a recipe for Ganja Brownies, but here's a recipe with a few added surprises, courtesy Aaron Sanchez.

½ pound cone piloncillo
  (unrefined Mexican sugar)
6 ounces unsweetened chocolate
6 ounces Mexican chocolate
½ pound butter
5 eggs
2½ cups + 1 tablespoon sugar

1 teaspoon vanilla extract
1 teaspoon almond extract
3 teaspoons espresso
1½ cups flour
½ pound walnuts
1 cup cream
1 tablespoon ground cinnamon

Preheat oven to 425F. In bowl over double boiler, melt piloncillo, both chocolates, and butter. Allow mixture to cool. In another bowl, whisk the eggs, 2½ cups sugar, both extracts, and espresso until well mixed. Then pour cooled chocolate mixture in the egg mixture. Mix well, then add the flour and walnuts. Add this mixture to a greased 9- by 9-inch baking pan and bake for 25 to 30 minutes until brownies are well set.

Whisk cream until stiff, then add 1 tablespoon each sugar and cinnamon. Cut a wedge of brownie and serve with dollop of canela crema.

Prep Time: 30 minutes
Cook Time: 30 minutes
Yield: 27 brownies

DAISY AND THE MINCE PIES
by Anne Perry

Anne Perry is the best-selling author of two acclaimed series set in Victorian England. Her William Monk novels include Death of a Stranger, Funeral in Blue, Slaves of Obsession, *and* The Twisted Root. *She also writes the popular novels featuring Thomas and Charlotte Pitt, including* Seven Dials, Southampton Row, The Whitechapel Conspiracy, *and* Half Moon Street. *Her short story "Heroes" won an Edgar Award. She recently wrote a novel set during World War I, entitled* No Graves As Yet. *Anne Perry lives in Scotland.*

There have been a lot of changes recently, otherwise none of this sorry business would ever have happened. Willow and I—she is my half sister, rather more spaniel, whereas I am a trifle toward the smooth-haired collie—used to live with Boss. However, things get different as one gets older, and now we live with Friend, just across the driveway. And Tara, who is all Labrador, which is at the root of the problem, lives with Boss and Bell. Bell is so long and thin she doesn't look like a proper dog at all, and she can run faster than anything else I've ever seen. She goes round and round and can't stop, so she has to jump clean over you. It is disconcerting, to say the least.

I thought I wouldn't like the arrangement, but I find I do. We all do. Which doesn't change the fact that if I had been at Boss's house, the thief would never have got away with it and Tara wouldn't have got into nearly so much trouble.

It began just before Christmas when the weather was all bright and sharp and full of sparkling edges. A man came to the door, selling mince pies and cakes and other things to eat. We weren't allowed any, of course. "Mince pies aren't good for dogs!" That's always the excuse. Anything people really like for themselves isn't supposed to be good for dogs. I'm sure they don't do us any more harm than they do them.

He came to my new house as well, but Friend wasn't in, so Willow and I barked at him a lot, and he went away. You would think that would be all there was to it, but two mornings later, Bertie, the blackest of Boss's black cats—I've lost count of how many there are—came flying over here with his tail in the air and a lot to say. That in itself is not so unusual. Bertie's often over here, and he often has a lot to say, but this time he was very upset. The very first occasion somebody opened the door, he slipped in between their ankles and up the stairs like a shot.

Willow and I were in the study, with our front paws on the sill, watching the world. Actually it is high and a big window, and on a clear day you can see halfway across Scotland right to the mountains in the middle, if mountains are what you like. They are all white and glittering at the moment. I prefer people coming and going on the driveway.

"You shouldn't be in here," I said, but I couldn't be bothered to get up and chase him.

"Somebody came in the night and stole a hundred pounds from Boss!" Bertie replied, ignoring my remark.

A hundred pounds is a lot of money. It would buy a hundred of the very best bones, the ones that last a week or so, if nobody steals them or loses them. Puppies, like Bell, tend to bury them and then forget where.

"She must have lost it," I said reasonably. "If anyone had come in, Tara would have barked and Boss would have heard her and got up." Bell sleeps upstairs in Boss's bed. I don't know why. I was never allowed to that I can recall. I suppose it has something to do with her being so thin, and rescued, and all that. Although we all were, at one time or another—except Thea, the Siamese cat.

She was bought . . . I can't imagine why! Apparently she came from Fort William, which is hours away, and screamed all the way home. She has a voice that would break glass. I've always been surprised the chandeliers haven't fallen off! But she's clever and beautiful, and Friend seems to like her a lot.

"But Tara was asleep, Daisy!" Bertie said sharply. "That's the problem! She stole all the mince pies, except one, and fell asleep so hard and so long she's still only half awake now and Boss is furious with her. That money was going to be for turkey and Christmas cake and pudding and all sorts of things. And Tara's in terrible disgrace. Nobody'll speak to her, and you know how she hates that! She's going to be left alone all Christmas, shut out and crying inside herself."

I thought about that for a few moments. Tara is greedy, but Labradors are like that. I think they can't help it. Usually Boss knows better than to leave anything where Tara can reach it!

"She ate nine mince pies," Bertie added miserably. "I don't know how she slept after that! I'd have been sick."

"Tara is a very large dog, you are a very middle-sized cat," I told him.

He glared at me, but he *is* middle-sized compared with Humphrey.

"What are we going to do to help?" he asked plaintively.

"We will have to detect," I replied. We have done this before on several occasions, with great success, in particular the matters of the Silver Quaich, the Archaeologists, and the Christmas Goose. "What do we know . . . exactly?"

"Very little," Bertie replied. "There were ten mince pies and a hundred pounds of money when Boss and Bell went to bed, and they were gone in the morning, all except one mince pie. And the utility room door was open instead of closed. Tara was in her basket in the utility room, and so sound asleep she didn't even wake up for breakfast. And the mince pie plates were on the floor."

"And the tenth pie?" I said curiously.

"On the bench," Bertie replied. "Boss saw it before Bell could reach it."

"Just a minute! You don't live in the kitchen! What were you doing there when Boss first came down?" I had an excellent point in that.

"I wasn't there!" Bertie said crossly. "Dexter told me!" It is a sore issue with him that ever since his accident, Dexter, a rather handsome grey tabby, has lived inside, along with the two wild kittens, Rufus and Star, who are the most recent rescues. To begin with, they were very frightened. She is called Star because she only comes out at night. All day she hides, and since she is black and gets under things, she is very difficult to find. People don't know how to look with their noses.

I haven't a lot of patience with kittens myself. They knock things over, especially Christmas trees, which they will climb up; they leap out at people; they do a lot of spitting and jumping; and on the whole, they talk nonsense. But cats are all right as long as you keep proper control of them.

"Well, didn't they see or hear something?" I asked. "Where was Dexter?"

"Curled up asleep on the couch," Bertie replied with disgust.

Since I had been curled up asleep on the couch in Friend's bedroom at the time myself, I did not comment.

"But Star and Rufus were awake," Bertie went on, not looking straight at me.

I waited.

"They saw him," Bertie continued, his green eyes staring over my left shoulder.

"Saw him? Why didn't you say so? That's excellent! What was he like?"

"That's it." Bertie blinked. "They said it was the fat red man on the cards."

"I beg your pardon?"

"Father Christmas," he said quietly. I swear, a black cat can blush.

I was plunged into disappointment. I had really hoped for something useful because I had no better ideas myself, but what should we expect of kittens, and wild ones at that?

"I considered arguing," Bertie went on. "But Dexter got very upset. Anyone would think they were really his kittens, not just adopted. I dare say he feels responsible. It is very awkward having relatives, even pretend ones."

I knew what he meant. I feel mildly responsible for Tara simply because she is a dog and sort of family.

Bertie got up and took himself off just before Friend returned, and after I had given Friend a suitable welcome, I sat down to think very hard. I talked to Willow about it. She was very upset too, for Tara's sake, but she had no clever ideas.

It was going to be a terrible Christmas.

Sometimes if she makes a fearful noise, Thea gets let in. Friend is very softhearted that way, or else Thea hurts her ears as much as she does mine. Anyway, in the afternoon, about four o'clock, just after sundown, I was in my basket in the hall, under one side of the stairs, feeling close to despair, when Thea walked by, thoroughly pleased with herself because she was inside.

She regarded me with curiosity. "Why are you lying in the dark like a wet Sunday?" she asked. She always wants to know everything.

I told her about the missing money and that Tara had stolen nine mince pies and fallen asleep on duty.

Most cats are thieves, and Thea is one of the best. Unlike dogs, they have no sense of property at all. She thinks everything is hers, even the house!

"I don't believe it," she said simply, twitching her tail in the air. All her natural sympathies were with Tara. Thea will take anything she can reach, if she likes it, and she hates being shut out, even though she—like Archie, Humphrey, and Pansy—has a perfectly good utility room with a fleece-lined bed next to the boiler. She says that isn't the point, it is the principle of the thing. Nobody should shut her in or out of anywhere.

"I wish I didn't believe it," I replied. "But it's true. A hundred bones worth of money, and Tara's in disgrace. Or is it the Father Christmas part you don't believe? Nobody does! There's no such person, but you can't tell kittens that."

Thea gave me a cold, blue look. Siamese cats are the only creatures in the world with eyes that colour, like circles of sky with a brain behind. "I don't believe Boss left nine pies on the bench and the utility room door open," she replied patiently. "If she had, Tara would have been in there and taken them before Boss was into the hall. She hasn't the sense to wait until no one is looking. Tara used to live over here, before you and Willow came. I know her!"

It was true. Tara has an endless appetite. She will eat anything that will fit into her face! But she is not devious and she never holds a grudge. I began to think very hard and rather more clearly. I know the utility room in Boss's house. It closes very well, very firmly. I can open bar handles with my paws. All you have to do is pull on them. But this one is round, and it takes fingers to hold and turn it. That means people!

"The kittens said it was Father Christmas," I said.

Thea, who had gone to sleep on the old pew, uncurled herself long enough to give me a blue look that would have frozen a teapot, and put her nose back into her tail.

"No, they didn't!" I realized suddenly. "They said it was someone who looked like the man on the cards!"

Thea uncurled herself again very slowly. "Why would he let Tara into the kitchen to eat the mince pies?" she asked. "That's stupid!"

"It is!" I agreed with a sudden surge of pleasure. "Because if he came in through the back door and the utility room, she would have barked before he got to the mince pies to bribe her with—or if he came in through the front door, then. . . ."

"She would still have barked before she let him in to give her the mince pies," Thea finished for me. "So the whole thing is nonsense. Tara is innocent!"

"No, she isn't. She ate the pies—or why was she asleep all this time?"

"I don't know," Thea admitted. "Go and ask the kittens again. You should speak to everybody."

"You go," I replied. "You can get out, and you can get in through the cat flap at Boss's."

"I'm asleep," she answered. "Go yourself!"

There was no point in arguing with a cat that's asleep, so I went to the door and barked until Friend let me out. She was busy working, so she didn't watch me, which was a good thing. Friend has outside lights on over the driveway, and scrambling over stone walls is very undignified, especially at my age. But getting into Boss's garden is more difficult. It is supposed to be dog-proof to keep Bell and Tara in. Tara just mooches around looking for anything to eat, but Bell gets the wind in her nose and runs for miles before she ever stops to take a breath and wonders where on earth she is.

I got fed up waiting and tried the side gate with my claws. I'm rather good at gates, and I managed to open the latch and push. The gravel was all frosty and stiff and made no noise when I walked on it. The yard gate was open anyway, because the back door was closed, but as soon as Tara heard me she came to the other side. She was feeling very lonely and miserable, and she was just glad to hear anybody at all who wouldn't tell her off.

Bertie came out of the cat flap. "It's no good," he said grimly. "I've asked the kittens again, and all they will say is that it was Father Christmas, and Dexter boxed me around the ears for doubting them. He really is very difficult these days. Adopting strays isn't good for him."

I explained to him what Thea and I had worked out about the kitchen and the utility room and the mince pies, and he took the point immediately. Then I started to bark because I was fed up with standing outside. I don't like the cold—it is nearly as bad as the rain. I am not a water dog!

Because I was barking, Tara started to bark as well. Bell joined in, although neither of them had any idea why, they just like to make a noise. Actually, so do I.

Boss came to find out what it was all about and told us we were silly, but I shivered frantically, so she let me into the kitchen, where it was warm and bright and full of nice smells. But she still shut Tara in the utility room again, which made me even more determined to clear her name.

Star was sitting under the Welsh dresser. She is a very odd little black kitten. Cats take a lot of understanding. She has a beautiful face and a short tail. Boss said that when she was born, her mother accidentally bit a piece of it off.

When Boss went out of the room I lay down on the floor and looked at Star. "Were you there when the man on the card came and took the money?" I asked.

She blinked at me several times.

I waited.

"Yes," she said at last. Perhaps she was a little jumpy after having been told so many times that she was talking nonsense.

"Which door did he come through?" I asked.

"That one," she said, looking toward the utility room.

"Past Tara? Are you sure?"

"Yes." She blinked again, but she did not waver in the slightest.

"What about the mince pies?"

"He put the money into a bag, and then he put all the mince pies in as well, except one."

I was very puzzled. It made no sense. "He came back and fed them to Tara?"

She blinked again. "No, he went out the front door," she replied.

"With the mince pies?"

"I told you!"

"He wore a red coat?"

"*Yes!* And red trousers and a hat with white fur on it, and fur on his face, lots of it."

"Like a sheep?"

"A what?"

Of course, I had forgotten that she had probably never seen a sheep, although there are some quite near here. I get shouted at every time I go to bark at them.

"Thank you." I waited until Boss came back and let me out through the utility room. I stopped and very gently asked Tara if she had actually eaten the mince pies at all, because it was beginning to look as if she hadn't.

She looked embarrassed but didn't stop weaving around. "Yes," she admitted. "And they sent me to sleep."

I treated that with the disdain it deserved.

She went back to her bed and rooted around; a moment or two later, she uncovered half a mince pie that she'd somehow missed. She picked it up and dropped it quickly. Perhaps she'd had enough of mince pies for a while.

I went over to it. It smelled very odd.

"What have you got, Daisy?" Boss asked me, bending down to pick it up. She was about to throw it away, when I barked. She looked at it more closely, then sniffed it. "That's odd!" she said with a frown. "It smells like whisky." She sniffed it again. "It smells like a lot of whisky. Tara?"

Tara looked hopeful and wagged her tail.

"Where did you get this? It's not one of mine! Were you drunk, girl? Is that what happened? Who fed you these?"

Father Christmas, I thought, but how could I tell her that? I couldn't, but Bertie could! Where was he? He could get into the house and knock down one of the cards with a picture of Father Christmas on it. But would she understand?

"It looks just the same as ours," Boss said thoughtfully. She bent down and pushed Tara out of her bed, feeling in the blanket, and a moment later she came out with a little silver and green piece of paper. "It is the same! It was the salesman from the bakery van, wasn't it! He fed you those in the afternoon, and then came back when you were so drunk you slept right through it! You didn't steal them after all! You just didn't look at what you ate! But then you never do." She turned to me. "Well done, Daisy. You'd better go home, and I'm going to call the police. I don't suppose we'll get our hundred pounds back, but we'll manage. At least Tara isn't in disgrace any more."

But she didn't call the police straightaway. Friend came to fetch me, and they talked about it together in the sitting room in front of the fire and decided instead to call the company that sold the mince pies and find out where the salesman was at the time.

Then we all got in Boss's car, which is very large. A four-wheel drive they call it, but I thought they all had four wheels. "All" was Tara, Bell, Willow and me, and Bertie—who loves cars a lot, far more than I do, unless they are going to the beach—and, of course, Boss and Friend. We didn't take Thea. She howls all the way, and if you have ever heard a Siamese howling, you will understand.

Boss drove in the dark over to the next village to look for him. They said he would be out late, because of Christmas. We found him down on the beach, on the other side of the peninsula, and pulled up next to him.

There were coloured lights all over the place, and music played from some-body's open door. Boss and Friend both got out and let me out, too, because they knew I wouldn't go haring off.

The man looked a little startled when he saw them under the street-lights, and rather uncomfortable. "Hello, ladies," he said a bit awkwardly. "What can I get for you, then?"

"How about a dozen mince pies?" Boss said icily.

"Preferably not laced with Glenmorangie," Friend added with a sar-castic lift of her voice, pulling her coat a little more tightly around her. "That can make you pretty drunk, if you eat enough of them."

"Drunk enough to sleep right through a burglary," Boss added.

He went rather red in the face but denied it before he was really accused. "That's a nasty thing to say! I wouldn't speak like that if I were you. It could be taken as very offensive!"

"It could indeed." Boss nodded her head. "Actually she's rather a valu-able dog, that Labrador. Got a pedigree as long as your arm."

I never thought pedigrees were worth anything, but it sounded good, and it was true that Tara did have one.

The man swallowed hard. "Is it really?"

"Yes," Boss answered, staring hard at him. "And actually she didn't eat all of them. Still got half of one left in her bed. Enough Glenmorangie in it to light a fire."

"*Yours,*" Friend added with rather a hard smile.

"Oh no they weren't!" he said quickly. "You look at the ones I gave you, miss. No whisky in them at all." He smiled back.

"Exactly!" Friend snapped. "The ones you left were straight—but the ones you fed Tara when you came back were 100 proof."

"You . . . you can't know that!" he blustered a bit.

"Yes, I can," Boss answered with confidence. "Same pattern on the cases, same cutter of pastry."

"You . . . you can't prove I did anything wrong." He looked very unhappy now.

"I can't prove you took my hundred pounds," Boss agreed. "But I know you did. I can prove you came back and fed my dog mince pies laced with whisky. And why would any honest man do that?"

"I . . . I like the dog. . . ." he trailed off.

Friend and Boss both gave him a look Thea would have been satisfied with, cold and blue as the winter sea.

"How about if you give your word you won't ever do it again," Boss suggested, "and we don't complain about your trying to poison my valuable dog? No one will believe you fed mince pies, fit to sell people for Christmas, to a dog you don't know. It would raise a lot of suspicion you don't want."

"Yes, yes, of course," he agreed too quickly.

"And you could also give her the hundred pounds you took," Friend added.

He hesitated for only a moment, then very reluctantly fished in his pocket and pulled out ninety-five pounds and fifty pence.

"That'll do." Boss took it quickly.

"You can make up the rest with mince pies," Friend pointed out. "Straight . . . no Glenmorangie! These aren't for the dog!"

He glared at her, but he obeyed.

"Thank you," she said graciously, taking them all and putting them into a carrier bag. "Merry Christmas!"

MINCE PIE

1 cup TVP granules
    (Textured Vegetable Protein,
    for vegetarian meals)
1 cup hot water
4 cups tart apples, peeled and
    diced

1 cup raisins or currants
½ cup apple cider
½ cup brown sugar
    (reduce if needed)
1 orange, grated rind and juice
1 lemon, grated rind and juice

Place above ingredients in a large kettle. Bring to a boil, reduce heat, and simmer gently until apples are soft, about 20 minutes. Stir in spices and nuts (below) and cook 5 minutes more. Keep in a covered jar in refrigerator until ready to use. Makes 1 quart. Have ready 1 double crust.

1 teaspoon cinnamon
1 teaspoon nutmeg
1 teaspoon mace

½ teaspoon allspice
½ cup chopped walnuts
    (optional)

Line a 9" pie plate with the bottom crust, fill with mince mixture, top with crust, seal edges by crimping together, slash top in 6 places. Brush a little soy milk onto the crust. Bake at 375F about 1 hour until nicely browned. If pie begins to brown too soon, lay a piece of foil lightly over the top.

A SPOONFUL OF SUGAR
by Janet Laurence

Janet Laurence is the versatile and accomplished author of the Darina Lisle mysteries, as well as the recent novels of Canaletto, the Venetian artist. Additionally, she shows her talent for cuisine with a series of cookbooks she has penned.

The kitchen was warm, far warmer than the rest of the house. There was a sleek cat named Mouser that sat in a rocking chair and never ventured elsewhere. A huge, green-painted dresser was comfortably cluttered with gaily patterned china, moulds in bright copper and white porcelain, and a round tin that looked as though it might contain biscuits.

The cook was a tall, spare woman, her face severe, her hair neatly bound up beneath a triangular white head covering. "My name is Mrs. Twitterton," she told James. He had found his way down to the kitchen the day after his mother and Mr. Porter had collected him at Tonbridge Station.

"So, my boy, welcome to Beacon Lodge," Mr. Porter had said with expansive warmth, as the horses completed the long haul up the steep lane. "You'll be right and tight here with your ma and me, long as you remember I'm your father now."

"Oh, Jimmy, darling, it's lovely to see you again," his mother had said, hugging him to her.

James had disentangled himself from her enveloping arms as her soft furs and potent perfume threatened to muddle his brain. "Did you enjoy your honeymoon?" he asked politely.

James's real father had been a military hero, decorated in the Crimean campaign. He'd lost an arm there, which meant he'd never been able to hold James properly. It hadn't mattered, though, because Colonel Gilstrap had the knack of talking to small boys and finding things to do with them, like fishing and riding and hunting for birds' eggs. He could even throw a ball for cricket practice; he'd learned to do most things with his left hand.

James had been outraged when the colonel died from typhus fever; it had seemed a personal betrayal. His mother had been devastated, too, but not in the same way. She hadn't blamed her husband for dying, but she'd cried and cried and said it wasn't fair. Then James had come home from school for the summer holidays to find his mother was once again smiling and getting excited about trivial matters, like going to some stupid dance or on an excursion that didn't include boys.

At first he hadn't realised what the increasingly common visits of Mr. Porter might mean. But when his mother explained that James was going to have a new father, he'd stared at her in horror. "That's stupid," he'd shouted at her. "You can't mean it!"

Her face had crumpled and he'd felt awful. Afterward he'd thought maybe he'd reacted like that because he'd started the fever that meant he couldn't go back to school for the winter term. There'd been a long period of bed with nurses and his mother holding his hand and stroking his forehead. For a time, he'd thought Mr. Porter had been forgotten.

By early spring, though, when he was beginning to feel almost better, he learned they were to marry, then he was to go and stay with his guardian while she and Mr. Porter went on their honeymoon to Harrogate. "Arthur says it's very nice there," she told him gaily. "And you'll have a lovely time with Uncle Peter."

The colonel had told James once, "Always assess situations, my boy. Stand back, see how the land lies and where the enemies' forces are. Then work out your tactics. That way you remain in control."

Was Mr. Porter the enemy? He certainly didn't have the trick of talking to ten-year-old boys. He got all sort of jolly and said things like, "You'll be glad to see your mother happy again," or, "You and I are going to be chaps together," and cuff him lightly round the head. But not lightly enough.

And James felt uncomfortable at the way the man would place a hand on his mother's shoulder, his fingers pressing into the soft flesh. And he felt unhappy about the smile his mother would give to Mr. Porter. "Arthur," she'd breathe, and the sound made James angry—it was too like the way she'd spoken to his father.

Mr. Porter looked nothing like the colonel. He was short, for one thing, and his face was round and podgy with eyes that were small and dark, like currants in fruitcake. He smiled a lot, but James watched and studied Mr. Porter and finally decided that it was only his mouth that smiled; those little brown eyes were as bright and cold as those of a cat waiting to pounce on a mouse.

"Here's your nursery," said Mr. Porter, taking him upstairs. It was at the top of the house, and James felt dizzy as he looked out of the window and saw the ground fall away, down, down the hill. He was higher than birds flying over the tops of tall trees.

There was nothing welcoming about the nursery. It had a table and four upright chairs. There was a cupboard and a set of empty bookshelves. On the floor was a threadbare rug.

"Soon our things will come, and then we can make it homelike for you," James's mother said hurriedly and took him downstairs again.

After exploring, James decided he didn't think much of Beacon House. It was much smaller than his old home, and there weren't nearly as many servants. Their previous ones had been friends, and he missed them. Only his mother's maid had come with her.

"Fine comedown this is," Maisie sniffed to James as she helped him unpack in a bedroom not much more welcoming than the nursery. "What would the colonel have said, that's what I wonder."

James remembered something he'd overheard Uncle Peter say to Aunt Mary. "The fellow's a bounder. I tried to talk sense into Louise, but it was no use."

"You can't know that," Aunt Mary had protested. "He seems harmless enough, very pleasant in fact, makes a woman feel, well, cherished. Just because he's not quite our class. . . ."

"Not quite our class!" Uncle Peter had exploded. "An out-and-out social climber. All he wants is Reggie's money. I told her so, but—"

"Oh, Peter, you didn't!"

"It's James I worry about most. The trust fund's safe enough. I retain control of that until he's twenty-five—unless he dies, of course. Then it reverts to Louise, but she has a tidy penny herself, and what's to become of the boy under that bounder's influence? Eh? Answer me that!"

Then Uncle Peter had seen James standing in the doorway.

"What's a bounder?" James had asked.

"How long have you been listening?" Uncle Peter had said, very sternly.

"I wasn't listening," James protested hurriedly. Uncle Peter could make him feel very small. "I just heard you say something about a bounder's influence, and I thought it sounded funny, that's all."

Uncle Peter had looked at him very hard, but James had kept his expression quite innocent. Then he'd told him a lot of nonsense about the way a cricket ball could bound and how it could influence a batsman. James had known it was all a fudge.

"Where are the horses, please, sir?" asked James his first morning after breakfast. This was taken in a small room off the hall, with just James and Mr. Porter. James's mother always had hers in her bedroom. "I like riding," he added politely.

"We don't keep horses for you to ride!" said Mr. Porter sharply. "There's the carriage pair and my mount, that's all."

"What about my pony?" asked James despairingly. He'd missed Blackie so much in London. "When is he coming?"

"Sold," said Mr. Porter bluntly. "No room in the stables."

James felt his underlip quiver. After finishing his breakfast very fast, he asked the copy of the *Times* that hid Mr. Porter's face if he could get down, and then he scampered up to his mother's bedroom.

"You haven't really sold Blackie, have you?" he burst out, flinging himself on the soft bed, where his mother reclined amongst lace pillows.

"James!" she exclaimed, rescuing the coffee cup that threatened to upset on her breakfast tray. "Darling, do be careful!"

He slid off the bed, chastened. "But Blackie," he insisted, thrusting his hands into his trouser pockets.

"Oh, darling, you're too old for a pony now. When you're really better, then we'll get you a proper mount."

James was torn between the loss of his beloved pony and a sense of excitement at the prospect of acquiring a full-size horse. "But I never said good-bye," he protested, the loss overwhelming him again.

His mother held out a hand. "Darling, I'm sorry. We just had this very good offer, and Mr. Porter explained that his groom is also his gardener and he wouldn't have time to look after another animal until proper arrangements have been made. Now, what are you going to do this morning?"

"Perhaps we could go for a walk together?" James asked hopefully.

"Darling, I'm sorry, I have so many letters to write. You find something to do on your own."

James went up to the nursery and looked at the empty shelves. There wasn't even paper and pencil so that he could draw. And no books! The colonel had said once, "You can learn everything from books, my boy, remember that. Never know what life will bring. With knowledge you can cope with anything thrown at you."

James went downstairs. Mr. Porter was coming out of the breakfast room. "Books? Books?" he repeated, looking dumbfounded.

"I like reading," James said.

"Do you, indeed?" Mr. Porter made it sound something not done in polite society. Then he went back into the breakfast room and opened a glass-fronted cupboard, took out a couple of heavy volumes, and handed them to James. "There, they'll keep you going."

James took them back to the nursery and opened the first. *Home Chat* it said. Above the title someone had written "Jane March" in the sort of writing that James managed. He found this encouraging and opened the book expectantly.

Ten minutes later he put it down again. Nothing but a bound collection of magazines with home hints and stories about girls who lived in horrible homes and met handsome young men. Nothing James could be interested in. It was jolly cold, too, in the nursery; the fire was tiny and gave out very little heat. He thought of going for a walk on his own, but it was pouring with rain and, anyway, he was still exhausted from yesterday's travel. That was when he went downstairs and found the kitchen.

Mrs. Twitterton was taking a batch of biscuits out of the oven, and a warm, sweet, slightly spicy aroma filled the air and made James's mouth water. "Gosh, those smell good," he said longingly.

"You look like you can do with some feeding up," she said. "But they should cool for a moment."

The two of them stood looking at the biscuits for what seemed an age to James. Then the cook took a broad knife, slid it under one, and offered it to him. "Careful, though, it's still hot."

He took it gingerly, then wolfed it down. It was crisp, buttery, and totally delicious. "Gosh, that's good!" he said. Mrs. Twitterton looked pleased and gave him another.

"Haven't you had any breakfast?" she asked after a third, but there was a smile in her voice, and her twinkling grey eyes and wide mouth softened the effect of her angular face, all sharp cheekbones and bony chin.

"I didn't feel like eating then," he said. Since he'd been ill, he'd almost never wanted to eat.

"I can see we'll have to tempt you. What do you like best?"

"Porridge," he replied at once. "And I like it with sugar. At Aunt Mary's I had to eat it with salt, and it wasn't nice at all."

The cook nodded. "Got a sweet tooth, you have, like Mr. Porter."

James didn't want to be like Mr. Porter in any way. He almost cancelled the porridge, but the thought of the thick, creamy oatmeal with sugar and milk running over the top stopped him.

"What do I call you?" he asked, then blushed as he realised he was speaking through a mouthful of crumbs.

"Mrs. Twitterton's my name, but you can call me Mrs. Twit."

"You've made a hit with her," said a large man coming in through the back door. "She doesn't allow many to call her that." He wore heavy boots, shabby brown breeches, and a huge green apron. His face was weather-beaten and his eyes a faded blue under fiercely hairy brows. His voice was surprisingly soft. Over his arm was a basket full of vegetables: leeks, cabbage, and curly kale. "Here's what you ordered for today, me dear."

"Don't you bring your dirty feet into my clean kitchen, Bob Frattle! You can leave the vegs in the scullery."

"Go on with you! Man needs a cup o' tea and a bite o' bread and butter in this sort of weather, don't 'e?" Bob's broad face split into a wide smile, displaying a large gap in his front teeth.

Mrs. Twitterton sighed heavily, but James got the impression the gardener was quite welcome. "Sit down, then, but mind where you put those large clodhoppers."

As soon as the man was seated, a cat appeared from nowhere and settled on his knee. A huge hand, lined and ingrained with dirt, started to stroke the animal, and loud purring filled the room.

"Who be this, then?" Bob asked, looking at James. "You the new missus's little boy?"

"Not so much of the little," the cook said sharply. "James is a young man."

"Why, of course he is," said the gardener. "You'll be wanting to see my onions, I shouldn't wonder, young James."

"Do you have a lot of them?" asked James politely, leaning against the table and helping himself to another biscuit. "And are they very large?" Their last gardener had won prizes for his onions—they'd been huge.

"Indeed they are," Bob said. "When the squirrels and the rats leave them alone. Mr. Porter said he'd get me some arsenic to deal with the little b—, uh, with the dratted vermin." He changed his word in midstream as he saw James.

"That'll be it over there." Mrs. Twitterton pointed her wooden spoon at a brown wrapped package on the sideboard. "Brought it home yesterday and said it was for you."

"An' if I'd gone when you said, I'd never 'ave got it," Bob complained, but James could tell he was laughing. It was as if they were having two different conversations, one with their words and another with their looks and tone of voice. Yet Mrs. Twit sounded much more like his mother than she did the gardener.

"Stand by for her ladyship's tray," sang out a new voice, as the kitchen door opened and in came Alice, the maid. She saw James and stopped. "Sorry, didn't realise you'd be in here."

James didn't quite understand why she should be worried, any more than he understood why she should call his mother "her ladyship," since she had no title. But grown-ups often said puzzling things.

"Glad to see everything's gone," said Mrs. Twit cheerfully, as the tray was dumped on the table. "Cup of tea, Alice?"

"Yes, indeed." Alice sank into a chair beside Bob. "Could do with getting off me feet for a moment." She ran a finger between her lisle stocking and the inside edge of her lace-up shoes. "Up and down, up and down it's been this morning with Miss 'Igh-and-Mighty asking for first this and then that. Needs a maid of 'er own, she does, but it's not going to be me! I've got enough to do."

James stifled a gurgle of laughter, then grinned as Mrs. Twit looked at him in a very understanding way. "The colonel said Maisie was autocratic," he said, pronouncing the word with care.

"The colonel?" Alice said.

"My father," he said proudly. "Maisie's been with my mother since forever. The colonel said she thought she owned her."

"Well, she don't own me!" Alice said crossly. "And if she wants morning tea, she can come down and get it."

"At home, she was always waited on," James said, a little shyly, not at all certain if he should be talking like this. But he liked Mrs. Twit, and Maisie had never been particularly friendly to him.

"Well, she'll 'ave to learn different 'ere," declared Alice robustly. "What 'appened to your dad, then?"

"He died," James said briefly.

"'Ow did Mr. Porter meet your ma?" asked Alice, slurping eagerly at her cup of tea. "'Er upstairs was distinctly sniffy when, making conversation like, I asked."

Mrs. Twit and Bob said nothing, but James could sense that they, too, wanted to know.

He thought for a moment. How, exactly, had Mr. Porter come into their lives? "I think he was at my father's funeral," he said at last. "I think he said he'd known the colonel in the army. Something to do with pro . . . pro . . . procurement?"

"My!" said an impressed-sounding Alice. "Didn't know Mr. Porter had ever been involved in anything like that."

"What is he involved in?" James asked.

There was silence in the kitchen. Mrs. Twit looked from Alice to Bob. "Well?" she demanded. "Aren't you going to answer the boy? No good asking me, I've only been here five minutes."

Bob's face had lost its genial openness. "Comes and goes, 'e does. And lives like a gennelman."

"Gentleman, huh!" snorted Alice. "When I think 'ow 'e and Mrs. Bright carried on! She was cook 'ere," she added for James's benefit.

"Said she was a cook!" snorted Bob. "But 'er cakes never rose. Now, Mrs. Twitterton's a proper one, angel food is what she produces."

"What happened to Mrs. Bright?" asked James, watching the little smile of acknowledgement Mrs. Twit gave to Bob.

"Left when Mr. Porter married your ma," Alice said promptly. "Right up to the end, she thought she'd 'ave 'im!"

"Don't you go letting 'im 'ear you speak like that," Bob said with a note of warning.

"Didn't you say the other day that Mr. Porter had been married before?" asked Mrs. Twit in a friendly way. "What happened to his first wife?"

"Died," said Alice gloomily. "She never got over her daughter's death. That was her daughter by her first husband. They both came 'ere, just like you and your ma," she added to James. "Such a shame it was, Jane was a nice little thing."

"Was her last name March?" James asked, a trifle nervously because children weren't supposed to enter their elders' conversations.

"'Ow d'you know that?" asked Alice in surprise.

James explained about *Home Chat*.

"Always 'ad 'er nose in a book, never 'appier than when she was reading," Alice said.

"What happened to her?" Mrs. Twit fetched a loaf of sugar from the kitchen dresser and started to scrape it down with the back of a knife. Glittering crystals gathered around its foot.

"Got some sort of wasting disease. Awful sick she was, weren't nothing the doctor could do, and finally she died. The heart went out of the missus then. Master tried to jolly her along but it weren't no good."

"Did she take sick too?" Mrs. Twit poured the grated sugar into the pan of her scales, shook her head at the weight, and scraped again at the sugar loaf.

James seemed to have been forgotten. He'd long ago learned the art of sitting quietly and not calling attention to himself. Could any of this explain what Uncle Peter had meant when he called Mr. Porter a bounder? He sneaked another biscuit and listened hard.

Mrs. Twit approved the amount of her sugar, weighed out butter, and then started to beat them together in a bowl with a wooden spoon, the butter and sugar paling into a creamy mass.

"She had an accident," Alice said shortly.

"I found her dead at the bottom of the steps," Bob said sadly. "Neck was broke. Lord knows what she was doing going down that way in the dark."

There was silence for a little, as though no one liked to take the conversation further.

Mrs. Twit vigorously whisked eggs with a fork, then started to beat them into her mixture bit by bit.

"How old was Jane?" James asked at last.

The three grown-ups looked at him in surprise. They had obviously forgotten he was there.

"Eleven," Alice answered.

Only a year older than himself! "Was she too old for toys?"

"Oh, you mean as 'ow there ain't none in the nursery? That's 'cause her grandmother came and took everything after Mrs. Porter died. Said Mr. Porter didn't need them, 'e 'ad all 'er daughter's money, what she 'ad from 'er first marriage, and who knows, but 'er other daughter mightn't want them someday."

Mrs. Twit beat her mixture even more vigorously, as though she was on the side of the unknown grandmother.

How sad, thought James, both that Jane had died and that her toys were gone. He watched Mrs. Twit add chocolate powder to her cake mixture. She tasted a little, then added a bit more chocolate.

"You can lick the bowl," she promised him with a smile, and James realised that, even if there weren't any toys in the Beacon House nursery, there was a welcome for him in the kitchen.

The next morning a bowl of creamy porridge appeared at breakfast. In front of James's place was a silver-topped, cut-glass bowl.

"Now," said Mr. Porter, putting down his paper as James pulled out his chair to sit. "That's your own sugar bowl; you help yourself to as much as you want. I like to see a boy enjoy his food."

Perhaps things were going to work out all right after all, James thought. He opened the bowl.

"That'll put hair on your chest," Mr. Porter said encouragingly. "You'll soon be running around."

James ran a hand over his upper torso, so slight beneath his shirt, and wondered how many hairs Mr. Porter had on his. Then he dug the silver spoon into the coarse, sparkling grains and sprinkled a generous amount on his porridge. He added milk, richly creamy, and ate a spoonful.

It was good! Hot, with the swollen grains soft and satisfying, a faintly clean smell coming from them as he spooned them into his mouth, the milk a cool contrast, the sugar sweet and crunchy. But after the first couple of spoonfuls, he felt so full he put down the spoon and laid his napkin beside the plate.

Mr. Porter was not pleased. "Boys should finish their food," he said sternly.

James tried to explain how he didn't have much appetite since he'd been ill.

"Stuff and nonsense, boy, you will finish your plate."

James looked at the porridge and then at Mr. Porter. He shook his head.

Mr. Porter's face grew red. "You will sit there until you've finished, you understand?" he hissed at James.

The boy stared at him. Mr. Porter stared back. James folded his arms and sat back in his chair.

Eventually Mr. Porter closed his paper and snapped it down on the table. "Until you've finished," he repeated as though he'd just spoken. Then he got up and left the room.

James continued to look at his porridge and felt no more desire to eat it than when he'd first laid down his spoon.

Alice came in and cleared the rest of the breakfast away. "Aren't you the one?" she said as she took the last of the cutlery off the table, but there was an admiring note in her voice.

James was left at the table with his plate of half-eaten porridge. He looked at the window. If he opened that, he could dump the rest of his porridge outside and be released. He continued to sit in front of the plate.

Sometime later his mother swept in. "My darling!" she exclaimed. Arthur has told me you won't finish your porridge, but you love porridge! Are you ill?"

By then James had begun to feel decidedly unwell and had to make a hurried exit.

After he'd finished being sick, his mother put him to bed. Gradually the stomach cramps subsided and he was able to eat a little of the delicious chicken soup Mrs. Twit sent up for his lunch.

Later, feeling better and learning from Alice that his mother had gone out to a tea party and Mr. Porter was on some business in nearby Tonbridge, James got up and went down to the kitchen.

Mrs. Twit was sitting in a rocking chair by the range, the cat on her lap, a cup of tea in her hand. "How are you now, James?" she asked. "Feel up to a biscuit?" He nodded and she waved a hand at the dresser. "There's the tin, help yourself. As you can see, I'm a prisoner in my chair." She stroked the cat and it purred loudly.

James took a biscuit and came and sat on a chair at the other side of the range, grateful for the heat.

"Didn't you like my porridge?" Mrs. Twit asked.

"Oh, yes," James said eagerly. "It was just that after a bit I wasn't hungry anymore. I haven't been eating much, you see."

"I see." Mrs. Twit rocked a little in her chair, and the cat purred even louder. "Maybe you weren't feeling well."

"Oh, I was!" James said earnestly. "I felt better this morning than for a long time."

"Until you ate my porridge," Mrs. Twit said gently.

"I was all right until a long time after I'd eaten it," he said. "It can't have been anything to do with the porridge. I expect it's because I was so ill before."

Mrs. Twit smiled at him, and for a while they both sat and listened to the big clock high up on the wall as it tick-tocked the minutes away.

The next morning James's plate of porridge was much smaller and he managed to finish it. But later the cramps returned and he was sick again.

It was the same the following day, and Matt, the boy who helped Bob in the garden and stables, was sent to fetch Dr. Birch.

The doctor was an elderly man with rheumy eyes and hands that trembled as he fitted his stethoscope in his ears. He examined James, asked about his previous illness, then said that rest and a light diet should do the trick.

After he'd gone, James lay in his bed, feeling miserable and sick. He longed for his old bedroom with all its toys and books and wanted very much for his mother to come and entertain him, but she'd asked if he'd mind very much if she went to a luncheon. James did but didn't like to say so.

At lunchtime Alice arrived with a tray. "There, eat that and you'll soon be bright as a button."

There was a slim fillet of fish under some frothy pink sauce. Beside it was a little mound of pale green puree, which turned out to be leek, and a small potato sprinkled with chopped parsley. It all looked delicious. James took a few mouthfuls, then realised he hadn't unwrapped his napkin. It was rolled up inside a silver ring that had JANE in a plain cartouche on the patterned silver.

James's appetite disappeared.

Alice tut-tutted when she came back for the tray. "Your ma said you might want to get up if you felt better, but looking at what you've left, I shouldn't think you'll be doing that," she said severely. The white frill threaded with black that she wore round her head had slipped toward her eyes, altering her whole face from its ordinary plainness to something more sinister. James shrank back as she leaned forward to take the tray.

After she'd gone, James couldn't bear the boredom any longer. If he got up, he could sit by the fire in the drawing room, then his mother could play a game of cards with him when she returned from her lunch.

Feeling weak but thankful the cramps had once again gone, James dressed and went downstairs.

No one was around. James went into the morning room to see if there was something more readable in the bookcase than the bound magazines. He struggled with the catch of the glass door; it was stiff and he had to pull at it. It opened so suddenly that the cupboard rocked slightly and the cut-glass sugar bowl fell off the top. Broken glass was everywhere, and the spilt sugar lay like glistening snow on the dark red carpet. James was appalled.

He went in search of Alice.

In the kitchen, Mrs. Twitterton was cutting thin slices of buttered bread. She smiled at James. "Feeling better? I'm sorry you couldn't eat your lunch," she said in a matter-of-fact way that managed not to make him feel guilty.

"I've broken the sugar bowl," he blurted out. "It's all over the carpet. Mr. Porter is going to be very cross."

"Oh, dearie me," Mrs. Twit said. "Then we'd better clean it up so he doesn't know."

"I can't find Alice."

"It's her afternoon off." Mrs. Twit went to a cupboard and took out a pan and stiff brush. "Now, let's see the damage."

The cat was licking at the sugar as they entered, and Mrs. Twit shooed it off. "Oh, dear," she said. "Such a nice looking bowl, too." She picked up the silver top and laid it carefully on a chair seat. "Might be able to do something with that."

"Mr. Porter said it was my special bowl, for my porridge sugar." James felt even more upset.

"Well, well," said Mrs. Twit. "Your own sugar bowl, fancy that." She started to pick up the larger bits of glass and put them in the pan. "I think I've seen a mate to this in the kitchen. We can fill it with more sugar and then no one will know."

"Shouldn't I tell Mr. Porter?" James asked anxiously.

"It was an accident, wasn't it?"

He nodded.

"Then why get everyone upset?"

James thought the colonel would not have approved. "But—" he started.

"No buts," Mrs. Twit said very firmly. "You're not going to get away with it completely, though. You're going to have to scrape the sugar loaf to fill the other bowl." Somehow that seemed to make matters better, so James quelled his uneasiness as he watched her brush up the sugar. When she'd finished, you'd never have known anything had happened.

Back in the kitchen, Mrs. Twit emptied the pan, then went into the pantry, hunted around a cupboard filled with glassware, and brought out a cut-glass bowl with a silver top.

"It's exactly the same!" said James excitedly.

"All it needs is a bit of a polish, and you'd never know the difference."

Then Mrs. Twit got out the sugar loaf and arranged James so that he was kneeling on a chair. She showed him how to scrape down the hard, conical pillar, releasing a shower of sugar. From time to time, he spooned this up and put it in the bowl. While he worked, he watched Mrs. Twit making sandwiches. There were meat paste ones, cucumber ones, and ham ones. "Is Mr. Porter coming back for tea?" he asked nervously.

Mrs. Twit nodded and went over to riddle the coals through the grate of the big, black range, making them glow brightly. She took off the cover of a large black stew pot and tasted the contents. Then she added something and stirred it in.

"Is that dinner?" asked James, starting to feel hungry.

"Beef done the French way," Mrs. Twit said. "You'll like it."

"What did you put in just now?"

"Salt. It brings out flavour. I added some at the start, but everything needs tasting as it cooks, to see if more is required."

James thought that, good as the dish smelled, it would be no fun having to eat it in the cheerless nursery all on his own. That evening, though, his mother said, "Mrs. Twitterton suggested that you might eat more if you had your supper in the kitchen with her. It's not comme il faut at all for you to eat with the servants, but Mr. Porter has said he doesn't mind. Would you like that?"

James nodded eagerly.

The beef done in the French way was delicious. It had been cooked with carrots and turnips and onions, and there were whole peppercorns in the thin broth. The slices of meat were so tender you almost didn't need a knife. While James tucked in at one end of the table, Mrs. Twit bustled about the kitchen, slicing meat, arranging it on a large serving dish with the vegetables around it, pouring some of the broth over, and then adding more to a sauce boat. A big mound of creamy mashed potatoes was placed in a vegetable dish, then Alice took it all up to the dining room.

There'd been fish to start with for his mother, done the way James had had his for lunch. "Sauce rose, I call it," said Mrs. Twit. "It's made with tomatoes." And Mr. Porter had had mussels. James knew that his mother didn't trust shellfish ever since the colonel had had a bad oyster many years ago and been very ill. But James loved all the different sorts, particularly mussels.

"Have you lived in France?" James asked after Alice had taken the food up to the dining room.

Mrs. Twit nodded. "I learned a great deal. The French appreciate food in a way we don't. Over here, as long it looks impressive, no one cares how it tastes."

Pudding was chocolate mousse. James loved it but found he couldn't eat much of it.

"Very rich," Mrs. Twit said gently as she took his half-finished dish away.

"Where's Mouser?" asked James, looking around for the cat, as Alice took the coffee tray up to the drawing room.

Mrs. Twit's expression changed. She rattled plates as she dumped them into the sink, and James knew something awful had happened. "Bob found her dead in the garden just before supper," she said shortly.

"Oh, how awful," said James. "How did she die?"

After soda was added to the water and the plates mopped clean, rinsed and placed in the rack over the sink, Mrs. Twit finally said, "Old age," in a much softer voice, and James felt a bit better.

"I had a dog that did that," he said. "Rover was ever so old, and the colonel said he needed a long, long rest. Perhaps Mouser did too."

"Perhaps," agreed Mrs. Twit.

Alice brought more dirty china down from the dining room and helped with the washing up. James expected to be told it was time for bed, but nothing was said. Instead Alice was telling Mrs. Twit all about a young man she'd met in a shoe shop in Tonbridge.

Finally the kitchen was all cleared up and Alice sat down with a sigh. "Ooh, me feet! You going to make us some hot chocolate, cook?"

"That I am. I have to prepare it for Mr. Porter anyway."

It was true, it had soon become a joke with James's mother how much Mr. Porter liked hot chocolate. "I have merely to look at the stuff," she laughed once, "and my waist doubles in size!"

"Would you like some?" Mrs. Twit asked James.

Hot chocolate was a great favourite with James, and he said, "Yes, please." It was long enough after his dessert for him to feel just a little hungry again.

"You should be in bed," Alice said, yawning.

A small pan of milk was put on the stove to heat. Mrs. Twit chopped up a slab of chocolate and added the small pieces to the pan, stirring it well. Then she poured some into three cups. James marveled that it could all melt together into the smooth, sweet, deeply flavoured drink he so enjoyed. He watched Mrs. Twit as she carefully tasted her cup. "Just a little sugar is what it needs," she said.

James took her the bowl from the coffee tray. But Mrs. Twit put it beside the stove and found a pair of wicked-looking tongs. "We don't want to have to grind more, we can use pieces for this," she said, retrieving the loaf from the dresser and hacking some bits off the top. She added one to James's cup. "Stir it in well."

James stirred his small cup and watched Alice add several pieces of sugar plus cream to her much larger one.

She drank deeply and smacked her lips. "That's the ticket," she said happily.

Mrs. Twit added sugar grains from the bowl to the chocolate that remained in the pan on the stove and stirred it carefully in. Then she gently poured it into a porcelain cup, added a matching lid, placed it on its saucer, and handed it to Alice. "There you are, last job of the day."

Alice groaned but got to her feet, placed the cup on a small tray, and took it out of the kitchen.

"And you, my lad, should be off to bed," Mrs. Twit said. "I'm surprised your mother hasn't sent down—she must think you're there already."

In the morning James came down to find that Mr. Porter was not at his accustomed place.

Sitting on a spirit-warmed hot plate was the customary bowl of porridge, and in front of James's place was the bowl of sugar. He sprinkled a generous amount over the creamy mixture.

It was strange sitting at the table on his own but very peaceful. Then Alice came in, her face light with an awful excitement. "Oh, Master James, what a to-do!"

James felt very frightened. "What's the matter, Alice? Is it Mama?"

"No, it's the master, dreadful he is. Up half the night, doctor sent for, missus in such a tizzy!"

"Is Mr. Porter ill?"

"Ill? I'll say he is! Near to dying, I shouldn't wonder!"

"That's dreadful!" said James, then caught himself thinking that, actually, the prospect of Mr. Porter disappearing from his life wasn't dreadful at all. But thoughts like that were wicked, and anyway, he didn't really want Mr. Porter to die.

James got down from the table and went to find his mother. But she was with Mr. Porter.

In the kitchen later in the morning, Mrs. Twit was calmly cooking lunch: roast chicken with stuffing and bread sauce, James's favourite.

"Did you hear?" James asked breathlessly.

"That Mr. Porter's sick, you mean?"

"Alice says he's near death!"

"And you believe her?"

"Well. . . ." James leant with his elbows on the table, watching Mrs. Twit taste the bread sauce she was cooking.

"You don't want to trust everything you hear."

Her matter-of-factness encouraged James to think things mightn't be that bad.

Suddenly the door to the kitchen was flung open and there stood the doctor. "Tell me what the family has been eating," he demanded, his little goatee beard quivering while his watery gaze looked from Mrs. Twit to James.

The cook ran through the previous day's menus for him.

"You forgot the mussels," James told her.

"Mussels?" enquired the doctor sharply. "Did everyone have mussels?"

"No," said Mrs. Twit slowly, "just Mr. Porter."

"Ah!" exclaimed the doctor, looking relieved. "That's what it'll be then. I always say you can't trust shellfish."

"They were only delivered yesterday," Mrs. Twit said sharply. "And I was told the supplier has an excellent reputation."

"Can't trust tradesmen," said the doctor briefly, turning to leave the kitchen.

"How is Mr. Porter, sir?" asked Mrs. Twit.

"Poorly, very poorly indeed."

Mrs. Twit and James looked at each other after the doctor left the kitchen. "Doesn't sound too good," she said levelly.

"No, it doesn't," agreed James soberly.

Mr. Porter died that night. After, said Alice with gloomy relish the next morning, agonies of pain.

The arrangements for the funeral were lengthy and involved Mrs. Twit in preparing a great deal of food.

The service was long, but James was interested to see that the only person who really mourned Mr. Porter was his mother. The atmosphere afterward was almost lighthearted as the mourners tucked into Mrs. Twit's food. After nearly everyone had left, James went to the kitchen.

As he entered, Alice rose hastily to her feet. "All gone, 'ave they?"

"Not quite, it's just Uncle Peter and Aunt Mary. I think my mother's going to ask them to stay the night."

"Oh, my lord, no end to the day," Alice complained.

"Supper's easy enough with all the food that's in the house," Mrs. Twit said easily. "Where are the mistress and her guests?" she asked James.

"In the little sitting room."

"So you can clear the drawing room," Mrs. Twit said to Alice.

She groaned but went.

James sat in the chair he had come to think of as his. As he watched Mrs. Twit cutting ham and arranging the slices in a dish, he asked, "Did the doctor decide it was the mussels that killed Mr. Porter?"

"I think so," she said.

"Was that because nobody else had any?"

"That would be it." Her knife laid another slice of ham on top of the others.

"I had two," James said quietly.

Mrs. Twit looked up. "You did?" she said in an odd voice.

"Yes, when you were in the pantry. I hid the empty shells under the others," he added, shamefaced.

"Well, aren't you the one." The knife began to cut the meat again.

"But I haven't been ill."

"Nor you have," she agreed.

"So, do you think it was something else that killed Mr. Porter?"

"Maybe you didn't eat enough mussels," Mrs. Twit said calmly.

James thought about that. It made sense, in a way. But after a little, he said, "I saw you add sugar from the coffee tray bowl to Mr. Porter's hot chocolate, Mrs. Twit."

"You did, did you?" Mrs. Twit went and collected some parsley from a bunch sitting in a glass of water on the windowsill, snapped off the stalks, and arranged the leaves in the middle of the ham slices. Then she began to skin some cooked potatoes.

"Yes, I did," he said, emboldened by her calm attitude. "But you added pieces from the loaf for Alice and me. And there's something else. Since you found that new bowl with the silver cover and I scraped the sugar for it, I haven't felt ill at all."

"Is that a fact?" Mrs. Twit sliced the peeled potatoes into a dish.

James nodded earnestly. He would have said more, but at that moment the back door opened and Bob came in. He put a small basket of carrots on the table, sand clinging to their skins. "Them's the last," he said. "Nothing more left in my locker." He took off his cap and sat down without asking. "Devil of a day it's been, what with the master being buried and all me curly kale invaded by aphids. And the dratted rats 'ave been at me spring onions again. And there's the darndest thing. You know that packet of arsenic the master got me to deal with the danged things? Someone's been at it!"

"Never!" said Mrs. Twit without emphasis, rather as someone might exclaim at the fact that rain was forecast. "You're imagining things."

"Don't 'ave much imagination. Sure as I'm sitting here, the packet was full five days ago and today there's a good inch missing."

"Rats will have had it."

"Good riddance to them, then," Bob said indignantly. "I can do without them silly b—" He saw James and said instead, "silly varmints."

"I'll thank you, Mr. Frattle, to stop cluttering up my kitchen. I've a tidy bit to do, what with guests this evening."

Grumbling, the gardener rose. "You 'aven't been to see me onions, yet, Master James. Only thin sprouts at the moment, but they'll be prize ones, you see." Then he stopped. "What'll happen to the Beacon now, then?"

When Uncle Peter had arrived that morning, James's mother, who had done little but weep since Mr. Porter's death, had declared she wasn't staying here, Peter must arrange something. He'd patted her arm and said everything would be sorted out. James hoped that meant they could return to his old home.

"Any chives in the garden, yet?" asked Mrs. Twit.

The gardener looked slyly at the cook. "Might 'ave a few under me cold frames. What's it worth?"

"Go on with you! There'll be coffee in the kitchen tomorrow if you're around then. In the meantime, I'll be grateful if you could send young Matt up with a handful of them chives."

Still grumbling, Bob left the kitchen. Mrs. Twit spooned big dollops of mayonnaise onto the potatoes.

"Why did you do it?" James asked.

Mrs. Twit straightened her back and gave him the sort of look usually reserved for grown-ups. "Who's saying I did anything?"

James understood immediately. "No one," he said. "Anyone could eat a bad mussel." He sat and thought, as he'd thought so hard since Mr. Porter had died. Part of what had happened seemed clear—but only part—and how could he sort out the rest if Mrs. Twit wasn't going to say anything? Adults had so much power.

The cook tasted her mixture of potatoes and mayonnaise, then added salt.

"The girl who lived here before, Jane March," said James suddenly. "What exactly did she die of?"

"Her symptoms were the same as yours," Mrs. Twit said expressionlessly. "Except they were much worse and continued much longer. Eventually, after a lot of agony, she died."

James thought of the stomach cramps he'd had, the awful way he'd felt and the vomiting that he'd been afraid wouldn't stop.

"You said you weren't here then. Did Alice tell you all about it?"

Mrs. Twit said nothing.

"You knew Jane March, didn't you?"

Mrs. Twit started slicing tomatoes.

James began to get excited. "Was she a relation?" he persisted.

The knife was put down and James realised that Mrs. Twit was fighting tears. "She was my niece, God rest her soul. I was abroad at the time, working in France. I couldn't get back until after her mother, my sister, had been buried."

"Golly," said James, trying to imagine it all. "And you vowed vengeance, was that it?"

Mrs. Twit looked at him with a peculiar expression. "Tell me, young man, what makes you think I had anything to do with Mr. Porter's death?"

"It was the cocoa," said James. "You didn't taste it after you added the sugar. You always taste everything, but you never did that."

POT-AU-FEU

This long, slow cooking of one of the cheaper cuts of beef produces a marvelously tender result that is full of flavour. It is a traditional French dish that is always impressive and a great way to serve a lot of people. The meat can take as much as five hours to cook properly (more if it's very large) but is almost impossible to overdo. It needs a good piece of meat—don't try with one less than 3 to 4 pounds (1½ to 2 kilograms). It is excellent cold. Mrs. Twitterton would have served not only Mr. and Mrs. Porter but also all the indoor staff of the household and then would have used the leftovers for salads and maybe hash. The secret to its success is to keep the temperature well below the boiling point. As long as the odd bubble rises to the surface of the liquid, the joint is cooking.

The following recipe will serve 8-10 people.

4- to 5-pound (2- to 2½-kilogram) piece brisket of beef

flavouring vegetables—3 carrots, 3 medium-sized onions, 2 parsnips, 3 celery stalks, 3 leeks—all scraped or peeled, the celery and leeks cleaned and trimmed (leeks should be split for cleaning, then the leaves tied together again for the pot)

a bunch of parsley tied together with a bay leaf and a good sprig of thyme

5 crushed garlic cloves and a teaspoon of black peppercorns all tied together in muslin or cheesecloth

1 dessertspoon salt

stock—enough good meat stock to cover the meat and flavourings— this can be a mixture of beef and chicken or tins of bouillon or, at a pinch, really good stock cubes (make these up at half strength; they tend to be very salty)

vegetables to serve with the meat—a selection of carrots, onions, turnips and leeks (allow 1-2 of each vegetable per person). Have them all peeled or scraped, and half or quarter large carrots and turnips. Tie them in bundles or in pieces of muslin or cheesecloth so that they don't get mixed up with the stock vegetables and to help you remove them from the pot at the end of cooking

Trim any excess fat off the meat and tie, leaving a long piece of string hanging. Choose a cooking pan that will hold the meat and all the vegetables comfortably, then tie the end of the meat string to a handle. This will help to get hold of the meat when you need to test if it's done.

Add the flavouring vegetables, herbs, garlic and peppercorns, and salt, then cover with the stock to a point about 6" (2½ cm) above the ingredients. Bring steadily to simmering point, skimming as necessary. Then lower heat, half cover pan with a lid, and allow to cook very, very slowly for two and a half hours. Keep an eye on it, adding more stock if necessary, and reducing heat further if the dish shows any tendency to come to the boil. Skim again if required.

After two and a half hours cooking, add the vegetables to be served with the meat and raise the heat to bring back to simmering point. Then lower again and continue to cook as before for about another one and a half hours. Then test the meat with the prongs of a carving fork or a skewer to see if it is tender. Return for cooking a little longer if necessary. Everything can stay in the hot liquid if ready ahead of time.

When the meat is done and you are ready to serve, remove the beef from the pan and fish out the vegetables to be served with it. Drain all well. Slice the meat and arrange on a large dish surrounded by the vegetables, which should have been released from their cooking ties. Pour over some of the juices, and garnish with fresh parsley before serving. Or carve at the table and have the vegetables arranged separately in a serving dish.

If liked, a fresh tomato sauce or a herb mayonnaise or a Béchamel sauce with cream can accompany the meat. However, it is excellent just with the strained juices in which it cooked.

The remaining meat juices will make marvelous soup, either with the cooking vegetables pureed in it or using with others.

CINNAMON BISCUITS

Mrs. Twitterton would have made these biscuits by creaming the butter and sugar together, then adding the flour sifted with cinnamon. Today, though, we can use a food mixer to beat everything very gently together in one easy process, and that's the method given here.

1¾ cups (10oz/275g) self-rising flour
2 teaspoons ground cinnamon
pinch salt
1 cup (8oz/225g) butter, softened
⅔ cup (4oz/100g) caster sugar
vanilla sugar (optional)

Sift together flour, cinnamon, and salt. Combine with butter (the butter must be very, very soft) and caster sugar in the bowl of an electric mixer, using the "K" beater on a low setting. As soon as the mixture has amalgamated, stop the beater.

Form small balls with the mixture and place on a greased baking sheet, allowing room for spreading. Flatten a little with the back of a fork.

Place in a preheated oven at 375F (190C, Gas Mark 5) for approximately ten minutes or until biscuits are a deeper gold. Sprinkle hot biscuits with vanilla sugar and allow to cool for a moment or two before lifting off the tray to a wire rack. Store in an airtight tin.

Variations: Press biscuits flat with the back of a spoon or palette knife and add half a blanched almond instead of the vanilla sugar before baking. Instead of the powdered cinnamon, use the grated rind of a lemon or 2 tablespoons of sifted cocoa powder or 2 tablespoons currants.

ANOTHER ANTHOLOGY BY JEFFREY MARKS

Magnolias and Mayhem

Several of today's top Southern mystery writers spin yarns of murder and mischief south of the Mason-Dixon line: Jeff Abbott, Deborah Adams, Noreen Ayers with A. B. Robinson, Carolyn G. Hart, Beverly Taylor Herald, Dean James, Andrew Kantor, Toni L. P. Kelner, Jeffrey Marks, Margaret Maron, Taylor McCafferty, Elaine Fowler Palencia, and Elizabeth Daniels Squire.

— Magnolias and Mayhem is a 2001 Anthony nominee —

"Take your mint julep out to the veranda, then get ready for murder and moonlight—tempered with soft Southern charm."
—*Meritorious Mysteries*

"Bravo to this eclectic group of authors digging deep into the heart of the South. Their stories are rich in suspense, humor, and charm."
—Sujata Massey

"From urban Louisville, Kentucky, to the beach resort of Wilmington, North Carolina, and back in time to the Battle of Vicksburg, the authors render a South rich in Place; teeming with characters both quirky and complex; and punctuated with dialogues whose rhythms make me want to dance in praise."
—Anne Underwood Grant,
author of the Sydney Teague series

"Each story provides a full picture of the area to include powerful characterizations and many amusing scenarios. . . . Fans of the Southern crime story will fully enjoy this anthology intended for leisure reading over several cold nights."
—*The Midwest Book Review*

Hardcover ISBN 1-57072-112-2 $24.50
Trade Paper ISBN 1-57072-128-9 $15.00

www.jeffreymarks.com

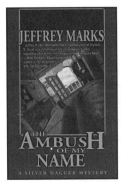

ALSO BY JEFFREY MARKS
The Ambush of My Name

Ulysses S. Grant returns to Georgetown, Ohio, after the Civil War, expecting parades and praise. Instead he finds the body of a man in his hotel room, and the evidence points to a connection with Lincoln's assassination. The reappearance of his childhood sweetheart only complicates matters. Delving into the town's secrets, Grant realizes that not everyone wishes him well in the upcoming presidential election. With the help of a Pinkerton agent and an ambitious reporter, Grant has to discover who wants to turn a triumphant homecoming into a deadly trap.

". . . a tasty little mystery . . . . [Marks] juggles suspects as expertly as a circus performer, right up to the last chapter."
—The Cincinnati Enquirer

"In general, and with no pun intended, *The Ambush of My Name* is an interesting and entertaining addition to the growing number of Civil War mystery novels."
—Civil War Book Review

"Jeffrey Marks has achieved what every writer hopes to do; he's penned a novel that grabs the reader on the first page and doesn't let go."
—Cameron Judd, historian and Civil War author

"Jeffrey Marks illuminates the forgotten years of Ulysses S. Grant in a debut novel full of intriguing history, appealing characters, and a very clever, climactic twist."
—Mark Graham, Edgar-nominated author of the Wilton McCleary series of Old Philadelphia

"It's a fascinating story, with both suspense and humor and a most surprising ending."
—Sharan Newman, author of the critically acclaimed Catherine LeVendeur medieval mystery series

Hardcover ISBN 1-57072-184-X $23.95
Trade Paper ISBN 1-57072-185-8 $13.95

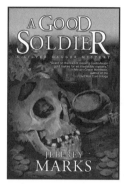

ALSO BY JEFFREY MARKS
A Good Soldier

In the second installment of the U. S. Grant mystery series, Grant, along with his wife, son, and father, visits friends in Bethel, Ohio, a sleepy hamlet which has begun to recover from the Civil War in a way quite different from other places of its kind. The church has a new steeple, and Grant's pals—men who had shared time in Andersonville, the worst prisoner of war camp the Confederates had to offer—were building stately homes. When his friends unexpectedly begin to die one at a time, Grant is left with a puzzle that has only one clue—a sparkling gold coin in the hand of his young son. Will it be enough to help Grant save the rest of his friends from the fate they so narrowly escaped in the war?

"With *A Good Soldier*, Jeffrey Marks captures an intriguing new side of General U. S. Grant. . . ."

—Jan Grape, author of *Austin City Blue* and
"Julia Dent Grant, a.k.a. Private Eye,"
a short story in *The First Lady Murders*

"An intriguing walk in American history with one of its finest generals—Ulysses S. Grant on the trail of missing Confederate gold makes for an irresistible mystery."

—Miriam Grace Monfredo,
author of the Civil War Cain trilogy

"In *A Good Soldier,* readers observe Ulysses S. Grant, as a person who has known the horrors of war and still grieves for the men that were killed and the nation that remains divided in principle. The audience also sees an individual who adores his wife and youngsters. . . . Though a strong historical mystery, the key character enables the author to make his mark as a gifted storyteller who makes history come alive."

—*The Midwest Book Review*

Hardcover ISBN 1-57072-215-3 $23.95
Trade Paper ISBN 1-57072-216-1 $13.95

TAKE A STAB AT THESE MYSTERIES COMING SOON

When Andy Carpenter stumbles across a body, he finds himself in the middle of a murder investigation. With his best friend, Maggie McLendon, he tries to figure out who the killer is, while also working out his feelings for Rob Hayward, an old friend who has suddenly reappeared in his life.

Death by Dissertation

by
Dean James

Derby Rotten Scoundrels

a SinC anthology

The Ohio River Valley Chapter of Sisters in Crime has compiled these mystery stories surrounding one of the world's greatest sporting events—the Kentucky Derby. Amidst the glamour of fast horses, beautiful women, and great bourbon is the underlying current, as deep as the Ohio River, of danger and deceit.

Reporter Kate Kelly masquerades as a friend's fiancée for a weekend adventure at a beautiful Kentucky horse farm. But when a deadly explosion rocks the farm, Kate quickly learns that planning a wedding involves more than wearing a huge diamond ring and picking out china patterns. It might just be the death of her.

Otherwise Engaged

by
Laura Young

SILVER DAGGER MYSTERIES

WOULD YOU LIKE TO WRITE A REVIEW OF A SILVER DAGGER MYSTERY? VISIT OUR WEB SITE FOR DETAILS

www.silverdaggermysteries.com

ALL SILVER DAGGER MYSTERIES ARE AVAILABLE IN BOTH TRADE PAPER AND HARDCOVER AT YOUR LOCAL BOOKSTORE OR DIRECTLY FROM THE PUBLISHER
P.O. Box 1261 • Johnson City, TN 37605
1-800-992-2691

8-04

Culpeper County Library
271 Southgate Shopping Cent
Culpeper Virginia 22701
825-8691